T0108705

THE
Trophy
WIVES

Dear Reader:

The Trophy Wives is an interesting spin on the concept of women marrying for money. Usually, women who yearn to marry into money end up basking in the lap of luxury, "doing lunch" with their like-minded friends, and enjoying a carefree existence. Such is not the case with Amber, Kyle, and Shayla. Yes, all three of their husbands are wealthy: a real estate broker, a professional athlete and an owner of multiple businesses. Yes, they have money to spend on a whim. Yes, they live in mansions, have household staff, and are afforded every luxury imaginable, including birthday parties thrown on multi-million-dollar yachts. However, they all have serious issues to battle and tackle themselves. Everything is not as it seems, and that is usually the case when it comes to wealthy couples that the world envies.

Charmaine R. Parker has done a magnificent job of examining why money truly can never buy happiness in *The Trophy Wives*. With vividly fleshed out characters, an edge of suspense mixed with an edge of sensuality, this novel will surely be a source for numerous discussions about love, relationships, and the part that finances play in them. Parker has laid the ground for what hints at a sequel to see where these group of women will end up next, after all of their secrets hit the proverbial fan.

As always, thank you for supporting the authors of Strebor Books. We strive to bring you the future in literature today. We appreciate the love and look forward to continuing to bring you cutting-edge voices in the industry. You can find out about our other authors on www.zanestore.com and you can find me on Facebook @AuthorZane and on Twitter @planetzane. Or you can email me zane@eroticanoir.com.

Blessings,

Zane

Publisher
Strebor Books
www.simonandschuster.com

ALSO BY CHARMAINE R. PARKER
The Next Phase of Life

ZANE PRESENTS

THE *Trophy* WIVES

CHARMAINE R. PARKER

SBI

STREBOR BOOKS

NEW YORK LONDON TORONTO SYDNEY

Strebor Books
P.O. Box 6505
Largo, MD 20792
http://www.streborbooks.com

© 2013 by Charmaine R. Parker

ISBN 978-1-59309-465-2
ISBN 978-1-4516-9655-4 (ebook)
LCCN 2013933643

First Strebor Books trade paperback edition September 2013

Cover design: www.mariondesigns.com
Cover photograph: © Keith Saunders/Marion Designs
Wedding rings: © Shutterstock Images

10 9 8 7 6 5 4 3 2 1

Manufactured in the United States of America

For information regarding special discounts for bulk purchases, please contact Simon & Schuster Special Sales at 1-866-506-1949 or business@simonandschuster.com

The Simon & Schuster Speakers Bureau can bring authors to your live event. For more information or to book an event, contact the Simon & Schuster Speakers Bureau at 1-866-248-3049 or visit our website at www.simonspeakers.com.

DEDICATION

To my parents, James and Elizabeth, for emphasizing the importance of education and exposure; for being positive role models; for demonstrating the true meaning of family and friends. Your love is endless. I love you for being you.

To my husband, Ricardo, thank you for your love and support.

To my daughter, Jazmin, you are truly a blessing. I am proud of your accomplishments. Never give up.

To my sister, Zane, who would've thought when you asked me to edit the manuscript for *Addicted* that it would become a No. 1 bestseller? Or that a decade later, you'd evolve into a nationally bestselling author of thirty-plus books and write scripts for two popular TV series? Congratulations on your success.

To my sister, Carlita, a superwoman who mirrors many lifestyles as a wife and mother of four with a full-time career. Hats off to you.

To my brother, Deotis, may you rest in peace.

ACKNOWLEDGMENTS

I'd like to thank God for providing me with good health, mind and spirit. Through You all things are possible. You are the reason I was able to complete this novel despite a heavy workload and busy lifestyle as publishing director, editor, wife, mother, event planner and the list continues.

To daughter, Tangela, and your daughter, Savannah, hugs and kisses.

To Aunt Rose, congratulations on turning ninety-five. You are an amazing spirit and we celebrated your life with pride. You are truly the epitome of an angel, and we all are blessed to have you in our lives. We appreciate your huge heart, wisdom and love. May you continue to experience great health.

To Aunt Margaret, you are a wonderful aunt and mother. You and Aunt Rose represent North Carolina royally: kind spirits and good cookin'. My youth memories will always be cherished.

To Grandma Cardella, rest in peace. You were such a positive influence for all of your grandchildren. You were the pillar of the community and we loved you dearly. Thanks for showing us the meaning of kindness.

To all of my grandparents, you were special.

To my in-laws, Richard and Pearl, thank you for treating me as your own. To brother-in-laws, David P. and Jerry.

To my brother-in-law, David M.

To Sharon, since age thirteen, we have called each other "bestest" friend (you say I created that word). Although the distance keeps us apart, the bond continues. Your sisters, Lisa and Gail, are like my sisters.

To my "girls" ("Hey, girl"), Rhonda and Lena, we've celebrated years of our unique bond. I'm fortunate to have true friends from elementary school. To the other "girls": Donna, Susan, Myrna and crew. What's up, ladies?

To my friends (there are so many; please forgive me if I didn't include you as it was not intentional), Mamie, Sheila, Cheryl, Ardith, Deb, Teri, Tomi, George, Rico, Yvette, Reggie, Vicki (we go way back); Patricia, Maria, Noelle, Ola, Sandra, Eddie, Dwayne and Joyce T. Denise D., may you rest in peace, girl.

To my L.A. friends, Joyce and Curtis, China, Carolyn, Ruth, Diane and Sharon.

To my nieces and nephews, Andre R (you were like a son during childhood; thanks for being like a brother to Jazmin), Elizabeth, Jaxon, Arianna, Ashley, David, Aliya, Jewell (rest in peace), Andre J, Jonathan, Nicolas, Zachary, Malik, Greg, Stephanie, Brandon, Danielle, Aaron and Audrey. To my great-nieces and great-nephews.

To my godson, Brian, and his brothers, Adam and Nicolas.

To all of my extended Sherrill and Caldwell family.

To cousins Percy, Franklin and Alan, you are truly like brothers. Carl, you are a gem. Fidelina and Terry, Ronita, Debbie, Beverly and Nick, Francesca, Gloria Jean, Janet, Karen, Thomasina, Derek and Retha, Shirl and Ed, Jackie, Tamu, Isha, Zakiya, Rashida, Sunday, Kwesi, Dana, Jimmy, Melinda, Mercedes, Stephanie, Gregory and many more. To the "younger cousins," Trey, Bo, Alex, Brittany, Benza, Karlan, Dean, Ray-Ray, and all of the others too numerous to name.

To all of my extended Roberts family. Lewis (you left us in D.C. to return to N.C.), Erica (much success on your Asali Yoga Studio in Harlem), Sheilah Vance, Esq. (congratulations on your success as an author and publisher; it's running the family.) Dennis, I look forward to meeting you someday.

To my "new" family, on the Parker and Brooks sides. Aunt Pat, you always remember the special occasions. You do too, Aunt Mary.

To Aunt Barbara Ford, thank you for your advice and wisdom.

To Aunt Olivia, you were a joy. You always said I'd someday write my own book. I always remember your words about life: "If you ain't put nothin' in it, you ain't gonna get nothin' out of it." I can hear you laughing now.

To Uncles T, Carl and Cecil, thanks for you kindness.

To Jimmy, congratulations on your success; and Toni, great to connect with you.

To my godparents, the late Rev. L.C. and Myrtice Siler.

To my sisters' close friends, Pamela, Destiny, Pam, Cornelia, Dawn, Wanda, Debbie, Dionne, Tinera, Karyn, Michelle, Melba and Aurelia.

To the Strebor authors. As publishing director of Strebor Books, I have enjoyed working with you. Welcome to the family. Allison Hobbs and Cairo, you are special. Thank you for your continuous support. Allison, you are a true sister-author friend. It is a pleasure to do events with you. Special shout-outs to Strebor's Suzetta Perkins, Lee Hayes, William Fredrick Cooper, J. Marie Darden, Marsha D. Jenkins-Sanders, Rodney Lofton, Michelle Janine Robinson, Che Parker, Dante Moore, Earl Sewell, Oasis, Nane Quartay, Timothy Michael Carson, Shamara Ray, ReShonda Tate Billingsley, Pat Tucker, Harold L. Turley II, B.W. Read, Julia Blues, Stacy Campbell, Curtis L. Alcutt, N'Tyse, Brenda Hampton and Yolonda Tonette-Sanders. Curtis Bunn, this is our second time around (worked together in sports news). There are so many of you to name and the list keeps growing.

To Keith Saunders of Marion Designs, your talent is appreciated. Thank you for your incredible photography and design of our covers for Strebor. You are awesome. To Deb Schuler, thank you for your efficiency. You are the ultimate layout designer with an editor's eye. It has been a pleasure working with you both. I value our rapport as friends as well as business associates. Strebor is blessed to have connected with such professionals with wonderful personalities. As publishing director, I am in touch with you weekly and appreciate your quality work ethics and helping me make our deadlines.

To Yona Deshommes, my publicist at Atria/Simon & Schuster, thank you for all you do.

To my friends from the journalism world, Toni, Denise, Cheryl, Sunni, Richard, Ita, L'Taundra, Michael and Chris.

To fellow authors, I've met many of you through the years at Book Expo America, the National Book Club Conference and book festivals. Congratulations on your works.

To the HBCUs, particularly my Howard U. alumni; the North Carolina Central University crew (the fun continues); and Spelman, my sisters' former home. To Morgan State University, my daughter's second home.

To book clubs for showing your support to authors and appreciation for the written word. You are our backbone. Thanks to the clubs who hosted me and invited me as featured author.

To authors. After decades of working as an editor reading news stories, novels and nonfiction, I have even more respect for your craft and the process. Keep on writing. There will always be readers to appreciate your creative works.

CHAPTER 1
Shayla

Shayla Benson opened the glass doors and entered the elegant, brand-new building. She slipped off her sunglasses, stopped briefly to wink at the handsome security guard on duty, then sashayed across the granite lobby floor. Her cobalt-blue clingy dress was tasteful enough for office attire but flirty and attention-grabbing as it swayed with each of her steps. She headed toward the bank of elevators with her clicking stilettos and pretended to push the up button. Today she was riding solo. She'd given her private driver, Tony, the day off.

Suddenly, she faked that she had left something outside, reentered the lobby and walked in the opposite direction toward the rear of the building. Hopefully, no one had noticed. Mondays were usually light at New Visions, her public relations firm, where she spent several days each week. After all, she was the head honcho and could freely be off the clock anytime. Her assistant, Camilla, always managed to be on point. Her eight-employee office in Largo, Maryland was in capable hands.

Shayla exited out the building's rear doors where a black Town Car was waiting. She gazed to observe her surroundings before opening the car's back door. She gracefully slipped inside where a gentleman dressed in an all-black Armani suit kissed her lips, then offered her a flute of champagne.

She grasped the glass and the two toasted before they smoothly downed the refreshing Giaconda Chardonnay.

The driver pulled from the parking lot and eased toward the main street.

"Where are we headed?" Shayla inquired, snuggling up to Wilson and offering her best seductive smile.

"I'm not telling. I like surprises." Wilson placed his arm around her shoulder and pulled her even closer, caressing her tenderly. "You have to wait and see."

Wilson loved the shock factor. It was their ritual to meet in this fashion twice a month. Their adventures were unpredictable. He wasn't the bland type of guy and she couldn't wait to meet up with him whenever that time of month approached.

Shayla closed her eyes and relaxed her mind, eager to find out their destination. Would they be having each other for breakfast? *Hmmm.* She smiled to herself and then gazed into Wilson's eyes.

The account executive was precisely what the doctor ordered. Besides his handsome looks, he was suave and cool. However, his charming ways sometimes proved overbearing. Shayla had a nickname for him: "Mr. Class." It represented his gentlemanly demeanor. He made her feel like she was a reigning queen and he was a servant at her command.

The driver steered onto the main street and then the expressway.

Shayla felt her cell phone vibrate. She opened her purse and pulled out the phone to view the time. It was 9:10. She read the text message: *Good morning, my lovely. And how are you feeling? I trust all is well at the office.*

Shayla sighed, then her mind started racing on how to respond. *Having a great day. Miss you, sweetie. See you tomorrow. Will be wearing your favorite thong.*

Mmm-hmm…can't wait.

"What's all that sexting about?" Wilson asked, guessing the nature of her messages. "You're with me now. That's a little rude, don't you think?"

"What would you be concerned about? I'm with *you*." Shayla was defensive, then warmed up. "And, are you kidding? I can't ignore my *hubby*." She reached over and placed her right hand on his waist and snuggled even closer. "Can I?"

"No, I guess not." He relaxed his body and accepted her comfort. Shayla had Wilson wrapped securely around her pinkie. *Spoil me* were the words that bonded them. He was a sucker for a wild sexfest, especially mornings and afternoons. Both of them playing hooky from their offices was a stimulant for their sneaky rendez-vous. Wilson could easily slip away, claiming he was out on a sales call from his busy downtown D.C. securities firm. Whenever he didn't want snoopy trails on his own car, he hired a driver. He was willing to risk it all to be in the presence of Shayla, his dream bombshell.

Shayla gazed out of the window, the sun reflecting on her café au lait skin. Her piercing eyes were in deep thought. Her husband, Chad, was the ultimate spoiler who lavished her with expensive gifts and a luxurious lifestyle. Their custom-built, 8,000-square-foot estate with a brick and stone exterior and circular driveway nestled in the woods stated that she had arrived. Her enormous diamond ring had enough bling to be used as a flashlight.

Chad was a realtor extraordinaire, one of those multimillion-dollar sales folks who only had clients in a high-level tax bracket. His demanding position required him to travel frequently to serve clientele on both coasts. Today he was in Beverly Hills where his college classmate, Pierce Collins—born Dennis Jones—had hooked him up with home sellers that he'd met through his cosmetic surgery practice. It was a viable connection and Chad was reaping the benefits. In fact, so was Dr. Collins, who received a commission for each deal that Chad turned from his patients.

Shayla was aware that Chad was the ideal husband that any young girl would desire. He seemed to literally worship her and live his life to provide a comfortable world for both of them. They had recently celebrated their fifth wedding anniversary and the one missing link was a child. At thirty-three, Shayla felt the second hand quickly moving on the clock, but she was skeptical about being a parent. She was determined to keep her figure and she wasn't certain about dividing her time. Not that she was self-ish but despite the pressure rising from Chad, she didn't find that now was the right moment. Maybe somewhere down the line, she would realize it was time to succumb and welcome a child into their prestigious world.

The driver steered off the expressway, then proceeded along twists and turns on rural roads before stopping at a private entrance. A "No trespassing" sign awaited them as they crept slowly on the long dirt driveway surrounded by trees. Shayla gasped at the sight of a landmark in the image of a castle. The massive stone façade was jaw-dropping.

"Wow! What in the world?" she asked in disbelief of the story-book setting.

"Now this is what you call a *home*. Breezy Bend belonged to my great-grandfather who was a successful farmer who amassed a fortune," Wilson explained as they slowly approached the spectacle. "We've kept it in the family for a century. Yes, you could call it a plantation but we razed it to a castle. My grandmother was obsessed with *Cinderella* and *Sleeping Beauty* and all those tales, so she wanted to create her own fantasy."

"*Fantasy* isn't the word."

The driver parked in front of the awesome palace's circular driveway. Wilson walked around to open the door for Shayla. She stepped out onto the steps as he led her to the huge ten-foot double doors. Once inside, Shayla truly felt like a queen. She walked through the foyer in amazement, soaking up the classic features in the sprawling replica of a castle. Tall ceilings and candle-lit sconces were throughout.

Wilson clutched her hand and proudly led her up the spiral staircase and into one of seven bedrooms. This one he called the Grapevine, where three bottles of fine wine sat on a table. He motioned to them. "The choice is yours."

Shayla walked over and picked up each bottle, reading the labels intensely. Which one spoke passion? She was unfamiliar with them and chose a Riesling.

Wilson uncorked and poured the wine in two crystal glasses. He handed her one and they toasted again. "Cheers to the Grapevine."

"Cheers," Shayla repeated, then sipped. "Hmm, this is delicious."

Wilson led her to a corner loveseat opposite a huge window where trees formed a scene from a Southern romance novel.

"This place makes me feel back in the day. It also makes me feel like somewhere in the South, my homeplace, New Orleans. We had a lot of mansions and plantations surrounded by weeping willows. This really takes me back."

Shayla's mind drifted to her school nights and weekends helping her dad in his extremely successful restaurant, Chez La Vie, in the French Quarter. She, too, had a background where traditions were full of pride and a valuable property had been handed down. Her dad's father had opened the popular spot on the tourist map, and its Creole-Soul cuisine was worth waiting in long lines to experience. Shayla knew the family recipes by heart, although since married, she rarely spent time in the kitchen. If it were up to her, Chad might as well have put a sofa in it. However, her private chef, Natalie, was a talent to be reckoned with. Her dinners were prepared fresh with a creative spin, spoiling Shayla to evacuate from her own state-of-the-art kitchen. One day soon she would put her memory to test and show Chad once again that she still possessed her cooking skills.

Shayla was proud of her New Orleans heritage, although depending on her state of mind, her not-so-proud experience would ease its way in and block her thoughts. Shayla was the exemplary honors student at her high school. Even voted as the Most Likely to Excel. She also was the victim of an awful crime.

Being a standout cheerleader with a coveted, curvy figure had all the jocks craving for her attention. Only one player, tight end Rod Richardson, would be able to woo her as his girlfriend. The six-foot-five athlete at 235 pounds reminded her of a bodyguard who would protect her to no end. Girls often proved jealous and gritted on her for being the center of attention. Sometimes she was threatened and accused of trying to steal their boyfriends, or their so-called boyfriends. Shayla ignored their behavior and always held her head high with the utmost confidence. It wasn't that she was snooty, but she had to emit a hard exterior to avoid physical attack. The verbal assaults were devastating, but she never could show that her knees could buckle.

During her senior year, following a football team victory, Rod suggested they meet in their favorite spot, an abandoned house near the wooded area of the field. Shayla agreed and wrapped up in her light fall jacket. While waiting for Rod, she attempted to make herself warm during the cool evening temps. After fifteen minutes, Rod finally entered and closed the door in the bedroom where a few blankets were piled on the floor. They both undressed and as he stripped off his last piece of clothing, suddenly, they were barraged by five of his teammates. Shayla felt so ashamed as each of the five brutally raped her, one by one, taking turns as they ran a train on her. She was so frozen and shocked at eighteen that she couldn't get out a scream, only tears and whimpers. Rod, the only one whom she trusted, not only as a boyfriend but a friend, had planned the ultimate setup. She'd never said a word... to anyone.

"Are you okay?" Wilson noticed Shayla's mental state had changed, and he didn't think it was the effects of the wine.

"Yes, I'm fine," she lied, zooming back from her past. Now she wasn't sure she was in the mood. The sun was bright and peered through the windows, but at this moment, it didn't provide an uplifting mood. Her mind was in a dark place. But she needed this badly and she zoned out. This time, she led Wilson by the hand and headed toward the four-poster canopy bed. *Mr. Class, take me away from darkness. I need a dose of sunshine.*

New Visions was abuzz. It was always the case whenever a celebrity was expected in the office. Word spread like wildfire that a local and hopeful national hip-hop star was due for a 2:00 appointment with Shayla. In fact, whispers on the previous day alerted the staff from the youthful and fashionable to the wannabe cougars to the prudish, seventy-five-year-old Joan who refused to retire. So all had arrived in full force in their pick-me-up outfits, with heels reigning supreme.

When the clock struck 1:50, the ladies started to emerge and place themselves strategically along the burnt-orange and olive-green sofas. Some stood in the hallway or pretended to cross back and forth between offices. Shayla's male staff members were cool and visibly smirked at how this visitor brought out the wolves. All were aware that Shayla had a tendency to arrive barely before her scheduled appointments. Today was also a Wednesday when she often was late.

Shayla stopped in the ladies room on the first level and freshened up. She smoothed on her lipstick and straightened her hair to ensure each strand was in place. Satisfied, she left and walked to the elevator. When she entered her office suite, everyone quickly maneuvered to get in their respective places. Little did she know that it had been a chatfest before she'd arrived.

"Good morning...sorry, good afternoon. I'm still confirmed for my two o'clock, right?" she asked Camilla.

"Yes, ma'am," Camilla responded, smiling about the prior scene, direct from a beauty pageant lineup.

"What did I tell you about calling me 'ma'am'?"

"Mrs. Benson," she corrected. "How's your day so far?"

Shayla looked to see who was present. "It's been wonderful." She smiled. *Yes, Class made sure of that. He keeps me satisfied. Pleasure comes before business.* Despite her scheduled appointment, Shayla had ensured that her hump day started with a taste of Class.

"I'll be in my office when Mr. Harrison arrives. You can bring him back." Shayla strutted toward her office.

"Wow, you got a lotta pretty ladies up in here." Blaze looked over at his bodyguard who nodded in agreement and then continued to peruse a magazine. "I wouldn't get *any* work done."

"Thank you and I'm sure you are used to pretty women wherever you go." Shayla smiled at the tall glass of chocolate who was displaying his muscular physique in a form-fitting, black T-shirt.

"You know it. That's one of the best things about performing. They follow me and my entourage," he admitted, nodding toward Tory, who resembled a henchman. "But sometimes you can get tired of the groupies and wanna settle down, nah what I'm sayin'?"

"True, I understand." Shayla unconsciously rubbed her ring finger. Marriage was a blessing, but sometimes you wanted a fling— except in her case, it was *always*. She cleared her throat. "How may I assist you, Mr. Harrison?" she asked, putting on her A-game.

"Please, call me Blaze."

"Mr. Blaze," she corrected.

He explained how he had become an Internet sensation, a popular D.C. artist whose style was a mix of homegrown go-go and hip-hop. The younger staff already had informed her of his crowd-pleasing antics. He incorporated gymnastics in his act. He was eager to move on to the national scene with live performances and expand his career. He didn't want to become a one-hit wonder like so many of those who had inspired him. A makeover could assist in turning his world around. He needed sponsors and distribution.

Blaze, aka Robert Harrison, had grown up in Northwest D.C. where drug dealers attempted to recruit him to no avail. His mother had put the fear in him at a young age after her older son had been gunned down in the streets. She was overprotective of Blaze and encouraged him to pursue a natural talent. At sixteen, Blaze hooked up with neighborhood kids and formed a band. He was the lead singer and they performed regular gigs throughout the city. Now he was on his own and ready to continue the ride.

New Visions and Shayla Benson had a reputation for not only

salvaging images but creating positive ones. As he shared his life story with her, he was uplifted by her vibe—smooth and assuring. Shayla jotted notes and promised she would come up with ideas for a future discussion.

"Ooo, baby, baby! Aw, right there. Yes, baby." Shayla bit her tongue to keep from being a screaming fire alarm, waking up the hotel's residents. Blaze continued to pound her as she was positioned on the wet bar of his lavish suite at the Marriott. His thrusts penetrated deeply as she gripped his back and pulled him toward her with a vengeance. She tossed her hair from side to side as sweat dripped from her forehead. She didn't want to end up looking like a scarecrow and would be reluctant to see her fresh do gone limp. *Oh, well, I can make another trip to the salon, but I can't always get this kind of young loving.*

Blaze was ten years her junior and it was rare for her to connect with a younger man, especially one with a taste of thug. She mostly hooked up with mature, established men whom she encountered in her upscale world. But it was something about Blaze that was raw and real and she *loved* it. She had a penchant for creating nicknames for her side jobs and decided she would call Blaze "Raw." After their initial meeting, they had decided to meet at his hotel suite two days later. Shayla was about her PR business, but she also was on a mission for a sexual adventure. Why not mix business and pleasure?

"Ooh, I like it rough…keep going, baby…" Shayla was almost breathless while Blaze was quietly being fulfilled. Blaze was like a determined quarter horse in a race to the finish line. He banged her intensely and was all about satisfaction. Finally, they both exploded and she collapsed onto his shoulders.

CHAPTER 2
Kyle

"May I get you another drink, miss?" the beach bartender inquired.

"Yes, thanks. I'll try your Lava Flow." Kyle Andrews was working on number four, sampling various tropical drinks, as she bathed in the brilliant sun. She was beginning to feel her head spinning like she was on a merry-go-round. She'd need to stabilize herself so she wouldn't look dizzy or ditzy when she arose. Her once light caramel tone had turned to copper after the chaise lounge had become her home for the day. It had started with the most exclusive massage on the spa menu. Jamaica was by far her favorite island, but she had ventured to Tortola in the British Virgin Islands.

The hotel staffers had vied for her attention. Kyle was thirty-two, gorgeous with natural hair and a figure with curves carved from decades of ballet and jazz dancing. Her smooth, silky skin resembled a newborn's. A week's worth of continuous flirting and compliments had made her realize that a Caribbean adventure had been a wise choice. And she appreciated that she had made the trip alone.

Kyle and her husband, Bryce, still considered themselves newlyweds after two years. The honeymoon had continued and seemed to end abruptly after Kyle had miscarried. Bryce had decided he wanted a child with his lovely wife. She had desired to work toward her lifetime career goals, then parenting would be an option. However, Kyle gave in to Bryce's wishes and after discovering she was expecting, her interest heightened. She was excited about experiencing motherhood. She would put opening up a dance studio for youth on hold.

Then her world came crashing down two months ago when she lost her baby. Now here she was on the serene sand, sipping on drink after drink to ease her mental pain. Since the incident, Bryce had become distant and his personality had turned sour. Maybe it was his way of dealing with their darling's departure from the world before even entering. She had decided to let him have his mental and physical space, venture to a tropical destination, and when she returned, hopefully, they would be off to a fresh start.

Instead of focusing on the miscarriage, when she returned home, she would move forward positively with her plans to help youth through dance. She actually had toyed with incorporating modeling and etiquette in her curriculum. So many young ladies needed a bright outlook on life, and it was her dream to share her lifelong dedication to dance. All those years of vigorous training and performing on New York stages would benefit others.

"Is this your first time in Tortola?" The bartender set the glass on the tiny table planted in the white sand.

"Yes, but I guarantee you it won't be the last." Shayla smiled, then picked up her drink. *I think I deserve a lobster dinner tonight.*

Bryce was nowhere in sight at the terminal at Thurgood Marshall Baltimore-Washington International Airport. Her instinct was that he was late since that was his M.O. She was totally the opposite and insisted on being on time. She would wait outside for another fifteen minutes and then call him. A half-hour was over the top. She had talked to him via Skype the evening before and he promised he would be at the airport. *I hope this isn't one of these days he disappears.*

As she reached in her purse for her cell phone, a black Mercedes rolled up and its driver parked and stepped out. "Mrs. Andrews?" he asked, identifying her by a written description.

"I'm Mrs. Andrews and you are—"

"Bryce, your husband, sent me for you." The driver opened the back door to allow Kyle to get inside, then placed her suitcase in the trunk. He had been puzzled why Bryce didn't want to alert her to look out for his car.

"I see. Why did he make this arrangement?"

"Sorry, ma'am, I can't answer that. I'm only doing what I was hired to do."

And here I was trying to show off my Caribbean-baked body. Kyle was prepared to tease Bryce by wearing a sleeveless, low-cut, fuchsia dress. She had even opted to wear stilettos in lieu of her standby travel flats. It was all to be foreplay before she turned him out in the bedroom.

She leaned back and sighed. *Maybe he has a big surprise in store for me, or maybe it's another one of his vanishing acts.*

CHAPTER 3
Amber

Amber strutted throughout the aisles of Lord & Taylor in Tysons Corner. Her voguish attire exuded that she had walked off the cover of a high-end fashion magazine. Her black raw silk dress with chunky jewelry and large dangling earrings made her a standout. After making her favorite stop in the women's shoe department, she selected one of the latest trends on display. Her regular salesclerk spotted her and already knew her size. She was aware how her weekly visitor rolled: she would want the identical shoe in all available colors.

These would be added to her overstocked closet designated simply for her shoe collection. Sure, it was over-the-top with more than 500 pairs, but she had it like that. Shoes, clothes, handbags and jewelry gave her the ultimate high.

Today she had decided to bring her personal assistant, Zodi, a sweet, patient twenty-something who was raised in D.C. and still in search of her destiny. Zodi was her confidante and truly was a savior when it came to hiding the truth from Amber's wealthy husband, pro-baseball first baseman Trevor Trent. The Washington Nationals considered him among their top lineup, and he had been voted Most Valuable Player when they'd earned their division championship title.

Zodi would often stash Amber's brand-new purchases in hidden compartments throughout the house. It wasn't that Trevor chastised

Amber for her shopping sprees; he thought they were excessive. He loved her style and basking in the limelight with a trophy wife by his side. So if shopping to look good was her priority, then so be it. The reality was that he wouldn't be young and athletic infinitely. At some point, it made sense to focus on saving instead of spending. They planned to start a family soon, and he would set the children financially for life.

Their palatial mansion, designed by a popular local architect and featured in the *Washingtonian* magazine, was proof of their upscale existence. He was a country boy from the rural suburbs in Maryland and had grown up on a farm. He learned the necessity of hard work and how it would always pay off in the end. Fine things in life were not his goal. If he'd had it his way, he would have settled for a moderate-style house surrounded by acres of land. To satisfy his lovely wife whom he simply adored, Trevor agreed to build a dream house for his bride. He often wondered if it had been a mistake. Amber was obsessed with adding decor to their already magnificent home and definitely her own closets. It was overkill. Sure, he had bank with his multimillion-dollar contract, but he'd heard about pro athletes ending up broke, and he was determined he wouldn't join them in the ranks.

After returning from her shopping spree, Amber felt a pang of guiltiness as she climbed the spiral staircase. She turned around and looked down at Zodi. "Thank you, Zodi, for having my back," she whispered.

"No problem. I got you." *Boss lady sure has an obsession. She's a closet over-the-top shopper.* She stealthily walked to an area in the sunroom where she hid Amber's latest possessions.

CHAPTER 4
The Wives

A mber made her grand entrance into Canyon restaurant after valet parking her convertible. It was her knockaround, every-day ride that she cherished. At thirty, she was a thrill seeker who found joy zipping through the suburbs on back roads. It appeared she was first to arrive.

She asked the maître d' for a table for three and was seated by a window. The sunlight's reflection on the copper walls provided a peaceful ambience. She smoothed out her turquoise dress and crossed her legs to show off her latest sandals.

"May I start you off with something to drink?" a waitress inquired.

"Water with lime for now. I'll wait on the others. Thanks." Amber pulled out her iPad and started perusing her favorite retail online sites. *Gotta have these.* A new line of spring dresses was featured in a special. She clicked her size 8 and pressed to order all six colors. She ensured the delivery address was at her neighbor's house. Her girl, Jaslyn, would cover for her. After all, Amber usually showered her with routine gifts, throwing in an extra order occasionally.

"Hey, girl." Shayla approached and startled Amber, who quickly closed her tablet. She never shared her shopping sources. "Hope we didn't keep you waiting too long."

"Oh, no, you're right on time." *Damn, I didn't get to finish my order...*

Shayla, dressed in a tan dress, and Kyle, sporting a bronze strapless dress, sat and then grabbed their menus. Amber placed her tablet in her purse and then checked out the menu.

Amber, who sometimes practiced a vegetarian lifestyle, ordered a Greek salad. She veered from her diet when she attended parties with Trevor. Seafood and steak were the norm at these high-end events and she had no issues giving in to temptation. Shayla ordered a chicken club sandwich and Kyle decided on linguine. A bottle of wine graced the table, then another bottle and another.

"So, ladies, how are you? And how's everyone's hubby doing?" Amber asked teasingly.

"I'm sure yours is getting ready for the playoffs soon," Shayla responded knowingly.

"Oh, yes, they were spectacular this season. I can't wait until they *win* the whole shebang. We plan to have a grand party at the house."

"You mean *mansion*. You are quite the entertainer," Kyle added.

"With help, of course. Jaslyn always volunteers to help since that's her forte." Amber enlisted her assistance, not only to sneak shipments to her home, but she owned her own event planning firm and had such clients as the Washington Redskins, local celebrities and politicos.

"Chad's due back tomorrow. He's been gone two weeks now." Shayla perked at the thought of seducing her husband in a sexy drama. "I can't complain though. He's turning the deals. Real estate is thriving on the Coast."

"I'm sure you'll be jumping his bones." Amber laughed.

"*Knockin'* his boots," Shayla teased.

Amber looked at Kyle. "So, tell us about your Tortolaaaaa island adventure."

"It was faaaannntastic. Guess you could tell I was still thinking

I was there, lying on that white sand and sipping on mojitos," she responded, snapping back from her faraway gaze.

"Well, tell us about the eye candy 'cause that goes hand in hand." *Hmm-mmm*, Shayla thought.

"Girl, what you doing asking about eye candy?"

"It doesn't hurt to look." *Especially when I'm always on the hunt.* Shayla smiled and downed another glass of wine. She needed not get too tipsy or she'd say a little too much. Her girls were her girls, but she hadn't revealed that she was one horny chick forever in search of a sexual fix.

"Hey, but I will say there was this one native guy who definitely caught my eye all right." Kyle licked her lips playfully and smiled. "I was naughty but nice…teasing him a little, enough for him to keep the flirting on. I made sure I wore my cutest bathing suit and had my skin all shiny and glistening in the sun. Humph, I gave *him* some body candy."

"Like I said, there's nothing wrong with looking. Just don't touch, huh?" Shayla was even fantasizing about the islander's image.

Amber felt awkward but decided to turn the conversation in a serious direction. "Kyle, did the getaway help your state of mind?"

"It's okay to say it…I lost the baby, and yes, Tortola did take me away to another place. It opened up my mind to see that perhaps it wasn't meant to be. Maybe it wasn't my time." Kyle sipped her wine. "I'm a newlywed, still young, and I can prayerfully give birth in the future."

"How's Bryce? Is he acting better, more understanding?" Shayla inquired.

"He's cool." Kyle thought back to her arrival home a week ago and how Bryce wasn't there to meet her with a loving hug and kisses. She direly needed to be in his embrace after her loss. "Although, he didn't even…" She paused after realizing she wasn't ready to share details of his behavior upon her return. That night he'd acted indifferently, and after offering a lukewarm hug, they slept in the same bed, but it was like a petition divided them. She simply chalked it up as his way of coping with grief.

"What was that?" Shayla sensed there were other thoughts she was holding back.

"Nothing." Kyle paused. "He didn't even say he was sorry," she lied, realizing she almost slipped and told them about his absence at the airport.

"Awww." Amber touched her hand and nodded. "It'll be all right."

"Thanks." Kyle resisted the eruption of watery eyes. She had shed enough tears. It had meant the world to Bryce to welcome a child under his wing, and she believed that it would secure their relationship. She still had newlywed jitters and didn't feel a hundred percent that their bond was solid. Bryce's sometimes strange behavior possibly would change for the better if a child were in the picture. She had learned that money truly didn't always bring you happiness.

"I'm here for you. Feel free to call me anytime," Amber reassured. She looked at Shayla, then Kyle. "We need to regroup. So, what about a ladies' night? Hell, maybe a weekend."

"I'm game." Although she was only a week away from returning from Tortola, Kyle immediately felt her tension ease. She could use another getaway.

"And I'm in, too," Shayla agreed.

"Well, chickadees, where and *when*?" Amber was eager to get the ball rolling with their plans.

"Since I just came back from Tortola, I'll let you two decide. As long as there's a bar, a spa and food, it doesn't matter to me," Kyle stated.

"And shopping…I *must* get some souvenirs," Amber added.

"Souvenirs?" Shayla teased. "Girl, you won't be in the gift shops; you'll be in the designer boutiques."

Amber and Kyle laughed.

"True, but I won't be selfish. I'll bring back gifts."

"Let's go someplace where none of us have been." Amber closed her eyes and reopened them. "What about the Poconos?"

"Sounds like a plan," Shayla agreed.

"I won't be able to shop for cute heels in those mountains." Amber chuckled.

CHAPTER 5
Shayla

T he calming scent of lavender and chamomile penetrated Shayla's nostrils as she immersed in her Jacuzzi. She was so comfortable she'd have to be careful not to drift to sleep. She looked at the time and calculated when Chad would arrive. It had been two weeks and she could feel the tingle between her thighs. It was all she could do not to jump in his arms and wrap her legs around his waist when he opened the door.

Her plan was to prepare a delectable dinner, then unleash her desires to make up for his time away. Suddenly, she felt a tinge of guilt. She had fulfilled her needs multiple times during Chad's absence. She trusted he had not played around while on the West Coast. She always considered herself an infidelity detective. There would be some clue.

Shayla softly smoothed the washcloth while Kem played in the speakers. She stepped out and gracefully layered her skin with lotion before spritzing on his favorite perfume, Euphoria. She slipped on her latest investment, a hot pink halter babydoll, and layered it with a sheer black lace kimono. Her strappy black sandal heels showed off her fresh pedicure. She would greet him at the door like she was auditioning for the Playboy Club.

Shayla glided down the stairs and headed for the gourmet kitchen with tall black cabinets and granite countertops. It was a chef's dream. Tonight's New Orleans menu reminded her of evenings after school helping out in her dad's restaurant. And one of her experiments, red velvet cheesecake, was already in the refrigerator.

The preparation triggered thoughts of how cooking was no longer her best friend. It had become her enemy. How shameful since she was from a family of chefs. Sometimes she realized that Chad was a hot catch, and one of the reasons she had snagged him was her kitchen skills.

Tonight she wanted to make Chad feel super special, pulling out all stops to make him feel like a king. She had given their chef/live-in housekeeper, Natalie, the night off. Her darling hubby would be all hers, and if she wanted to swing from the chandelier, she could do that. If her wish was to play naked tackle on the sunroom floor, it would be fine, too. Tonight, their mansion in Prince George's County, Maryland was all theirs.

Shayla was familiar with Chad's schedule as he routinely took the same evening flight from L.A. on Fridays. She paced back and forth from the kitchen into the formal dining room, ensuring that her fresh, brilliant-colored flowers were creatively placed and the scented candles were all aglow. Ambience and structure were extremely important to Chad. He was a stickler for everything in its place.

A graduate of the prestigious Wharton School's MBA Program, Chad was raised in a prominent Philadelphia family. The Bensons were big in politics and socialites who were popular on the party scene. He never suspected he would unite with a Southern girl as he'd only dated Northerners. It was something about her innocent smile and gorgeous looks that captivated him. Her twang was also appealing and cute, although much of it had diminished through the years of living in the D.C. area.

The key in the lock sounded off her body alarm. She giggled as she realized she was acting like a teen newlywed. She would tame down and appear humble. It had been six years ago when she'd laid eyes on him at a gas station and he offered to fill her tank. Her mother and grandmother had always told her that church was the ideal place to find a man of substance. She'd found it amusing when she found her soul mate at the pump.

Chad opened the front door and was pleasantly surprised to find Shayla waiting in the foyer. His chocolate skin radiated as he looked piercingly at his wife's sexy ensemble, undressing her with his eyes. He sported a navy, custom-made Italian suit with a butterscotch-colored tie. He set his luggage at the door and closed it.

"Lady, you look marvelous. I see what I've been missing." He embraced her and then kissed her lovingly. They released their locked lips.

"Thank you, Mr. Handsome. I really missed you, sweetie."

"I missed you, too."

"Smells delicious. What did Natalie prepare?"

"I gave her the night off. I fixed dinner."

"You did what?" Chad was in disbelief. "You, Miss-I'm-Not-Wearing-a-Chef-Hat, how did you decide to cook?"

"I figured you'd be surprised. It's been a while."

"At least six months, but twice a year is good. I'll take it." He laughed.

Shayla grabbed his hand and led him to the formal dining area. "Let's eat. I'm starving."

"Can't wait." He followed her, checking out her sensual vision. "That's if I can finish the meal. You're looking *good*. I'm not sure I'll last."

She glanced back at him and smiled. "Oh, we have alllll night."

"That we do." *I soon will feel the jetlag, but I can't deprive myself of any treats. Plus, I'm sure Shayla has been itching for this lovin',* he thought proudly. Chad pulled out a chair and sat at the table with sparkling china and crystal wineglasses. In the center was a chilled bottle of Shiraz. "Hmm, you've added a new brand to our collection."

"Oh, yes, you're gonna love this one." Shayla changed her disposition and guilt spread over her face. Thankfully, she was still in the kitchen where Chad couldn't see her expression. *I'll never let on that Mr. Class turned me on to the wine.* Thoughts drifted of her morning at the castle and how she would love to repeat that visit in the near future. *Shame on me.*

Chad entered the kitchen and approached her from behind, wrapping his arms around her waist. "Hmm, that looks scrumptious," he noted, watching her slowly stir the aromatic seafood gumbo.

"Oops, better not make me burn myself." Shayla was startled and almost jumped out of her skin. "Thanks," she said, relaxing and acknowledging his compliment. "It's rare to see me with a fork and spoon unless I'm eating." She laughed. "My grandparents are probably turning over in their graves after they shared all the family recipes with us and their granddaughter is rarely utilizing her skills."

"Well, I'm sure Natalie is enjoying her break. She's a great cook, but my baby can burn even better."

"Awww, that's sweet of you." She grabbed a large bowl from the cabinet and scooped gumbo into it.

Chad walked to the sink, washed his hands and placed the garlic bread in a basket lined with a silk napkin. He removed the wine cork device off the counter. They carried their meal and placed it on the dining room table.

Throughout dinner, they made small talk and caught up on what had transpired during Chad's absence. Shayla was tickled that she couldn't rest her mind from thinking about sex.

"You have room for the red velvet cheesecake?" Shayla asked, rubbing her abdomen. "I'd better plan on a Zumba workout tomorrow."

"Sure. Now you know I'm not turning down dessert."

Shayla went to the refrigerator and returned with the cake.

"You did your thing." Chad tried a forkful. "Deelicious."

"Thanks. This was my first time trying the recipe." She tasted a piece of her slice. "Not bad." She looked at Chad. "So business went well this trip?"

"Definitely. And I'm working on some new clients for you." He looked at Shayla. "How's your business going? Any more clients? You told me about the hip-hop guy. What's his name again?"

"Oh, it's Blaze."

"Blaze? Yes, it's Blaze." *And boy, is he on fire.* "He's local and looking to expand."

"Out in L.A., that's all day long. I've met a few music gurus and can do some networking on my next trip."

Chad was extremely supportive of Shayla and her entrepreneurial role. When they'd married, he considered her a trophy wife and would have loved to have kept her home. Take care of her and treat her like the queen that she was. But her desire to own a PR firm wasn't simply a dream; he could finance her project. So New Visions was born. He easily extended his bankroll for start-up costs as well as the furnishings of her elegant office suite. Chad was proud that her venture had been a success and he was committed to helping her build a future.

Some of his buddies bragged about their stay-at-home wives

who relished their picket-fence lifestyles. Chad adored that Shayla was not only beautiful, but she had a driven personality and could hold her own. He viewed her as fearless and take-charge. The only missing link was the patter of tiny feet in their home. Maybe someday that dream would also come alive.

Chad stood in the shower and revitalized so his energy would be up for Shayla, who had unbelievable stamina in the bedroom. After he stepped out, he dried off and smoothed lotion over his body. He could hear the sounds of Miguel's "Adorn" floating from the bedroom's ceiling speakers. Shayla truly was the queen of seduction, a vampire temptress between the sheets. Sometimes they'd act out their favorite TV and film characters. Tonight, it would be straight, no-chaser.

Wrapped with his towel around his waist, he walked into the bedroom. *Oh, maybe not. Looks like it's game time.* Shayla was sprawled across the bed on her back. She'd stripped off her cute babydoll and top.

"Come here," she demanded enticingly. "I had to think of a new game for us. I'm going to test your senses—your nose and your tongue—smell and taste. Oh, that's a cute name. Smell and Taste. Better yet, Sniff and Taste." She giggled.

Chad approached and removed his towel, dropping it on the floor. He stood above the bed where Shayla had rolled back their comforter and lay on their 1,200-count Egyptian sheets. The lighting was dim and as the crooner's voice wailed in stereo, it was time to get the party started.

"Okay, so tell me how to play." He sat on the sheets and stared at her lovingly.

"I have some new oils and I've rubbed a different one on each breast, one on my navel and one in my coochie. You have to sniff and guess the scent, then enjoy the flavor."

"You have a hell of an imagination." He shook his head playfully. "I never know what to expect." He reached over and massaged her left breast, bent over and sniffed. "Lemon?"

"You're right. That's an easy one."

Chad licked her breast gently and then lowered his nose over the right one. "Peppermint."

"Correct again."

He suckled her nipple tenderly, then released his tongue. "Now the navel." He lowered his body and breathed in the tantalizing scent. "Hmmm…this must be lavender." He tickled her navel with his soft licks.

She jumped slightly. "You are too good at this game."

"Well, let's see if I can guess this one." He moved toward her cat as she wiggled it teasingly. "Babe, I think you got me this time."

"Finally," she teased, satisfied he hadn't guessed all of the scents. "It's a mix: mandarin and vanilla."

He entered with his tongue and stroked her clit. "Oh, yes, oh, yes." Chad continued to enjoy her nectar, then raised his body up, slowly inserted his joy rod, then plunged deeply inside her. He rocked Shayla's world before they both reached a peak and came in a burst of heated passion.

CHAPTER 6
Kyle

Kyle lay on a cushiony chaise longue in the sunroom of her master bedroom of her Prince George's County home. She munched on Oreos and downed them with sweet tea. The flat-screen TV was simply on for background noise. She was fidgety and fighting insomnia. She looked at the clock: 12:30 a.m. *Where in the world is Bryce? He told me he'd be home early tonight.*

Determined to stay awake until he arrived, Kyle continued to stuff snacks at this late hour. She was aware that it was bad for her figure and if caught, Bryce would get on her nerves with his complaints. He consistently irritated her whenever she enjoyed her sugar and fatty foods. If she found herself gaining a few pounds, she'd go on a crash diet and schedule workouts with her trainer.

When she heard the garage door open, she immediately cleared all evidence of her snackfest by stashing the wrappings under her chair pillow.

Bryce walked in the bedroom and was caught off-guard when he spotted Kyle.

"Well, I didn't think you were ever going to come home. Started to call out the National Guard," she teased, faking humor. Instead of appearing pissed, she did the reverse.

"Hey, sweetie, I apologize. I really do hate it when I promise you and don't deliver."

"You said you'd be getting here by ten." Kyle untied her bathrobe to seductively reveal her freshly lotioned body, still rich in tone from the island trip. "I'm sure you can't resist this."

Bryce walked over and sat at the foot of the chaise and played with her toes. "Babe, I've gotta be on the real. I am whipped, exhausted. I couldn't get it in if I tried." He sighed and then reached over and pecked her lips. "Rain check, okay?"

You have a lot of nerve. "Okay," she complied, then gritted when he stood up and walked into the bathroom to shower.

"Kyle, apologies again about last night." Bryce bit into his slice of wheat toast as he then scooped up a forkful of his cheese omelette. Kyle had prepared him a hearty breakfast while she limited hers to oatmeal and low-fat yogurt. After her midnight snack attack, she figured a light meal was in order.

"It's happening so frequently, though. You are away while I sit here playing the waiting game. What's up with the repair business? I thought it would be a low-maintenance venture. I realize it's new, but that's what managers are for."

"Right, but I have to stay on top of things. The only one I truly trust is myself."

Six months earlier, Bryce had opened three auto repair shops in D.C. He was from the city and it was ideal for locations to be convenient to his former neighbors, family and friends. With an already established clientele, he wouldn't need to rely on advertising. Word-of-mouth was always the best form.

Kyle had toured the shops when they'd first opened, but grease and glamour didn't mix in her eyes. It had been four months since she'd stopped in.

"I was hoping we could finalize plans for the studio."

"Shoot," he responded.

"Well, once I hire the contractor to do the build-out, I'll be all set. I already have teachers for jazz, ballet, tap, Zumba, and need to find one for hip-hop. The girls are going to love it," Kyle added dreamily.

Bryce opened *The Washington Post* Metro section and flipped through the pages.

"Bryce, are you listening?"

"Of course. That's cool. Glad you're moving ahead." He scrolled down the page. "I was checking the numbers."

"I want your opinion," she insisted. "I'm thinking about adding an etiquette class. Teach the girls to act like ladies: how to walk, dress, set a table—I may even add modeling."

"Wonderful." Bryce looked up from the paper and smiled. "Do what your heart tells you to do. I'm all for it and will support you all the way."

Kyle soaked in his tender words. It was rare for him to show compassion. Often she viewed him as selfish and only in to his own pet projects. However, Bryce was as eager as Kyle to launch the studio. In his mind, it would offer something for her to focus on and steer her eyes and ears away from his own business.

In addition to a healthy investment her parents had provided, he had added funds to the project. While Kyle had attended Columbia University, graduating with a dual bachelor's degree in business administration and education, her life had been a challenge. Growing up in a modest home in New York with five siblings, her parents worked tediously to provide for their children. Top grades in high school had landed Kyle a full four-year scholarship to college. Her dad had toiled for decades as a railroad worker, and her mom was forced to retire her waitress job of forty-five years after she'd started having trouble with her knees and legs.

Lately, Bryce's track record was declining with his incognito moments.

"I'm meeting with Shayla and Amber tomorrow evening. They're going to help me finalize the end phase and plan the grand opening."

"Where?"

"Amber's house."

"You sure you don't be meeting up with some of the players in that camp? They have a lot of parties. Ballers be stopping through—"

"Bryce, I've been to a holiday party and a fund-raiser." She recalled that he had been invited on both occasions but had declined to attend without explanation. "Be for real."

"I am for real. I know what's up, *Mrs.* Andrews," he added suspiciously.

"No comment." Kyle was one to avoid confrontation, and she didn't feel up to being defensive. She couldn't imagine why Bryce occasionally hinted that she was a flirt or possibly involved in a side relationship. If she were Shayla, she could understand why he'd be suspecting. Shayla flaunted her figure and had a wandering eye. *Sure, I had a little fun flirting in Tortola, but that's not my thing. I was on vacation solo and figured there was no harm in working my new bathing suit. I couldn't wait to flirt with you when I returned, but you didn't even show at the airport.*

CHAPTER 7
Amber

Amber curled up her toes and wiggled them to tease Trevor. Lying on their king-sized bed, Trevor reached over and tenderly massaged her feet, exposing her fresh pedicure. He leaned up and suckled each breast, trailed his lips to her navel and then to her heated patch. Her waft of Clive Christian No. 1 perfume created excitement as he breathed in its tantalizing scent. She gently laid his body back and climbed on top of him, slowly inserted his manhood and then started grinding, imagining she was a cowgirl. She picked up speed and swirled her hips, then leaned over while Trevor enjoyed lapping her breasts. Their two drenched bodies continued with extreme force and uncontrollable passion before erupting into a breathtaking climax.

Needing to keep his strength for the playing field, Trevor could strategize his sessions and looked forward to making love with his adorable wife. Amber considered sex like a nonstop shopping spree.

What a way to start my morning. Amber headed to the bathroom to shower before cooking a gourmet-style breakfast, her favorite meal.

Growing up in a wealthy household in Oakland, California, she rarely had an opportunity to prepare dishes as the family's private chef was in-house. On weekends, she would create waffles and omelettes for her parents and younger sister, Autumn, whose unstable personality had led her to major in psychology at Stanford University. She hoped to someday extend her education to an advanced degree to open a practice as a therapist.

Amber had always described herself as a free spirit, a true Cali girl, laid-back and stress-free. She had spent years traveling up and down the Coast, from San Francisco to San Diego, soaking up all the West had to offer. The scenic and cultural experiences had provided a wealth of opportunities. Her traveling lifestyle led her to L.A. along with her best friend, Desiree, also a psych major, whom she had met in college. There Desiree had met a Dodger, who invited them to a Dodgers-Nationals after-party. Amber had locked eyes on Trevor. They maintained a coast-to-coast relationship for a year before Amber relocated to D.C. Their private wedding ceremony became public when a local magazine centerfold featured their lavish exchange of vows.

"Lady, breakfast is scrumptious. Thanks." Trevor kissed her on the lips. "You have to get ready for tonight with the ladies."

"Yes, Kyle wants our assistance with her studio opening. I'm also going to get their feedback on our project. We can have an event right here."

"Great idea."

Amber and Trevor both had a love for the game. Baseball was embedded in their families. Trevor was trained at elementary school age by his dad and uncles in Maryland. Amber, too, had spent countless days on the bleachers watching her father, uncle and cousins playing baseball. Times had changed through the years and the sport had become a dying pastime for African-

Americans. Television rarely captured a player in the likes of Jackie Robinson or Ken Griffey, Sr. let alone Satchel Paige or Cool Papa Bell of the Negro Leagues. The couple believed young males continued to focus on basketball or football, which they felt sparked false dreams. They wanted to demonstrate that in reality, slots were limited.

"The deal is that where I attended at Howard, there isn't a baseball program anymore. The same is true for many of the black colleges. They had to close the programs. Couldn't find enough interested or enough to give away scholarships," Trevor had pointed out during their initial conversation about creating a baseball program. "And if you know the facts, baseball is the highest-paid sport, not football or basketball. I want to ensure that these young people are aware. They don't think baseball is cool enough. Truth is, size doesn't matter. You have to rely on your skills."

They decided to launch the Diamond Dreams Foundation, a nonprofit organization, to open doors for young African-American males to learn about baseball. They would provide training, form Little League teams, and offer scholarships to prospective athletes. Ideally, they hoped some of the discontinued high school and college programs would be revived. In addition to shooting the hoops and running a touchdown, young men would reap benefits from swinging a bat and sliding into home plate.

CHAPTER 8
Kyle

Kyle pulled her luxury vehicle into the garage. She never quite felt like it was her home. Bryce had it tailored as a bachelor's pad complete with a man cave in the basement. Walls were decorated with sports memorabilia and an eighty-inch flat-screen was locked on ESPN and Xbox heaven. After their wedding vows, he allowed her a room to call her own and she dressed it as a den with brilliantly colorful furniture. She needed to feel uplifted in an otherwise dull environment. He had bought the three-level Colonial and it would not have been her first choice. Her dream house was a rambler. She was moving in to his abode and had to settle for his purchase.

Often she figured her life would be ideal reflected on the screen, particularly the ID Channel's *Who the Bleep Did I Marry?* Bryce had been successful in concealing that he was a closet control freak. Kyle considered she was under the microscope at all times. He needed the 9-1-1 on her whereabouts at all times. She was shocked that he didn't drill her about going to Tortola. She later guessed he was giving her space to cope with the loss of their unborn child.

She opened the garage door and entered the house through the kitchen. She switched on the light and then set her purse on the granite counter. She had looked at her cell phone upon getting in her car in Amber's driveway. She had missed a couple of calls from Bryce and texted him to indicate she was pulling out to head home. She'd had her phone buried inside her bag while at Amber's house. *Wow, I never heard it vibrate. Guess I was having too much fun.* They'd brainstormed and come up with creative ideas for both her dance studio grand opening and Amber and Trevor's upcoming fund-raiser. *I bet he's sleep by now.* It was after one a.m.

Amber had given her a large container of fruit salad that she'd enjoy with yogurt for breakfast. She opened the fridge to place inside and closed the door. She turned to pick up her purse, then head to the bedroom.

"Nice of you to come home."

Kyle jumped to hear Bryce's voice and see him standing in the doorway leading to the dining room. "Whew, you scared me." She sighed with relief. "Please, don't do that again," she said shakily.

"So, how was your little pow-wow?" Bryce walked in and stood at the counter.

Kyle smiled. "I'm really excited about the studio—."

"Do you know what time it is?"

She squinted her eyes and looked at the microwave clock. "One-eighteen."

"Exactly," he snarled. "You're supposed to be in by midnight."

"What? You mentioned something crazy like that before we got married, but I didn't take you serious."

"Well, I meant what I said…midnight."

"You've got to be kidding," she responded sassily. "I didn't even do that in high school."

Bryce gripped her by the arm and slung her into the edge of the corner desk.

Kyle attempted to catch her balance and reached to hold her

outer thigh where it had contacted the sharp corner. She slumped over, speechless.

Bryce looked at her with disgust, unable to connect with her eyes. "Next time, you'll know when the clock strikes twelve." He turned and arrogantly walked out of the kitchen.

CHAPTER 9
The Wives

"Cheers! Happy birthday to me!" Amber lifted her glass to toast Shayla's and Kyle's as the limo driver turned into the entrance. A large wooden sign read: *Pinebrook Haven* in huge block letters. "Welcome to the Poconos, ladies!"

"This scenery is gorgeous. Amber, you're a genius. You do it with class." Kyle absorbed the atmosphere along the tree-lined road leading to the resort.

"I try," Amber bragged. "Never been here, but thought let's try something different. Easy access, smooth ride. This is the big one, so why not do it up in style?"

She had celebrated thirty during a private weekend with Trevor. He'd surprised her with a trip to Paris where she shopped to her heart's delight. This was one time he didn't complain and let her loose in the boutiques like a toddler in a toy store. Amber was ecstatic with her haute couture designs. Now it was her girl time to celebrate with her closest friends and a weekend of bonding.

It appeared that Kyle had faced a challenge getting away from her possessive spouse. Bryce had irked her once when he'd questioned her for details of the special outing. He'd drilled her like a sergeant, and she was close to scrapping the invitation. He treated her like she was a teenager and he were the parent deciding whether to let her out of the house. Or an escapee from lockup. How could she continue to live with such an insecure fanatic, she wondered. *We've only just begun*, she thought of her newlywed status.

The driver pulled up in front of the lodge resembling a log cabin. Amber stepped out of the backseat of the limo to head inside to the front desk.

Shayla jumped out to follow her. "I'll go with you."

"Wow, we're used to mansions, but honey, this place is a fantasy paradise." Shayla observed the spacious three-level suite featuring bedrooms on each floor, wood-burning fireplaces and a private heated indoor pool. "Now, this is what I'm talking about." She walked into the bathroom on the first floor and gasped at the romantic, heart-shaped, sunken bathtub. *And this is where I should bring one of my honeys on my next visit.*

Shayla headed to the living room area. "Girl, you really did your thing picking out this place. It's a haven all right."

"I'd heard about it and thought it had all the amenities we could ever wish for," Amber stated.

"Well, you picked the right one," Kyle complimented.

Amber sank into the soft leather sofa and kicked off her heels, then slipped on some ballet flats.

"I was wondering if you were going to trek around here in those all day." Shayla laughed and glanced down at her own flats. "You're better than me. No stilettos in the mountains, honey."

"Make yourselves comfortable." Amber headed into the kitchen where the driver had placed the party trays. "When you're ready, there's plenty of food." She looked at the tote bag she'd had the driver fill with liquor at a local store. "And alcohol." She laughed. "I wasn't going to be stuck in these woods without the good stuff."

After the trio had changed into their loungewear, they gathered in the den on the U-shaped sofa and munched from the platters of cheese, crackers, wingettes, veggies and crab balls. Martini glasses lined the coffee table and smooth jazz softly provided a cozy background. Amber had concocted her special martinis and they were making their rounds. She was subtly preparing them to get in the mood for a tell-all game.

Amber stood up and walked to a table where she had laid a stack of cards. She sauntered back over to the group. "You ladies should be aware by now that I like surprises. So, I created this little game." She placed the hot-pink, purple and yellow cards on the table and pushed the platters to the side. "I guess it's the psych thing about me; get in to your minds." She giggled.

"It's all good, girl. Go for it," Shayla remarked, tipsy and feeling the effects of the cocktails.

"Cool with me. I could use some mental foreplay." Kyle poured another glass from the pitcher and sipped.

"This is how it works. Each card has a question and each of us will take a turn answering it," Amber instructed.

"Oh, I get it. We're getting ready to get personal." *But only so personal*, Shayla thought, realizing she had a heavy load she was unwilling to share.

"And whatever happens at Pinebrook Haven goes with the wind." Amber laughed. "It's all in fun and women needing to destress."

"Turn up that music a little." Shayla motioned to the stereo. "Better yet, change it to something funkier." She swayed her head. "That jazz is okay, but it's breaking my mood."

"No problem." Amber stood and walked to place her iPod on the docking station. She had several of the devices, all loaded with different choices: jazz, pop, romantic ballads, R&B, hip-hop and funk. She loved music and was ready to pump it up anytime.

Jay-Z and Justin Timberlake's "Suit & Tie" streamed through the speakers.

"That's what I'm talking about. Partayyyyy!" Shayla stood up and gyrated her hips while balancing her drink in her hand.

Kyle and Amber decided to join her, creating their own dance floor. Kyle started spinning, showing off her ballerina skills. After singing and lip-synching, they all plopped back on the sofa. Shayla had polished off her drink smoothly.

"Okay, I've got to put on our anthem. You can guess what this is." Amber went to the iPod and found the song reflecting her mission. Whitney Houston's "I'm Every Woman" created hysteria as the trio continued their dance party. Kyle took the lead and broke into an old jazz routine she had choreographed and performed on stage.

"Whew! I needed that." Kyle thought about how her life had been drab lately, how Bryce was back and forth with his mood swings, and how romance was on vacation. *I hope it's eating away at him that I'm here having a blast with the girls.* Sadly, she wondered how he would react when she returned to their home, full of beautiful tangible items but empty on love.

"Okay, ready for refills?" Amber poured another round of drinks from the pitcher. "Back to game time." She stood in front of Kyle and Shayla. "As I was saying, we answer each question and then the next person answers." She picked up a card after shuffling the deck. "I'll be first." She read the card. "Ooo-wee. This'll be interesting!"

"Who created the questions?"

"Yours truly!" Amber smiled and looked back at the card. "'*Where is the wildest place that you made love in your younger years?*' Notice I am asking *younger* as in teens or twenties. Not as in present, because I know we are freakaleaks!" She burst into laughter.

"Okay. You know I'm a Cali girl from the Bay area. Well, guess what? I gave my old boyfriend some nookie right below the San Francisco Bay Bridge. Can you imagine? It was so cold with that wind blowing up my skirt. I thought I would die, but I did go to heaven! The skyline was so gorgeous at night, and the city lights made me feel like the stars were twinkling down on us." Her eyebrows rose. "And he was hung…like a horse!"

"Hmm. I bet he was." Shayla could only imagine. She was tickled as she loved nights like this, opening up and bonding with the ladies.

Amber sat down and looked at Kyle. "Your turn."

Kyle arose and immediately felt embarrassment. "Well, if I must…Mine was outside, too. When I was at Columbia, this cool guy I met at the theater invited me to an after-party in Manhattan. It was one of those scenes out of a movie where all these folks were gathered on the rooftop of this condo. He lured me to a dark, secluded spot around the corner from the group. He jacked me up against the brick wall and we got it on right there, on the spot."

"And me, you want to know the wildest place I ever got it in? I don't think you'll believe this." Shayla expressively used her hands. "Those college days were the best. I had this crazy-ass brother I was hanging out with. And yes, he was from New Orleans, too. He convinced me to screw in the cemetery."

Oohs and *aahs* flowed from Kyle and Amber.

"No, you didn't."

"Girl, you *are* insane."

"After a night of partying, I got the nerve. But I couldn't believe it after the fact, like the next day. We got down in the graveyard, surrounded by all the skeletons buried above ground."

"That's right. They don't bury underground there," Kyle said.

"No, have to bury above sea level." She sadly thought about Hurricane Katrina and how it had devastated her beloved city.

"Okay, next. That's a hell of a spooky story," Amber suggested. She turned to Kyle. "You pull a card."

Kyle picked up the next card and read aloud: *"Pretend you were trying to hit on a celebrity. Name him and what would be your pick-up line?"* "Hmmm. Idris Elba. 'Hey, sweetie. You are a *fine* chunk of Godiva. I'd love to sample the whole box.'" She beamed.

"You got that right!" Shayla agreed. "This is tough…Ladies, I love them all. Terrence Howard, Laz Alonzo…Blair Underwood, Larenz Tate… Michael Ealy…they're a range of colors. I'd say to them, 'Honey, you got it going on. Have a little taste of this café au lait. You won't be disappointed in this true Southern Creole mix, straight from N'awlins." She burst into laughter.

"Don't forget Shemar Moore and Boris Kodjoe. Speaking of Boris, he's starring in *Addicted*, the movie based on Zane's first novel," Amber interjected. "Ooo, how could I forget the p-h-i-n-e Amin Joseph! He's got all of those hot, hot, *hot* love scenes in her *Jump Off* show." She fanned herself swiftly.

"Girl, all those brothas are *phine!*" Shayla added. She popped a cherry in her mouth from the martini glass and sucked it off the stem. *Hmm-mmm.*

Amber picked up the next card from the top of the deck. "Ooh, I like this one. *'What is your favorite fantasy?'*" She cleared her throat. "I could see myself stretched out on an island," she leaned back, "in my best bikini. One handsome guy is feeding me tropical fruit, while the other is going downtown on me."

"Ooo, double trouble." Shayla laughed. "Now that's my kinda scenario." She added, "For me, riding all night making love in a limo."

Kyle smiled. "Now, that would be a blast, particularly if it's someone you adored. Nonstop loving. Well, I'd go for spending the night on the rooftop of a city skyscraper. That sky-high experience in the old days has me craving for more of that action."

Shayla picked up a card. *"If you could create a sex toy, what would it be and what would you name it?"* She thought briefly. "Pussy Tamer to calm down my kat when it's hyperactive and working overtime." She laughed.

"Hmmm, Super Soaker to make me cum indefinitely." Amber exploded with laughter.

"Maybe Lickety Split so I could do acrobatics in bed," Kyle suggested to utilize her dance skills.

After Amber placed *Bridesmaids* in the DVD player, their eyelids fought to stay open. After filling up on Amber's appetizers and downing drinks, the ladies found the film watching them peacefully asleep. So much for comedy.

Amber awoke and groggily looked at the clock above the fireplace. She squinted to view the time: 4:13 a.m. She looked over and smiled at her friends. Both were covered with throws she had pulled out when she started the film. Kyle's head peeked above the blanket and Shayla was buried underneath, her full head covered. *Should I awake them? Or let them stay crashed out here? No, we need to take advantage of this fabulous place.*

She walked over and lightly shook Kyle, who woke up with little resistance.

"Why don't you head upstairs? Might as well get relaxed. The bed is calling your name, girl."

Kyle sat up slowly and then arose. "You're right. I was cranked out, huh?"

"Be ready for brunch and the spa. Then we're going to a winery in the woods."

"Can't wait. I'm going to have to diet when I get back." Kyle grinned. She gathered her personal items, walked out of the room and up the staircase leading to a three-bedroom loft.

Amber took a few steps and pulled the cover. *Oh, my...where the hell is Shayla? Oh, whew, she must've gone upstairs earlier.* She headed upstairs and peeked in the bedroom that Shayla had claimed. She then looked in the room set to be hers, and Shayla was not present.

She picked up her cell phone and sent a text to Shayla. There was no response.

Well, she's a grown woman, and I can't be chasing her down like a child. I'm sure she's safe, she thought nervously. *Or is she? Hope she wasn't eaten by a bear.* She laughed to herself, then uneasiness settled in again. She lay on her bed and tucked herself under the covers. Serious thoughts infiltrated her mind and she prepared to contact the sheriff's office.

After a while of restlessness, Amber heard a soft creak and realized the front door of the condo was opening. *Must be Shayla, but where the hell has she been?* She heard light footsteps and figured Shayla apparently walked into the den first to see if they were still in there.

Shayla found the room empty and started the flight of stairs to stealthily enter into her designated bedroom. She closed the door, then headed into the bathroom to wash her face and shower. *That was some serious mountain madness I had tonight.*

Shayla had ventured out to meet with an on-site ski instructor, Brad, whom she had met when she'd made a brief walk to the concierge desk during check-in. He was a tall, chiseled specimen with a golden complexion from endless days on the sunny slopes. She had winked at Brad when she'd noticed his lengthy and alluring stares. When he approached her in the lobby and offered his cell and condo unit number, she vowed that she would visit him during the wee hours. Only if he'd promise to keep mum about their hookup.

When she'd knocked on his unit about 2:30 a.m., Brad lured her seductively into his abode. They'd made passionate love against the backdrop of a crackling fireplace. It was rare for Brad to mingle romantically with resort guests, but he'd found Shayla irresistible. Ideally, he wanted her to stay over, but she advised it was simply a one-time quickie. She was there to hang with her girls—point blank—and needed to return to the condo before sunup.

"So, how did everyone sleep?"

"Simply *vonderful*," Shayla quickly responded. *If only I could've cuddled up all night to my big, teddy bear.*

"Great." Amber looked at her suspiciously but avoided asking any questions. She could save that inquiry for a later date. Then again, they were all consenting adults and as long as Shayla was safe, it was none of her business.

"Fantastic." Kyle yawned. "I didn't want to get up, but I didn't want to miss out on anything. Was I half-asleep or did you say we were going to a winery today?"

"You heard right, after brunch and then we'll return for our spa treatments." She handed Kyle a spa menu. "Take a look and see which one you prefer. Three masseurs are attending to us during a special late-night session, simply for us."

"Now aren't *we* special?" Shayla crossed her legs. "You are always working some magic."

CHAPTER 10
Terra

"I'm telling you, Terra, these sistahs are the bomb. I scoped them out one time they stepped in the office." Blaze paced back and forth, puffing on his Cohiba cigar. "My rep, *Mrs.* Shayla Benson, is married to a cool dude. I've never met him, but from what I hear, he's got it going on. Pockets lined. Says he's in real estate, always brokering deals on the West Coast. But for real, for real, he'd better look out. She's one phat mother—" He caught himself, not wanting to refer to his classy chick on the side with crude language. His mind drifted to the ongoing sex sessions he constantly shared with Shayla.

"You always talkin' 'bout betterin' your life and thangs. This is your *in*, understand? You need to hang wit' the kinda folk you feenin' to be," Blaze continued, attempting to convince his best friend from the neighborhood to venture out. "You never know who can hook you up with a little sumthin'-sumthin.' So, sis, lemme get you on the inside track. I'm tired of hearin' yo complaints 'bout all the dudes, your stylin', everythang."

Terra Jones sank further in the chair niched in a corner in Blaze's Northeast row house. She observed her surroundings and her mind zoomed to a past of challenges and roadblocks. Her destiny was in her own hands, having grown up without parents when both had succumbed to the deadly streets. A lone gunman had shot them during an invasion when he'd mistakenly entered the wrong home in search of a stash of drugs. It turned out that the targeted house was next door.

Terra, the next to youngest of five, was left to embark on her adult life at age eighteen. She'd figured her future would work out, especially with older siblings to support her personal goals. But life took a downward turn, and her two brothers eventually went to the slammer on robbery charges. Her only sister had committed suicide. Only she and her six-year-old brother, Torian, were left in the household. Faced to move forward on her own after they moved in with her Grandma Elaine, she landed a job in retail and found that a low-end clothing store truly had its perks. It kept her looking sharp and in style—only the fashions were less expensive knockoffs than those of magazines. Now at twenty-five, she desired more than basic attire.

Terra was a standout with her model looks, ebony skin and a slender hourglass frame. Compliments were like a daily routine.

She closed her eyes and envisioned a life outside of her world. In a dreamlike trance, she sketched herself flaunting designer wear and pushing some luxury vehicle. Some of her friends were gold diggers; others traded their bodies for cash. She had vowed to attain her wares the honest way. Every time she thought of crossing the line, she'd hear the faint voice of her mother, Josephine, warning her not to follow the path her siblings had chosen.

Maybe Blaze was right. She could rub shoulders with the elite, and perhaps some of the wealth would rub off on her. Her desire to attend college was squashed after she'd starting working full time. A top student, her teachers and classmates had pegged her to be ambitious following high school.

"Look, I can hook ya up. Tell ya what, next time I go for my appointment, I'll let you hang out. Maybe introduce ya two and make it look like you had to come around 'cause you helping a brotha out. Feel me?"

"Okay, okay, Blaze, I gotcha." Terra perked up and lifted up from her slouch. "Why not? I could use some new friends."

"Yep, with benefits," Blaze teased. "So sit back and let your big bro work his thang."

Terra stood up and switched across the room to the kitchen. When she'd turned twenty-five on her last birthday, she'd promised herself to step up her game. Venture out of her comfort zone.

Blaze checked out her image, gazing at a silver navel ring drawing attention to her sculpted abs. Her skin-tight jean leggings accentuated a low-cut belly shirt and formed a portrait of a confident young woman who didn't mind showcasing her figure. "I'd suggest you not show that piercing and let your skin breathe from those jean things when you come around." He smirked.

"Look, I don't need you telling me how to hook it up. I know how to dress to impress, as they say. What you think, I'm some kind of country bumpkin or something?" Terra looked at him with disgust. "I got this."

CHAPTER 11
Kyle

"Good afternoon, everyone. I thank you being here on this gorgeous day to share in my lifelong dream. Magical Moves Studio is forever indebted to you for your support. I vow that my studio will give back to this wonderful community, providing the art of dance in the finest tradition." Kyle beamed with pride as she formally prepared to cut the ribbon at her studio. "Not only will we offer well-trained instructors for classes from A-Z, but Magical Moves will serve another purpose by hosting events to enhance the lifestyle of our youth.

"Now, without further adieu…" She held the huge pair of scissors and snipped the ribbon. "Cheers to Magical Moves Studio." Kyle stood at the outdoor entrance of her new facility surrounded by a horde of community leaders, board members, dance instructors, parents and students who had signed up for classes.

Standing directly next to her, she was flanked by Shayla and Amber, her dedicated friends who had encouraged her to follow her dream.

"I can't believe it." She hugged Shayla and then Amber. "Thank you both. I couldn't have accomplished this without you."

"You're welcome." Shayla looked at her watch and frowned.

"Everything okay?" Amber inquired.

"It's fine. I realize I'm cutting it close with my hair appointment. I'll call and change the time."

"Shayla, go ahead, we understand, you have to keep yourself looking good for your *man*," Amber teased.

"Girl, please, I do it for *me*. Most of the time, I don't even think Chad notices whether I've just gone to the salon or not. And don't let it be a deal in the works. He's truly blind then."

Amber scoped out the crowd, then whispered in Kyle's ear, "Where's hubby?"

A disappointed look crept on Kyle's face. Amber pointing out his absence had blown her uplifted mood. *Who knows where the hell he is? Always pulling a no-show. This morning, he promised he'd be here. No business dealings would stop him. This is getting old, and now my friends are noticing.* "I really couldn't tell you. Now that's trifling, isn't it?" She looked at her cell phone and there were no new texts.

"I'm sor—" Amber started.

"Don't be. I bet he'll say he had an 'emergency.' Always an 'emergency.' Huh, but it's all good. I have the both of you here and that's what matters," Kyle faked nonchalantly and moved full speed ahead with her celebration. She looked at her group of supporters. "Let's prepare for the tour," she announced, before opening the door and welcoming the guests inside. Youth hostesses awaited to showcase the 12,000-foot space, register students and provide gift bags to more than a hundred supporters.

Each room was highlighted in various colors to reflect the dance genre. The pink room was prepared for ballet classes, red for aerobics, orange for Zumba, purple for tap and hip-hop, lime for jazz, and butterscotch for yoga.

As guests strolled throughout, they were entertained by a live jazz band. Walls leading to the individual studio spaces were lined with poster-size, black-and-white portraits of famous African-

American greats, including dancers Judith Jamison, Debbie Allen, Alvin Ailey, Louis Johnson and Cab Calloway.

"Hi, baby. I apologize. I wanted to stick around. Remember my friend had her grand opening today? Couldn't get away. I misjudged the time. Can I get a rain check for this evening?" Shayla had stealthily stepped back outside to quiet surroundings to call Damien, the latest addition to her playgirl roster. The twenty-two-year-old, whistle-clean hunk was a fashionable catch, a model who'd soaked many women's panties from his appearances in calendars and local ads.

"I'll wait as long as necessary for you, babe." Damien offered his best phone sex tone. "You can cummmm anytime you like." He smiled, aware that Shayla not only gave up the luscious booty but often stashed dollars in spots in his condo. He never inquired but was certain she was the one leaving him change for his service. He would find bills in mysterious places like under a kitchen canister or stuck inside a magazine. Perhaps she observed that he could use some extra cash as he was heading back to college after a hiatus for a modeling contract. It was likely she was embarrassed to actually state she was leaving money for him, and she didn't want to appear that she was paying him. No, she had a classy image to protect and needed to cover that she was tipping with cash for sexual favors.

"Wonderful, Damien…*Smooth Jazz*," she corrected to the pet name she'd given him. "I'll text you when I'm on my way." Shayla ended the call and then placed the phone inside her purse. *Kyle, I love ya, girl, but Damien is one booty call that I can't resist.* She headed back inside the studio, satisfied the evening ahead would be sensational.

CHAPTER 12
Kyle

S itting at the kitchen table, Kyle munched on a Caesar salad with tomatoes, feta cheese, raisins and sunflower seeds. She had turned down an invitation from Amber to join her for drinks at a local bar/lounge in the city. It was a gesture to extend the celebration of the studio opening.

Shayla had disappeared, stating she had a hair appointment followed by a business meeting. If it were only the two of them for a post-celebration, Amber would drown her in a sea of questions about Bryce's absence. She would have preferred if Shayla were also present.

Kyle had the soothing music of Jill Scott in the background. She definitely needed a fix to bury her depression. Bryce had formed a pattern and it was getting worse.

She closed her eyes momentarily to reflect on better times, their first encounter. Kyle had met him in downtown D.C. along Seventh Street. She had enjoyed a performance by the Dance Theatre of Harlem at the Kennedy Center and couldn't resist hanging out on the gorgeous spring night. She stopped at Maze for a drink and was seated alone at a table before she spotted Bryce at the bar flanked on each side by a woman. He was modestly attractive, well-dressed in a suit and tie, and quickly his eyes locked with hers across the room. After both of his prospective pick-ups left the bar, he approached Kyle and joined her at the table. They shared several rounds of drinks and he was gentlemanly to offer her a ride home. Kyle assured him that she would be fine once she had a cup of coffee.

Her first impression was that he was kind and chivalrous, walking behind her chair to pull it out for her and escorting her by her arm to her car parked in a nearby garage. Months later, he contacted her. Kyle never believed in dialing digits after a first meeting. She always waited to receive the initial call.

It would not be long before the two were enraptured with each other. Now Bryce had become an enigma and she couldn't figure him out. He had made a 180-degree turnaround. Kyle refuted the advice her mother had offered to allow at least two years before jumping the broom.

She snapped out of her thoughts when she heard the front door. She picked up her fork to continue eating her salad.

Bryce walked into the kitchen and stood at the table. "I see you're eating that rabbit food again. I was expecting a nice hot meal."

Kyle looked up from her plate. "And I was expecting you to be at my grand opening." She shoved a souvenir program across the table.

"Don't be smart." He walked over to the refrigerator and opened the door. "Humph, nothing in this fridge worth eating. Thought you were going shopping."

"Bryce, you and I both know that I've been swamped getting ready for the studio." Kyle angrily stabbed her fork into a tomato. "So, where were you anyway? Emergency?" she inquired sarcastically.

"Look, I don't need you questioning me constantly. I'm still working out all the kinks in this business. It's only been six months. You feel me?"

"Hell, you haven't even asked me how the opening went. Shows you don't give a damn." Kyle stood up and took her dishes to the sink. She turned on the water to rinse them and then opened the dishwasher to place them inside.

Suddenly, she felt an abrupt shove from behind and her leg hit the side of the dishwasher.

Appalled, she turned around to see Bryce in her face. He pushed her harder into the top of the rack. "Owww!" She gripped her side in pain. "You bas—!"

"Dare you to call me a name!" he interrupted. Bryce turned around and walked out of the kitchen, stating over his shoulder, "I'm going out for dinner. Meet some of the boys. To hell with this!"

Kyle shuffled to the kitchen table, clutching her abdomen. She looked at the dishwasher in disbelief, now the source of bruises forming. She gazed toward the ceiling, begging for an answer to the madness. *God, please help me. Is it anger management? Mood swings? Is it curable or irreversible? Or do I simply need to move on?* She curled over and laid her head on the table, overlooking where she had shoved the studio program. Soon it would be wet with tears.

Finally drifting to sleep, Kyle had to down several cups of chamomile tea to become drowsy. She twisted and turned until she lost the battle and one of her favorite black-and-white films, *Sunset Boulevard*, watched over her. She wrestled with her pillow and suddenly sat up sweating intensely, awaking from a nightmare. *Whew*, she thought. *It was so real.* In the dream, Bryce had cornered her in the kitchen with violent threats. She laid her head back on the pillow and zoomed back on the film. After an hour, she heard Bryce's footsteps coming up the stairs. She quickly turned her body toward the window and away from the flat-screen. She closed her eyes and faked sleep, zoning in on his soft steps into the bathroom.

Bryce showered longer than his usual routine. The water cascading over his body gave him the feeling that he was washing away his sinful behavior. Rejuvenated, he shut the water off and stepped out of the shower, water trailing down his body before drying off. After round after round of Hennessy and Coke, he barely had made it home and had texted his friends after pulling into his driveway.

He had complained that Kyle was a constant complainer who demanded more of his time than he was willing to share. They reminded him that the honeymoon was still a viable reality after two years, and he needed to be more compromising let alone compassionate. Sure, any new businessman considered his venture his true "baby," but wives needed to be placed at the forefront.

Spritzing on his favorite cologne, he prepared to seduce his lovely wife. Regardless of her portrait as Sleeping Beauty, he possessed a take-charge feeling and figured it was long overdue. It had been months since a lovemaking session and to his body, it felt like years. His narcissistic attitude and priority on his business dealings had overshadowed pleasuring his wife. After thirty-eight years of bachelorhood, possessing the husband title had sunk in slowly.

Bryce often revisited his bachelor days and couldn't shake off his desire to be single at times. He didn't have to answer any queries of his whereabouts or his lifestyle. Bryce had been the coveted jock in high school and had worked as an auto mechanic for decades. It was a natural progression for him to move into owning a chain of repair shops.

His first car was a loaded, souped-up Camaro, replete with all the gadgets of the era.

Kyle would be honored to know how much he bragged about her smartness during shop talk with the fellas. She was definitely the trophy wife he admired for her brain power as well as her dancer physique. The few times that she had stopped by the repair shops, staffers took note when she stepped in looking like she'd arrived in a limo from a Hollywood set. Dressed in her finest, Kyle turned heads and stopped workers in their tracks. Bryce was admired for having such a charmer for a wife.

Now Bryce would have the opportunity to put the charm on her, despite the angst that he'd unabashedly portrayed earlier. *Damn, I can't believe I pushed up on her like that. But then again, she deserved it, questioning me like I'm some kinda flunky. I rule this house. And I ain't takin' no stuff off nobody.*

He stared at himself in the mirror and didn't like what the reflection revealed. He was an angry-looking man, now all set to be a flunky for a broad. Bryce always considered making the first move as a sign of weakness. But on this night, with the effects of the Henny, he was willing to be a weakling. His desire was over-powering and Kyle would have to deliver, regardless of her sleeping. He would apologize for his actions, then she would fall for his passion. It was a selfish move, despite his abusive behavior.

Images of cruel scenes from childhood invaded his thoughts. Frequent visits by police to his home on domestic violence calls. His dad's raging temper thrashing out at his mother. He usually sought refuge in a bedroom closet where he was comforted from the visual and vocal torture.

Bryce snapped out of his trancelike state and turned away from the mirror. He didn't like what he had become; the effects had trickled down. Surely, Kyle would forgive him; his mom always withstood his dad's behavior.

He stood in the doorway and stared at his wife before approaching the bed, picking up the remote and then turning down the TV. He slid under the sheets and reached over to caress Kyle, whose face was turned away from him. He whispered in her ear, "Hey, babe, I'm back. Sorry." He stroked her shoulder. "Miss me?"

Kyle ignored him, still pretending to be asleep. He forced her to face him, turning her body toward him and rolling her over like some object. She complied like a puppet—limp and speechless.

She lay coldly, resenting that she allowed him to enter her. He reeked of alcohol and she figured it was to blame for his momentary horniness. There was no feeling or emotion and she was relieved when he released, grunted and then fell asleep. It was all in one swoop—a loveless scene shaded by a dark cloud.

CHAPTER 13
Shayla

Shayla zipped down New York Avenue into D.C., turned onto Florida Avenue and cruised along U Street Northwest. The bustling corridor lined with trendy lounges, bars and restaurants was reminiscent of an upscale New York neighborhood. Amazed at the area's transformation, she recalled back in the day when she first relocated to D.C. Her family had warned her to avoid the once drug-infested and prostitution-riddled streets where she now cruised for a parking space. It was now a coveted address to land a renovated condo.

Damien was aware that she was a 'burbs girl and parking normally was a breeze. The warm air had driven out revelers to enjoy the nightlife. She circled several blocks before spotting a car pulling out. She immediately grabbed the coveted spot and parked. She cut on the interior light and pulled out her lipstick, glossed over her lips and puckered them. Satisfied, she unlocked the doors and stepped out. Walking along the sidewalk, she felt in the limelight as her voluptuous curves and cleavage in her tight-fitting, summery floral dress was a knockout. She had deemed her outfit a little risqué for the youth dance studio earlier, but it was necessary to look like a prized specimen whenever in Damien's presence. She had to be on her P's and Q's in order to maintain her boy toy, who she surely figured had groupies lined up. Initially, she had met him as a prospective client.

Reaching his building, Shayla adjusted her dress, smoothed it and glanced at her newly pedicured toes peeking through her sandals. She rang the doorbell and waited for Damien to buzz her inside. Once she entered the lobby, she walked to the elevator and pressed the key to the seventh floor. After exiting, she rounded the corner and immediately started to feel flushed and excited. She knocked on the door and Damien welcomed her inside his immaculate bachelor pad. A fifty-inch flat-screen, a navy circular sofa accented with oversized pillows and a coffee table with *GQ* and *Maxim* magazines offered a simplistic look.

Shayla settled back and looked around the room. Portraits of Damien's family members lined a sofa table. She particularly liked the one of his older brother.

He walked to his well-stocked wet bar and poured two glasses of Hpnotiq on the rocks. Sitting down beside Shayla on the sofa, he clinked his glass of the turquoise liquid with hers before tasting and then continued to watch sports. It was torture for Shayla to attempt to wait patiently for the basketball game to end. Her mind wandered as he intensely focused on the play by plays.

He doesn't think I came all the way here for a damn game. He's going to make me wait to satisfy my coochie. "Earth to Damien."

He batted his eyes and looked at her. "Say what?"

"All that sexy talk on the phone, I figured you'd be—"

"Forgot the game was on tonight."

"Ohh-kay."

She took charge and teased him with her tongue, inserting it in his mouth and then licking his neck. The two wrestled their way, entangled, into the bedroom. They landed on the king-sized bed.

Shayla's mind drifted with the effects of the alcohol. *I really need to get a reality check. This youngun and I have no conversation. It's not like Mr. Class. Even Blaze and I can talk PR language. The only thing*

Damien can share conversation-wise is the modeling world and I get tired of that. Hell, I'm way too old to think of a career. But hey, do I give up his King Kong rod to get some mental satisfaction elsewhere? Duh, I don't think so.

She climbed on his back, her vagina resting on his waistline. She reached over and placed on some soft gloves she had pulled from her purse. She had come prepared as Damien expected a full-body massage. She opened a small bottle of sweet almond oil and poured some on his back, then proceeded to knead his shoulders and back and continued down his body.

Would he reciprocate or was he simply selfish? A selfish lover… but an irresistible body.

It didn't take long for her to discover. Damien gently rose up and she climbed off his back. He laid her on her back and then inserted his rod, plunging deeper and deeper before she bit her tongue to avoid a scream in his thin-walled condo unit. She released in total satisfaction. Well, he was a little on the selfish side, no foreplay, but she considered that his young and strong stamina always compensated for the lack of affection.

Shayla tossed about as she was being massaged and teased by Damien. Finally, he had shown some loving gestures. Disappointedly, she awakened and grimaced; it was all a dream. The sunlight peeped through the mini blinds and she sat up straight, directed her eyes to his side of the bed and he was gone. She figured he was in the living room. *Oh, my, I didn't make it home last night. Yikes!*

No matter how often she shared playtime with any of her lovers, she insisted she spend the night in her own home. It would be disrespectful to Chad to share a bed with another man overnight. There is always a first time and she'd forgive herself, chalking it up as a one-time mistake. She was thankful that Chad was on the other coast.

She rested her legs on the side of the bed and glimpsed at a note on the end table. She picked it up and read: *Shayla, I apologize that I had to leave. Didn't want to wake you. Sleeping too good. LOL. Had a 10:00 photo shoot.*

The drinks and earth-shattering orgasm had knocked her out. She sighed and placed her hand on her forehead, rubbing it to ease a now throbbing headache. It spelled *hangover.* She rose up and walked into the bathroom. Damien had left her a set of towels on the counter. She showered quickly, thinking the warm water would ease her head. After dressing, she decided to search for painkillers. Surely, he had something in his cabinet. She opened the small cabinet door under the sink and looked inside. A frame placed face-down caught her attention. She pulled it out and looked in admiration at a photo of a handsome man who looked about mid-forties. She shrugged and placed it back in its original position. After combing through the cabinet, she found a bottle of tablets. She poured out a couple and put the bottle back inside, then closed the door.

Heading to the kitchen, she looked around the condo. It truly was a decorator's dream, a page out of a lifestyle magazine. She grabbed a bottle of spring water, opened it and took the pills with a swallow. She dropped the bottle inside her purse and headed out the door. She'd stop at her favorite pastry shop and grab a cup of coffee and muffin en route home.

I'm gonna get on Damien for leaving me like that, she thought as she walked to her car. *I never stay over. His place is a danger zone.* He had put the whammy on her. She was amused and smiled. She pulled out her cell phone and checked for missed calls and text messages. All was clear.

CHAPTER 14
Amber

Zodi pulled up to the gate of Poplar Ridge Estates in Annapolis, Maryland, waved at the attendant in the booth and held up the magnetic card. The gate lifted to allow entrance into the community of massive custom-built homes. She swerved along the curvy roads before pulling into a driveway. Jaslyn was Amber's confidante and protective neighbor.

"Let me give her a call to make sure she's home." Amber dialed her cell phone. It rang a few times before she answered.

"Hey, lady, what's up?"

"Forgive me, but it's delivery time...the usual deal."

"Come on in."

Zodi popped the trunk and the two stepped out. Amber, in a coral wrap dress, walked to the back of the car, her YSL pumps clicking. Pulling out about ten bags of purchases from jewelry to shoes to dresses to lingerie, she handed a few to Zodi. She closed the trunk and they toted them to the front door where Jaslyn awaited.

"Ladies, we're going to have to stop meeting like this." Jaslyn laughed heartily and motioned for them to drop the bags on a bench in the foyer. "I'll stash them away later." She directed them to her sunroom. "Thank goodness I'm an *ex*-wife or my hubby would think I was crazy, trying to rescue a shopaholic."

Jaslyn had acquired the gorgeous home in a divorce settlement.

A four-story knockout and a three-car garage later, she was living the life of a bachelorette. To continue the wealth established from married life to an engineer, she operated a lucrative, home-based art business. *Delivery* was a household word as she had arrivals almost daily.

"Have a seat. Can I get you anything?"

"If it's okay to say it, you make a mean strawberry daiquiri," Zodi stated in complimentary fashion, hoping it would prod her to whip up some drinks. As a personal assistant, she never wanted to overstep her boundaries. But she'd visited in the past and found the daiquiris irresistible.

"And that's fine; I'll take any kudos you want to dish." Jaslyn walked into the kitchen. "Actually, this will be good," she yelled, realizing they would have an extended visit. "Why don't we have an impromptu meeting about the foundation? I'd already volunteered to help in any way."

Amber leaned back and relaxed. "That's a great idea." She looked at Zodi. "Do you have your notepad?"

Zodi looked in her purse and pulled out a black tablet. "Always."

Several cocktails later, the trio had hashed out appealing plans for an upcoming fund-raiser for the Diamond Dreams Foundation. Jaslyn had suggested the initial event could be at the Trents' estate. It would make it personal and offer a more cozy effect. Guests would include the D.C. mayor, county executive, area politicos and local celebrities. Trevor's teammates and their guests would be star attractions.

Jaslyn was a genius at event planning and was connected to the best caterers in town and entertainers. She decided that a baseball-themed décor would be eye-catching with an ice sculpture in the shape of a baseball and bat. She would select ingredients to create original, signature cocktails such as Swing Time, Batter Up, Home Run, Strike Out and Grand Slam—which would be the ultimate blend of four types of alcohol. It would creep up on you and then trigger an enormous buzz. Hostesses carrying trays of hors d'oeuvres would wear cheerleader outfits to keep the sports theme—a creative idea although they weren't a staple at baseball games. She'd recruit some of Kyle's dance students to perform a routine. They'd wear baseball caps from various teams.

The launch of the foundation would form additional Little Leagues in D.C. and neighboring counties. Pro baseball athletes would be speakers for events, and retirees would volunteer to coach the teams. College scholarships would be offered to outstanding players from both low- and middle-income families. For starters, the main focus of the foundation would be to generate renewed interest in African Americans and baseball. The feature film *42* about the life of Jackie Robinson had affected the community and opened eyes that the number of African Americans playing baseball had dwindled significantly.

"Cheers!" Amber toasted and clinked glasses with Jaslyn and Zodi. All were pleasantly satisfied they had made progress with the plans to move the foundation forward. Amber would share the ideas with Trevor who was on a mission to fulfill his passion.

"Zodi, guess we should head out. Give Jaslyn time to stash away the goodies." Amber laughed and stood up. Zodi and Jaslyn followed and the three walked to the front.

Amber reached down and picked up a small bag. She handed it to Jaslyn. "This is for you. Thank you for your hospitality." She liked to present her with tokens for her hideaway assistance.

"No, thank *you*." Jaslyn beamed. "I guess you know I'm not much of a shopper, except what I need for my *biz*ness." She opened the bag and pulled out a shiny silver necklace with her birthstone in the shape of a heart. "Aw, thanks. This is sharp."

"You're welcome. I thought you might like it." Zodi opened the door for her and Amber to walk out. Amber turned around with a smile and winked. "We'll probably be doing a repeat next week."

No, boss lady, I hope not. You really need to slow down on your shopping tip. It's wayyyy over the top. At first, it was cool to hide a little here and there, but now I'm beginning to see that it's more than an addiction. You are obsessed. Zodi wondered if it would ever get to the point where she'd break her silence and betray Amber, enlightening Trevor to what was in his midst, but he was too blind to see.

Trevor was standing in the foyer when Amber walked in. Zodi had driven her own car and had dropped her off.

"Oh, I wasn't expecting to see you so soon."

He walked over and embraced her. "Well, the meeting ended early. Now I can have the whole evening with you." He kissed her gently on the lips. "Sound like a plan?" He peered around the corner toward the front door. "You're alone? Zodi drop you off?"

"Yes, we had fun today. The usual girls' stuff."

He softly grabbed her hand and led her up the stairs. "Uh-huh. Now let's go see if we can knock it out the park."

Now I wish I hadn't dropped off my new thong set at Jaslyn's, Amber thought. *Should have brought that piece home.*

CHAPTER 15
Shayla

"Can you please help with the zipper, sweetie?" Shayla had wiggled into her black dress, which accentuated her curves. Standing in front of the full-length mirror in her bedroom, she debated which jewelry would best complement her look of the evening.

"Sure thing." Chad, dressed immaculately in a black suit and burgundy tie, walked toward her and stood behind her. He zipped the dress and gazed into the mirror.

"Oh, and help me with this necklace, please." She went to the dresser, opened a hidden compartment and pulled out a diamond necklace. She walked back to the mirror and handed him the necklace.

Chad complied by looping the piece around her neck and clasping it. He kissed her neck, soaking in the fragrance while stealing glances in the mirror. "You look absolutely gorgeous."

"Why thank you, Chad." In her best seductive voice, she added, "And you lookin' good. As they say, you clean up nice." She admired him in the mirror.

He walked closer and wrapped his arms around her waist. They started swaying to Jill Scott's "Blessed." The tantalizing moves were growing more intense. "Hey, we'd better get out of here or we won't get past this room soon, the way you're making me feel."

"I agree. Save it for later." She removed his arms, turned around and kissed him gently on the lips.

Chad and Shayla were determined to arrive at Marvin restaurant before their celebrity guest, R&B diva Passion. She was in town for a concert at the newly refurbished Howard Theatre, an institution in D.C. where the likes of James Brown, Lena Horne and the Supremes performed back in the day. Her debut hit, "It's Real," had clinched the No. 10 spot on *Billboard* magazine's chart, and her goal was to ensure longevity at the top level. She hoped it would continue to climb to the top position.

Chad had told her Pierce Collins, Chad's Beverly Hills plastic surgeon cohort, had introduced her to him during one of his West Coast visits. Chad had promised Shayla that he would attempt to woo some clients from the entertainment world.

They had selected Marvin as they thought the restaurant honoring D.C.'s own native crooner Marvin Gaye was appropriate for an R&B invited guest.

Shayla sipped on her martini and scoped out the clientele. Chad tasted his Hole in One and flexed his muscles, noting that quite a few manly stares were zooming in on his wife.

Suddenly, when Passion walked in, conversations dropped and heads turned toward her, mesmerized by her commanding presence. She sauntered regally, and if anyone didn't recognize the celebrity, they still would have thought she was *somebody*. A teen hostess led her to the table but not before embarrassingly requesting her autograph at the booth. Her high school friends would be the picture of envy.

Passion projected the image of a runway model as she stepped lightly yet distinctly in her six-inch stilettos. Her tailored, form-fitting, ankle-length black dress highlighted her slender figure. Its plunging necklace showed plenty of cleavage. She gripped her tiny black beaded clutch with grace as she made her way to the table. The hostess stopped and motioned to her empty chair.

"Thank you, sweetie."

"You're quite welcome."

Passion touched the back of the chair when Chad stood up quickly. "I'll get that for you. Welcome and thanks for joining us."

After Passion sat and pulled up her chair, Chad introduced, "This is my lovely wife, Shayla. Shayla, this is Passion."

The two shook hands, both revealing a faux smile. Shayla shielded her slight jealousy of the youthful, twenty-one-year-old beauty who'd joined them.

"A waiter will be here shortly." The young hostess beamed about meeting and then seating her idol. Excitedly, she added, "Meanwhile, I'm going to get off my station and get you started with a drink."

"A Stiletto Sangria, please."

"Stiletto, I love the sound of that. I'm not familiar, but it must be a ladies' drink."

"Oh, definitely. It's actually made with Hpnotiq Harmonie."

"I see." *Hpnotiq, Hpnotiq. Now that's familiar. Oh, that's what Damien gave me. It's hypnotic all right. Maybe that's the hip, trendy drink of choice among the young folks. I had a little too many of those when I got turned on to it.* She recalled her latest adventure when she awoke at Damien's, thinking that she had driven home.

"Thanks for stopping by," Shayla offered genuinely. "How was the show last night?"

"Fantastic. I'm told it was a sell-out. From my view onstage, it definitely was a full house. We rocked it too." Her caramel skin glowed from the small lit candle atop the table.

"Great. You have already established a wide fan base, and I'd love to offer my services."

First thing I'd do is tone down some of that lion mane, Shayla thought. *But she is quite attractive and that always helps in entertainment.*

"I really hadn't planned on touring. Then when I released 'It's Real,' I suddenly had a runaway hit. It's every artist's dream to come out the door bangin'. But I don't want to end up as a one-hit wonder."

The waiter returned with Passion's drink and took their food orders.

Shayla analyzed her stunning features. "Did you ever model?"

"How'd you guess? Yes, I did when I was a teen. Of course, that wasn't many years ago. Only stuff like newspaper ads and a couple of store catalogs."

Passion was raised in L.A. in an ethnically diverse neighborhood where she lived with her mother and six siblings. Determined to chase her dreams, she had honed her voice skills by attending a school for the arts. She'd travel a long route on the bus in order to get the best vocal education the area had to offer. She'd appeared in musicals and talent shows before a record label executive discovered her talent.

"I see. I'm surprised you didn't pursue that career path. Modeling can be quite prosperous for someone your age."

Chad interjected, redirecting the conversation to business. "I agree, but it looks like *music* found her, and here we are."

Shayla realized if Passion agreed to hire her as a consultant, she would need to do a thorough interview to find out more about her background. She'd already searched the Internet prior to their dinner meeting and found little about the rising starlet.

CHAPTER 16
Kyle

"*Plié! Relevé!*" the ballet instructor announced to the room of fifteen girls. Lani caught the mirrored reflection of Kyle standing in the doorway as she led her practice class. She needed to impress the studio owner to become a permanent fixture.

Kyle smiled, satisfied that Lani was displaying competence and confidence. She walked down the hall and peeked in the jazz room where a group of dancers performed a routine to Michael Jackson's "Smooth Criminal," choreographed by their young teacher, Natasha.

These were the last two classes of the evening. Since opening Magical Moves, she found that the studio was more of her first home than her actual residence. It was also an oasis for her to seek solitude away from the troubled environment where she laid her head at night.

Bryce had become increasingly uncaring and arrogant, often at the brink of unbearable. Their sex life had diminished, and she accepted it as she had lost desire for the man she'd charmed into marriage. The honeymoon was not only over; it was demolished. Despite the abusiveness, she had persevered, figuring it was a matter of time before he'd cease. He'd blame it on his business and that when it was rocky, he'd vent and take out anger on her. Usually, he would apologize profusely and then attempt to win back her trust.

Wanting her short-term marriage to work, she vowed to give it another year—the physical and verbal abuse would have to end. The longevity of her parents' marriage had inspired her to deal with the ups and downs, but she didn't visualize hers for the long haul if he didn't improve. Perhaps once Bryce's business stabilized, he would be back to his original demeanor and behavior. Shayla's and Amber's marriages appeared to be on point from what she observed. She was the newlywed in the group and she wanted hers to blossom also. She was willing to go to counseling but hadn't broached the subject with Bryce—yet.

Kyle walked back to her office, proud that her instructors were talented and the students were receiving professional lessons. They would leave Magical Moves highly trained, prepared to enter the world of dance. Perhaps some would appear on Broadway someday or be a backup dancer on tour for a popular recording artist. She sat in her desk chair and decreased the sound of the DVD playing on her flat screen. It was a documentary on the history of dance. This evening, her manager, Sienna, was off, and she was running the studio solo. She pulled out a stack of paperwork to see the new registrants. Her discount special and mail-order coupons had helped to booster steady enrollment.

Kyle looked up and saw a figure out of the corner of her eye. She turned toward her doorway and smiled. "Hello."

"Hello, I was getting ready to knock. Hope I'm not disturbing you. I could see you were deep in thought." The dark-skinned, stocky man with a bald head nodded. He was neatly dressed in a crisp navy-and-white striped shirt and jeans.

"Please, come in." She stood up as he approached and shook his hand. "Kyle Andrews. Have a seat." She motioned to a chair on the opposite side of her desk.

"Thanks, I'm Erick Williamson. I was determined to meet you. I can't thank you enough for what you've done for my daughter, Merlan, in such a short time."

"Oh, Merlan, in ballet. Yes, she's such a sweetheart. She has the best attitude and I'm sure you're proud of her," Kyle offered. "I can see from her homework, she's also a great student," she remarked, gauging her observations from aftercare.

"It's ideal for me, 'cause on the days I work late, I pick her up from here. She's already done her schoolwork. She's lovin' the classes and all."

"That's what we're here for. We not only instruct dance, we express the importance of education and camaraderie. And our desire is for them to blossom into beautiful young ladies. We have a handful of young men, and we encourage them to be leaders." She looked down and rustled her papers, before stopping at a sheet and perusing it. "She's also signed up for my upcoming etiquette class."

"Definitely, when I saw the brochure, I figured it'd be a good thing." He looked down and fiddled his thumbs. "She lost her mom, so I'm raisin' her solo. Can't teach a girl everythin' she needs to know, but I'm doin' the best I can."

"Oh, I'm sorry to hear—"

"It's cool." He looked up at the clock. "Class is almost over. Guess I'll step out and get her." He stood up. "It was nice meeting you."

"Likewise." She smiled. "Have a good evening."

"Thanks, you, too," he noted and then walked out of the office.

Kyle opened a bottle of water on her desk, took a swig, then gazed up at the DVD. The segment featuring the Dance Theatre of Harlem was playing. After such a moment with an appreciative parent, it was times like this that made her project worthwhile.

CHAPTER 17
Shayla

"Good morning, ladies." Shayla, wearing a colorblock sheath dress, walked into New Visions. She looked at her watch. It was barely after twelve. "Or rather, good afternoon."

"Good afternoon," Camilla and Rachelle said in unison.

"Anything earth-shattering that I missed this morning?"

"Well, you did receive a call from Passion. She said she's that new singer—" Camilla started.

"Oh, she called? Did she leave a message?"

"Only that she had called. She'll wait to hear from you," Camilla responded.

"Please, give her a call. I'm heading to my office." Shayla walked to the back, bouncing with confidence that she was getting ready to seal a major deal.

"Okay, Ms. Benson. Dialing now." Camilla picked up the receiver and returned the call to Passion. Once she answered, she put the call through to Shayla.

Shayla sat at her desk and soaked up the positive ambience of the lovely flowers that Wilson, "Mr. Class," had sent to her office.

They'd had a fantastic morning the previous day. He'd taken her for a return rendezvous at the castle. This time they'd made love in a sunken tub in the King and Queen room, which had an adjoining 1,000-foot bathroom. He had decorated by sprinkling bright daisies atop the water enhanced with peppermint oil. Red and pink rose petals formed the shape of a heart on the cream duvet on top of the canopy bed. Shayla had found the décor a first-class show of passion.

Wilson had earned his nickname from his high-end actions. She simply adored being in his presence, let alone the skills he held down between the sheets. He was the oldest of her lovers and by far the best conversationalist.

The floral arrangement delivered yesterday was a reminder of how truly wonderful a morning she'd had with him. Wilson was wise to sign the card anonymously as "Thank You" with a simple message showing gratitude for her services.

The intercom buzzed. "Ms. Benson, I have Passion on the line."

"Please, connect the call. Thanks." Shayla picked up the call. "Hello, Passion, how are you on this glorious day?"

"Hey, I'm hanging in there. Just tryin' to hold it down out here in La-La Land. Gettin' ready to work on my next single, goin' into the studio next week."

"That's wonderful news."

"Well, after I left D.C., I thought about it long and hard, and I'm feelin' the deal. I think I'd like to hook up wit' you, and let it do what it do."

"That's even better news. I'll be happy to sign you on as a client. You will be my second recording artist," she responded, referring to Blaze, her private side dish. *Mmm-hmm, he's an artist all right. Talented in the right places.*

"Second?" she inquired with disdain. "I thought Chad—er, Mr. Benson—said you were rollin' in the music biz. Told me you were nothin' but the truth and that you had a list of clients."

"I do have a lot of clients, Passion. Here on the East Coast, I don't find music clients as often, that's all," Shayla offered honestly.

"All I can promise is that I'll do my best. If you're interested, I'll have my assistant prepare the contracts."

Passion paused briefly. "Well, I have nothin' to lose. I'd prefer to have a sistah representin', so I'm good wit' it. You have the info, and I feel like I need someone who understands *me*."

"Once you return the contracts, I'll want to set up a meeting in *person*. In these days of email, voicemail, Facebook and Skype, I still prefer one-on-one, the personal touch. And that can be on either coast," she suggested. "If you're returning to D.C. soon, that will be fine. If not, I can visit L.A. I'm due for a visit. After all, Chad is there as much as he's home." Shayla smiled. "It's about time I meet Dr. Collins, or Pierce, as Chad calls him."

"Oh, yes, Dr. Collins. He's the bomb." Passion rubbed her abdomen as she was proud of her recent liposuction. "I'd highly recommend him."

"So Chad tells me. I look forward to meeting him. Again, I will check my schedule and determine when I can get that way."

"Okay, I will look out for the contracts. Thank you."

"You're welcome. Goodbye."

After Shayla hung up, she reflected on the idea of a visit to L.A., the City of Angels. Her secretive thoughts drifted to what it could offer. *Shame on me, thinking about the hunks of Hollywood. I've heard they take care of their bodies, eat healthy and work out.*

CHAPTER 18
Kyle

Kyle arrived home and walked into her kitchen. She was exhausted and ecstatic it was Friday. It had been a challenging week at the studio with intense rehearsals. The students had been practicing for a dance competition in all genres. She was proud of their accomplishments and figured they had a realistic chance to take home trophies. She also had to give kudos to her exemplary instructors. Tonight they had capped off the week with a pizza party at a local restaurant.

She walked to the refrigerator and grabbed a bottle of spring water. On second thought, she decided to also pour a glass of wine. She mounted the stairs. Bryce had texted her the usual message. He'd be home late. She wondered when and if he would ever show support for her project. He'd stopped by the studio on several occasions and met the instructors and some of the students. During the planning stage, she always had figured that he would be more involved once her dream came to fruition.

It would be ideal for him to interact with youth since he always was involved with adults through his business dealings. She couldn't fathom why he was lukewarm toward children. Their visions of parenthood had been crushed with the miscarriage. With his recent erratic behavior, Kyle had become concerned if motherhood would ever be realized—with Bryce.

She was resilient but would not force herself to continue in a marriage that was abusive. For now, she resolved that Bryce was helping her finance her entrepreneurship. He offered monetary support but not personal comfort.

After all of her years as a prima ballerina with an image of strength and confidence, it was hard to fathom how she had let herself be downgraded to a punching bag. Often she thought of reaching out to her parents for mental support, but they had so much pride in her studio project. She didn't want to damper her progress by sharing her troublesome marriage. She preferred to believe that all would improve once Bryce's business smoothed out.

Kyle entered the bathroom and started to run bathwater. It was her way to rejuvenate and mellow out for the night. She sipped the wine while removing her clothing. Once the scent wafted throughout, she slowly dipped in the tub, reeled back and continued to sip from the wineglass. She took a deep breath and closed her eyes. The relaxing atmosphere would take her to a place she wanted to be.

After the bath, she climbed out of the tub and dried off, wrapping herself in a towel. She crossed the room and looked in her dresser for a T-shirt. Her days of adorning sensual lingerie and sleepwear seemed to be over. She'd lost motivation to entice her newlywed hubby. His mind seemed elsewhere on most nights. After pulling the oversized shirt over her head, she crossed the room, climbed in bed and clicked to watch an old black-and-white film. It, along with the warm bathwater, would be like an endless sleeping pill.

CHAPTER 19
Bryce

"Okay, Jarrett, lemme holla at you a sec." Dressed in a navy jumpsuit, Sam motioned for Bryce, aka Jarrett, to enter his office. Mechanic certificates lined the walls and stacks of invoices and paperwork decorated his desktop. He sat down at his metal desk and Bryce eased into a chair across from him. The two often teamed up for after-hours powwows after the shop had closed. "Look, I've been runnin' this camp for you about eight months now. You told me when we amped the bizness, you were gonna line my pockets a little more. We've had a steady flow and wit' these fellas I'm gettin' ready to bring in, we'll be rakin' in the dough even mo'. You feel me?"

"I got you, Sam. So what you sayin'? Out of the three spots, you already gettin' paid more than any of the others running things."

"I'm tellin' ya, I'm bringin' in some new cats who are the joint. They are slick, smooth and real wizards. Can work that magic when it comes to coppin' wheels. These thieves are the best around and promise they can reel in some luxes. Mercedes, BMWs, Porsches, you name it. And they know the best neighbor-hoods where folk be slackin'."

"Okay, okay, if we step up the goods, then of course, we can match the cash with the product." Bryce twitched as he looked Sam in the eyes, determining if he could truly trust his right-hand man. At forty-eight, the salt-and-pepper-haired manager was well experienced. He was always changing hands, with a constant rotation of employees. It wasn't certain if he had some of his own tricks in play. Sometimes it was tough trying to oversee all three of his auto repair centers in D.C., particularly this location that was actually a chop shop.

Business had started to look prosperous and the key was the managers at the helm of each shop. Sam was the best organizer, dismantling stolen cars to resell their parts. He had spent an incarcerated stint for his career as a car thief. In the neighborhood where he grew up, he was known as "Wheels" for the enormous number of cars he'd stolen throughout the city. Now he was wheeling business deals under the auspices of a repair business.

"Sam, I appreciate you, man. That's why I have you at the helm, even over the other locations. You are the *man*. Always have been, brother." Bryce stood up and reached over to give him dap. "You're like my big brother. We go way back in the 'hood. You were running things then and running them now. So I trust what you're saying."

"Yep, the crew is workin' out the plan now. You always gotta have some def operations in mind. And these fellas ain't nothin' but the truth. You'll see."

Bryce's cell phone vibrated. He pulled it from its case and read the text. *Heading home soon?* "Well, that's the missus. Checking up on me as usual. I keep telling her I'm working late and trying to ensure all flows smoothly with the new business."

Sam shook his head. "Man, you the one who's a true gamer, not me. I can't figure out how your sweetie is still in the dark." He smiled mischievously. "One thing for sure, you know how to pick 'em. Got ya self a New York chick. She's a beauty, too. I see why you married that pretty young thing. She be killin' it." He laughed.

"Hey, man, I told you about making those comments about my wife. Don't be disrespecting my queen."

"Sorry, I didn't mean to sho' no disrespect." He paused. "Let me try again, your lovely wife, Kyle," he stated with a hint of sarcasm.

"And remember, when it comes to here, I'm known as *Bryce*."

"Got you, man, your other name, *Bryce*," he complied. "I try hard to 'member it. Glad she don't come 'round here. Every now and then, I slip up and call ya Jarrett in front of others, but I'll keep on practicin'."

Bryce looked at his cell and texted: *I'll be there in 30.* He grimaced about his fake response. *But it's more like an hour*, he thought.

Kyle had awoken from a peaceful dream when she'd texted Bryce. She laid her cell phone on the end table and sighed. She turned around, clutched her pillow and gazed toward his side of the bed. *Looks like it'll be another lonely night.*

CHAPTER 20
Amber and Trevor

"Welcome," stated one of four hostesses at the door of the Trents' palatial estate. The female teen was dressed in a red-and-white Washington Nationals jersey with the homeowner's number. Her black, pleated above-the-knee skirt complemented the team look.

The day had finally arrived when Trevor and Amber would launch their Diamond Dreams Foundation before the 250 guests that had RSVP'd. Black luxury cars and white limos lined up in the circular driveway as drivers dropped off the fashionably dressed. Others who'd driven themselves parked along the private and secluded roadway.

Jaslyn had coordinated the entire gala with Amber and Zodi. Men dressed in tuxedos circulated the home with platters of crab beignets, shrimp rolls, mini Southwest chicken wraps, veggie balls and fried mozzarella skewers. Guests strolled sipping a variety of wines from the home's climate-controlled wine cellar, which held up to 1,000 bottles. Other guests tasted the signature cocktails Jaslyn had created from baseball terminology and attempted to guess their ingredients.

The fifteen-thousand-square-foot, custom-built home with a stone and brick exterior had eight bedrooms, six bathrooms, an elevator, three fireplaces, a basement theater room, and a library.

After the meet-and-greet hour, all gathered in the expansive room as the Trents made their grand entrance. Trevor, dressed in a black tuxedo with a red tie and cummerbund, walked arm in arm with Amber, who gracefully descended the spiral staircase in a red halter Versace gown. Her diamond drop earrings and necklace sparkled as she stepped lightly in her Giuseppe Zanottis. When they reached the bottom of the stairs, Trevor escorted her past tall plants and huge, exorbitant paintings from Amber's art collection until they reached a makeshift podium.

"Good evening and welcome to our home. Thank you for joining us in the launch of the Diamond Dreams Foundation," Trevor greeted the guests. "My beautiful and adorable wife, Amber, and I truly appreciate you supporting our project. Our mission is to provide opportunities for African-American males to play baseball: educating them about the sport and why it's important for us to continue the legacy established by the Negro Leagues. We plan to establish Little Leagues for the youth, offer funds to colleges to recruit outstanding high school players, assistance to those from disadvantaged homes with an interest in baseball, finance field trips to professional baseball and minor league games and tournaments. We have a wealth of ideas and creative activities in store for these promising young boys and men." He paused. "I have a tendency of taking over the mike, so I'd like to turn it over to Amber." He handed her the microphone.

"Trevor and I cannot thank you enough for attending our gala this evening. We decided to create the foundation to allow other fans of the sport to participate. We don't want to continue to lose generations involved in baseball. Many of our historically black colleges and universities no longer have baseball teams. Why? Because they can't find enough players to fill a team, let alone to give scholarships. We'd like to initiate the process to increase awareness here locally and then expand nationally.

"I'd like to acknowledge my wonderful neighbor and dear friend, Jaslyn, who spearheaded this event, and my assistant, Zodi." She nodded to both who were standing together, blushing with pride. Smiling at Shayla and Kyle, who both stood with their husbands, she continued, "And I must thank my special friends Shayla and Kyle for their continuous support." They nodded, thanking Amber for recognition. "After words from our honorable mayor and celebrity guests, there will be a performance by our cheerleaders who have choreographed a delightful routine I'm sure you will enjoy.

"And if any of you are able to join us, please do for a screening in our lower-level theater room of the film *42* about Jackie Robinson. We thought this would be appropriate for the cause, honoring the baseball hero who made Major League history.

"Thank you again and enjoy the evening." She motioned to a massive room overlooking the in-ground pool. "Be sure to step into the sunroom and indulge in the tasty desserts from pastry chef Claude Cavalier."

"Girl, you, Jaslyn and Zodi did your thing. This has been *fantabulous*," Shayla expressed with admiration in a huddle with Amber and Kyle by the baseball ice sculpture. Flaunting a low-cut, gold-sequined wrap dress, she sipped on her Grand Slam cocktail, gripping the glass with her gold sparkled nails. "And I must say there is plenty of candy up in here." She laughed.

"Shayla, you keep those eyes rovin', honey, even with your man in the room," Amber teased, then sipped on her wineglass. For the love of a shopaholic, she had returned upstairs and changed into a more casual red Calvin Klein dress and YSL strappy sandals.

"I always say it doesn't hurt to scope out the scenery," Kyle interjected. "That's exactly what I did in Tortola," she whispered cheerfully. Tonight, she was uplifted. She needed the boost of confidence provided by her short black dress, emphasizing her legs, chiseled from decades of dance. Feeling elegant and regal, she realized that she hadn't received that much attention from any man, regardless of her husband, since returning from the islands.

"Thank you both again," Amber said gratefully.

"We didn't do much—" Shayla started.

She held up her hand. "You helped me by being you. Your support. Surrounding me with positivity *and* creativity. Kyle, your talented dance students gave an awesome performance." She looked at Shayla. "And you used your PR skills to create that fantastic brochure. ...Wow, I realize I didn't bring them from the office for the hostesses to put in the gift bags." She looked down at her feet. "These babies are hurting. That's why I had to switch up."

"I'll get the brochures," Kyle offered. "Where are they exactly in the office?"

"Would you? That's sweet of you. I'm not feeling those stairs and don't want to kick these heels off in front of *these* guests." She giggled. "Not Mrs. Trevor Trent," she added, feeling the alcohol effects. "Should've put on the flats from the jump." She sighed. "Kyle, the brochures are on the left. They're on a small table to the right as soon as you walk inside the door."

"Okay. Wait here and then I can give them to the hostesses." Kyle turned and headed up a back flight of stairs away from the crowd, who were now well into their fund-raiser-turned-cocktail party mood. Contemporary jazz streamed softly in the background.

She reached the top of the staircase and turned to the right, not aware that she had mistakenly gone in the wrong direction. She'd recalled Amber saying "right" when instructing her. She walked down the hall and saw a door ajar. She opened it further and gasped in amazement. She crept inside and spun slowly around. It was like she was a child discovering Candyland. Suddenly, she was inside an upscale shoe store, engulfed by hundreds and hundreds of pairs in what seemed like a zillion colors and styles. *Damn, this is a fetish dream*, she thought, as she eyed the rows of shoes from floor to ceiling. *Prada, Gucci, Louboutin, Bruno Magli, Miu Miu… What doesn't she have? Amber is living like a celebrity. Well, she is married to a pro baller. She's a shopper and a shoe freak, but I didn't think she was a shoe* freakazoid. *But hey, girl, I ain't mad at ya.* She twirled around to scope out all the shelves. *Hmmm, wonder why she never mentioned she had this many shoes, though?* She quickly zoned out of her entrancement, delicately walked out of the room and closed the door. *Amazing.* She turned to the left, passed the staircase and walked into the first door. She had reached her original destination, Amber's office. Besides a tour when the home was first built, she had not been on the upper level. Normally, the ladies' favorite spots were the kitchen, great room, patio and theater room, where they'd enjoy chick flicks during their movie nights.

Picking up the red box of brochures, she left the room and walked downstairs. She searched for the lead hostess once she arrived to the main area and handed them to her. "Hi, Mrs. Trent would like you to ensure each guest receives one of these. Please have the others place them in the gift bags. Thank you." She headed back to Amber and Shayla who were still conversing by the sculpture.

"Girl, I was beginning to think you were up there crashing or something," Shayla surmised.

"No...at first I didn't go to the right room, and then I found it. This place is huge," she said uneasily.

Shayla looked over at Chad and Bryce who were holding their own pow-wow. Both were elegantly dressed in black tuxedos and drinking signature cocktails. *Hmm, my hubby is definitely handsome. I'm sure a lot of these sistas are checking out the goods. What's wrong with me? It's not that I don't appreciate what I have. Guess I must be greedy. Or do I simply have an issue?* She smiled. *But it's a good issue.* She turned her attention back to Amber and Kyle. "You don't think we disappeared too long, do you?"

Kyle glared at Bryce nonchalantly. "No, we're fine." She realized that her husband rarely noticed her anyway, except when he wanted her to strut around like a trophy wife in public. But behind closed doors, he was like a monster.

"Well, since I'm the hostess, I'd better get back to business, or rather entertaining. I don't mean to be rude, but most of them are strangers. I'm not trying to make a bad impression or give Trevor a bad reputation."

"Trevor is such a social king, I'm sure he's handling things," Shayla stated knowingly.

"You are right about that," Amber agreed, then walked toward Trevor who was surrounded by his team players.

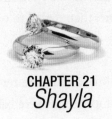

CHAPTER 21
Shayla

The hard rain drenched the streets and battered the glass of the expansive hotel window overlooking the skyline. The Capitol and Monument were in the distance and lit up with the crackling lightning. Thunderstorms offered a soothing and relaxing atmosphere. Gazing out into the sky, it reminded Shayla of nights in New Orleans when she visited her grandparents in their plantation-style home. The vicious storms were threatening, but yet they also offered serenity once all was calm. Thoughts then drifted to Hurricane Katrina and the devastation it'd had on her beloved city. She had relocated to the D.C. area, but relatives there had experienced the ugly side of Mother Nature.

She closed the sheer curtain and turned around. Wearing a bra and thong set, she eyed Blaze seductively. "You ready for round two? Looks like I won't be driving home in this weather."

"Yeah, babe, you right. Those streets can be treacherous." He looked at his watch. "Tell you what, want me to order some room service?"

"Good idea. I'm starved." She walked over to the bed, picked up a white hotel robe and slipped into it. He already was wearing one, opened up to reveal his buff chest. She sashayed to the desk and found the hotel's menu, then opened it for review. "I'll take the Gulf Snapper." She walked over to him sitting on the bed and handed him the menu. He decided on Rotisserie Chicken and picked up the room phone, then dialed to order.

She sat on the bed and picked up the remote, channel surfing until she found a show simply to provide background noise. She was only interested in Blaze for the moment and perhaps the TV would distract her from craving more gymnastics. He was a sexpert and knew how to bring it real and raw. After dinner, she hoped the storm would have subsided and she could drive home. Chad would be back in town the next day and she couldn't wait to get her claws on him. He'd said he needed to slow his West Coast visits and concentrate on more of the local properties for a while. He catered to multimillion-dollar homes and condos, and the number available in the D.C. area was steadily climbing.

Once the meals were delivered, they ate and then reclined in bed, propped up by pillows, awaiting the storm to ease. Blaze had opened a chilled bottle of Moscato.

"Shayla," he started.

"Yes, Blaze."

"I've been thinking…"

"Yes…"

"I haven't told you much about my personal life, right?"

"Right, what are you getting to? I can tell you're setting me up."

"What?" he responded defensively.

"Not like that. You're leading up to something."

"Oh, okay, that's better. I'm gonna come out and ask you." He sighed. "I have a baby sister," he lied. "Name's Terra. Looks like she could head in the wrong direction, and I don't want anything to happen to her. She's cool and all, but she truly needs some guidance, a mentor. Moms left us at an early age. So Terra was the only girl, and she's had to make her way through life solo—no females to look up to...except some of her girlfriends or folk she work wit'."

"And..."

"And I was gonna check if you and your girls wouldn't mind putting in some time wit' her. Show her the ropes. She needs to change up a little, feel me?"

"Yes, I *feel* you all right," she teased.

"No, on the real tip, I'd 'preciate if you'd take her under ya wings for a minute." He looked at her with goo-goo eyes and clutched her hand.

She set her wineglass on the end table and laid her head on his shoulder. "Blaze, I'm an only child, so I don't know what it's like to have siblings. I understand though how you could be concerned, especially if you sense she's taking the wrong turn." She caressed the soft white duvet. "I tell you what; bring her to the office on your next appointment. I'd be happy to meet her and we'll take it from there. Okay?"

"Yep, it's all good." He raised her head and looked her in the eyes. "Thanks, Shayla." He gently kissed her lips, then her neck and helped her ease out of her robe.

CHAPTER 22
Shayla

"Camilla, please bring in Mr. Harrison," Shayla announced as she buzzed the reception desk.

"Will do." Camilla stood up and looked across the room. She walked toward Blaze and Terra. "I'll show you back to Mrs. Benson's office now."

Strutting in her curvaceous figure and pulling down her clingy dress, she led them to the rear. When she reached Shayla's door, she opened it, allowing them to enter before she closed it and returned to the reception area.

Shayla stood from her desk and reached over to shake Terra's hand while nodding at Blaze. "I'm delighted to meet you, Ms. Harrison, and I've definitely heard good things about you. Please sit down."

It's Jones, not Harrison, but I've got to get used to this name, Terra thought. "I prefer Terra."

"Sure, Terra."

The two sat in the inviting chairs across from her desk. Camilla had placed cold bottles of water in each place on the desk.

"Blaze, to bring you up to date, I've pitched you for an article nationally in *Upscale* magazine and locally in the *City Paper*." Shayla tapped her desk with a pen. "I've also pitched you to open for Roz Monroe when she's in concert here. I'm waiting to hear now. It could lead to you going on tour with her," she stated, her voice heightening with anticipation about the popular R&B artist.

"Roz, now that's slammin'! I'm feelin' that move. That's a no-brainer there. When will you know for sure?" he asked eagerly.

"Likely in a week or so. Her manager and I have ties to New Orleans. Turns out she went to college there across town. So we consider ourselves homegirls."

"Cool, cool." He looked at Terra. "Why you so quiet?"

Terra looked down and twiddled the straps on her purse. She raised her head and then stroked her hair styled in a bob. "No reason. You were talking business."

"Well, I introduced you. Now that she's given me an update, perhaps you should enlighten *Mrs.* Benson," he emphasized, "about your up-and-coming desires."

Terra leaned toward the desk, her low-cut top showing plenty of cleavage despite Blaze's suggestion to dress conservative. "I'm not sure what all Blaze told you, but I feel like I've missed out on life. I was headed off to college but then I said the hell—" she corrected, trying to be professional. "I let that go for now. I've been working in retail since high school, and I'm ready for a change. Don't get me wrong. I love stores, but I could use a new space," she explained.

"I'd even be prepared to help you around here if you need it," she offered, trying to make herself sound promising.

"I understand," Shayla responded. "How's your English? I could have you do some proofreading and maybe some typing."

Terra cleared her throat. "Well, I'm okay in that department, but not necessarily a pro," she responded, trying not to lead Shayla in that direction after all. She wasn't interested in working or learning any new skills. Hell, she simply wanted to hook the kind of catch Shayla obviously had snagged: a man with lined pockets and a hefty bank account. That was her interest and something that had seemed unattainable. She had earned that right after all the dedicated years to her retail position and living life at the same level. Now, it was time to advance, and the only light she saw gleaming was to hang around those she aspired to emulate.

"I see. Well, we can find something for you, I'm sure."

Yeah, like a brother with dough you can roll my way, she thought.

"Shayla, she would love to get to know you and your girls," Blaze interjected, realizing that Terra wouldn't be a good fit in the office role. "I've only seen them once when I came up here, but I could see they had it goin' on," he complimented. "Terra promises to be a good student." He laughed.

"We simply enjoy life. None of us have any children—yet." She thought about how Kyle was the only one who had come close to parenthood since the three of them had met. Her unfortunate miscarriage had pre-empted that reality. "So we invest our time in our *husbands* and our friendship.

"I'm committed to Blaze and his endeavors, and I'll be happy to help you in any way that I can." She smiled at Terra. "Maybe we can get together soon in a different setting.

"Actually, one of my friends, Amber, has an assistant, Zodi, that's about your age," she offered. She looked at Blaze, who was frowning.

"Or we can welcome you to join us at one of our next ladies' events," she added, disregarding the suggestion she connect with someone on her age level.

Terra sat back and relaxed. "I would love to." Her mind sailed off to fantasize about a world in which she was unaccustomed.

"See, I told you it would be a breeze." Blaze reached over to give Terra dap while they stood outside of the office building.

"Yeah, I have to get used to saying the name Harrison…Harrison, Harrison." She grinned. "Thank you, brother, my *big* brother," she teased. "Good lookin' out."

"You'll be straight. Hang out with the ladies a little, get in the mix, taste a bit of the up and up, nah mean?"

Terra looked down with a worried expression. "You still think this is the right way to go?" She was beginning to feel slightly guilty, preparing to pretend she was someone that she wasn't.

"Well, you can keep on as is, struggling every day tryna make ends meet, working your day job—by the way, glad you got off today—or spend some time hanging out and grooming yaself for a different *lifestyle*."

She looked into Blaze's eyes. "Okay, cool, let's see what happens."

"Hey, you're young and yo' whole life is ahead of ya, so let it do what it do."

CHAPTER 23
Kyle

Kyle nervously sat the bar at the Tropics Lounge on Connecticut Avenue in D.C. She looked around at the slick surroundings. It reminded her of the islands when she'd gone to Tortola. Large palm plants lined the stone entrance and the dim lighting served as a shield for identification. It was helpful for those like her who were desiring shade. During the middle of such a sunny day, it felt like it was nighttime. Bright colorful paintings were peppered along the wood-paneled walls. It was definitely a Caribbean flavor. Nets holding seashells hung from the ceilings to resemble hammocks on the beach.

She checked her watch: 12:40 p.m. It was going on forty minutes since Erick was scheduled to meet her for lunch. After being prodded several times at the studio when he picked up Merlan, she finally had given in to simply have lunch with him. She considered it harmless in accepting the invitation from a parent. Erick alluded that he wanted to discuss any tips or advice for raising a girl without a mother. Although she didn't have children, he'd praised her on mentoring the female students.

Crossing her legs, she showed off her physique in a ruffled turquoise dress. She'd ordered a cosmopolitan and was ready for a second but didn't want too much of a buzz before Erick arrived. She nibbled on some honey-wheat pretzels to curb her appetite.

"Hello." She felt the warm breath on her back and turned around. It was Erick.

"Sorry, I'm late," he said, pulling out the barstool beside her and hopping on it. "The traffic was backed up. My apologies."

"Accepted. I've been here checking out this place. Feel like I'm in the islands someplace. I was in Tortola not long ago."

"Tortola? Never heard of it. Where is it?"

"British Virgin Islands. It's beautiful there." She emptied her glass and set it on the counter.

"What are you drinking?"

"Cosmopolitan, thanks."

Erick motioned toward the bartender who walked toward them and stopped.

"Another cosmopolitan for the lady, and I'll take Johnnie Walker on the rocks."

"So, how are you feeling?" Erick gazed into her eyes. "You look lovely," he added, checking her out in full force.

"I'm fine. It's good to have this break during the day. I rarely get away."

"How's that manager, Sienna? She's not working out?"

"Oh, no, she's great. This is my first foray into business, so maybe I'm one of those folks who's overprotective or it's hard for me to let it go, delegate stuff. Always wanting to have my hand in everything, and what do they call it, micromanaging?" She sighed. "Well, you said you wanted to pick my brain about raising a daughter. You're aware I don't have any children," she added sadly.

"I'm aware, but I feel like women still have a mother's intuition, whether they have kids or not."

"True...so how is it raising Merlan? Any grandmothers or aunts, cousins around? She's so adorable and such a sweet spirit."

"Sometimes she visits her grandmother down South. Otherwise, it's usually the two of us."

The bartender returned with their drinks. Erick downed his in a couple of sips and Kyle sipped hers graciously.

"My friend Amber was a psych major. Now she's working as a housewife." *And an over-the-top shopaholic*, she thought, recalling the surprise shoe store she'd discovered in her home. "She and her husband, Trevor—I'm sure you're familiar with Trevor Trent who plays for the Nationals—"

"Oh, definitely."

"They just launched a foundation to get more African-American boys interested in baseball."

"I'm feelin' that. We used to swing the bat, but all of a sudden, ev'body was tryin' to be the next Jordan," he noted, reflecting on his community team during middle school.

"Anyway, Amber's great with kids, and she's a people person. I hope she decides to return to school and then work with folks who need someone to listen. She'd be good at that." She bit into a cheese nacho.

"Well, we haven't had a chance to discuss it much. I'd mentioned it at the studio, but thought I'd invite you out to talk." He looked at her, trying to decipher her vibe. "Sometimes you look a little tense." He focused on her ring finger, then quickly averted his eyes. "Is everything okay?"

"Look, Erick, I don't know you like that," she responded defensively, unsure why he was checking her status. "What are you trying to say?"

"Oh, nothin'. Sorry, I didn't mean to offend you."

She became silent, looking at his piercing eyes. Despite the low lighting, she could see his smooth complexion complemented by a white shirt with an open collar. He always appeared handsomely dressed. With each cosmo, she noticed a new asset about Erick. If nothing else, at least he was paying her some attention. She missed such moments with Bryce when they'd first met. The dating phase had been memorable. He had been Mr. Wine and Dine. Now, except for the foundation fund-raiser, it had been a while since they'd had a true date night.

"No, you're fine." She thought maybe she had overreacted to his question. "I'm sorry. I'm a little on edge."

"About?"

She grabbed a piece of her hair and pulled it behind her ear. "It doesn't matter." A sad look appeared and she dropped her head.

He reached over and touched her chin, then lifted her face. "It'll be okay, whatever it is."

She looked into his eyes. "Thanks." She became tense. Here this strange man had reached out to comfort her and she kind of liked his gentle touch. "I'd better go. I'm not trying to be rude… We can talk about Merlan again. Say hello for me." She paused. "Maybe not," she added, indicating she didn't want her to realize they'd connected outside of the studio setting.

"No problem. Should I walk you to your car?"

"Actually, I used the valet. Have a good evening." She stood up and walked steadily out of the door.

She's a fine sista. And Merlan adores her.

Kyle replayed the actions at the bar in her mind as she navigated through the streets of D.C. She'd pulled into a local coffee shop and bought a cup, sipping it as she waited for her buzz to simmer. She definitely wasn't feeling Mr. DUI. Erick had provided an oasis albeit temporarily from the storm that she might face at home. She never could predict when Bryce would act like a calming sedative or when he'd burst into a flaming rage. It was a Thursday and he always was late coming home—like clockwork. Her stay had been longer than expected, and she needed to stop at the studio before heading home.

Since he was such a caring parent, she would take a special interest in Merlan. There wouldn't be any harm in taking her under her wing. She wasn't so sure that she needed to continue hooking up with Dad, or she might end up under his sheets. She quickly deleted the notion from her head, although it was quite a pleasant thought.

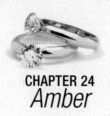

CHAPTER 24
Amber

"That feels wonderful," Amber said, relishing the masseur as he kneaded her shoulders with almond orange scrub. She looked over at Trevor, who was enjoying a chocolate mint treatment from a masseuse. The couple was set to have their his-and-hers massage session monthly in their basement gymnasium. When they'd met with the architect, Trevor pictured a home with a full gym. It would be a dream to accommodate his athleticism and to be able to work out anytime.

Trent turned toward Amber as the back rub took him to another level. "Yes, baby, doesn't it?" He was determined that he would stay awake this go-round. Sometimes he'd drift off into a light sleep after the hour-long intense but relaxing workout. It didn't help that the tables were cushioned and scented.

Chante Moore's "Wey U" piped through the room from ceiling speakers. Aromatherapy candles and raspberry lights added to the calm ambience.

"The fund-raiser was a success. I've heard nothing but good comments from the guys, our manager, everyone. They were impressed." Trevor turned his head to face the awaiting sauna where they would head next in their ritual.

"Yes, and I couldn't have been happier with the turnout. Jaslyn really should expand her event planning. She's the best." She relaxed as her massage deepened. "I'm going to plan another one but distance it out."

The Diamond Dreams launch also had been a winner, allowing them to clinch their initial financial goal. One of their first efforts would be to plan a trip for young males to attend a Nationals game.

After the massages, they thanked the massage duo who then headed upstairs for Zodi to lead them out. Trevor and Amber wrapped in oversized, fluffy towels and stepped into slippers. They plodded toward the sauna and walked inside.

Trevor turned on the timer and the steam seeped out and surrounded them, allowing their senses to release. Sweat drenched their bodies for ten minutes and then when the timer sounded, Trevor opened the door and they stepped out.

Next stop was the huge shower where they lathered each other with loofah sponges and vanilla cream. After rinsing off, he lifted her, wrapping her legs around his waist as he placed her against the granite tile. The water cascaded over them as he inserted his rod and penetrated deep, thrusting hard until they exploded beneath a waterfall.

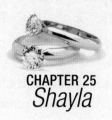

CHAPTER 25
Shayla

C had chomped on turkey bacon and a Cajun cheese omelette. "This is dee-licious, Shayla. I'm on the road so much, it's a treat to be able to sit at my own table for a change. And enjoy my wife's cooking, I should add." He bit into a slice of multi-grain toast and sipped his coffee.

Shayla looked up from her plate and wiped her mouth with her napkin. She wiggled the toes of her crossed legs. "Well, thank you, Mr. Benson, glad you could join me." She smiled. "So, you have some great news for me. You emphasized *great*. These ears are burning."

"Two things. It looks like the properties are picking up here with D.C. having a reputation as one of the wealthiest cities. The housing market is on the upswing and it's truly a seller's market. We can't keep enough listings because the buyers are buying them like wildfire. In fact, there's a shortage of available homes."

"I've heard that. It's a plus for the economy," she acknowledged. "I remember once Fourteenth and U was a buzz intersection for crime and hookers. Now it's the hangout for the up-and-coming." She reminisced about her jaunts to visit Damien in the area. "So I'm sure the neighborhoods have changed as far as housing. And they're building so many condos selling at high prices."

He put down his fork on his plate and looked into her eyes. "I have a pending deal for one of the most prestigious addresses in Glover Park. And another in the Foxhall area. Both are handsomely priced."

"Dare you tell?" she asked eagerly.

"One is eight million and the other five," he announced proudly.

"Wow, those are some West Coast prices."

"Right, and so if I can turn these kind of deals here, then I can plan to spend more time at home." He rose up, reached across the table and pecked her lips. "And that's better for the both of us."

"Yes, it is," she lied, selfishly thinking how Chad's increased presence would slow her roll with her ongoing hookups. *Mr. Class, Raw, Smooth Jazz and any newbies would have to take a backseat. Oh, I'm such a naughty girl.* She snapped out of her thoughts. "What's the other news you got for me? Can't get much better than that."

"I'm taking you on a vacation of your dreams for your birthday next year."

"Oh, where are we going?" she asked excitedly.

"I'm not saying. I'll ask you to pack your bags and then we'll be heading to the airport," he teased.

"That's not fair. How will I know what to pack? The weather?"

"I'd say prepare for the heat."

"Hmmm." Her mind started spinning as she guessed the location. "It's no need in me naming places, 'cause you're not going to tell me."

He nodded his head in agreement.

She playfully tapped him on the hand. "No fair. I don't like surprises."

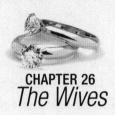

CHAPTER 26
The Wives

"That was a blast! I didn't know you had it in you," Shayla told Kyle, who had just sung Chaka Khan's "Sweet Thing" at the karaoke night. She'd worked the mike like she was a superstar, strutting back and forth across the stage as she belted out the hit.

"I was surrounded by music in New York and of course at the studios there. I spent many a dollar at Virgin in Times Square. I had a serious record and CD collection," Kyle stated. "I used to dream of being on Broadway permanently after I had a chance to appear a few times," she added, starry-eyed.

"Yeah, girl, we were glad to see you out of your shell you've been in lately," Amber added.

"I didn't get up there 'cause I would've emptied it out. No one would want to hear these lungs." Shayla laughed.

"So we're waiting to meet Terra. Did I say her name right?" Kyle asked.

"Yes, that's right."

They had stepped outside on the patio of the Channel Inn, a longtime staple of the D.C. Southwest waterfront.

"You say she's twenty-five? I know she wouldn't remember back in the day when this whole street was jumping. The Zanzibar, Hogate's, H2O, all those spots are history. This is the sole survivor of the party strip."

"Who would've ever thought those landmarks would've been torn down?"

"You got that right."

"We'll notice her when she steps in. Can't miss her."

Terra stepped into the lounge area when the band was taking a break. A customer with silver hair and a mustache sitting at the bar spotted her and turned his full body around. "Hello, sweetie, can I get you a drink?"

Terra, despite being dressed with bling-bling confidence, looked out of sorts. "I'm looking for some friends," she said, peering around him and then spotting them in the patio area. "I see them. Thanks, anyway." She headed toward the brick terrace, her flirty black skirt accentuating her toned legs as she flaunted her laced-up black sandals.

"Hi, Terra! We've been waiting on you," Shayla acknowledged as Terra pulled out a chair at the table. "This is Kyle," she motioned, "and Amber."

Terra reached out and shook both of their hands. "Hi, Terra Jones…Harrison," she quickly corrected to Blaze's surname. *Oops, I gotta keep practicing that name.*

"I was thinking you didn't recognize this strip," Shayla stated. "It was jumping a short time ago. Clubs were lined up and you could hardly find a parking spot."

"I always heard about it. Some of my older family members used to hang out down here," Terra responded. "I was too young— at the time. Guess I missed out."

"I'm sure the sugar daddies hopped on you when you walked in," Shayla announced.

"Well, one guy did offer to buy me a drink, but I kept on steppin'."

"I was telling Amber and Kyle that I'm somewhat mentoring

you for a while. Your big brother asked me to help out. You're the only girl and he said your mom passed."

"That's right." Terra shuddered about the deadly home invasion that resulted in the loss of her parents. "I miss Mom and it would be great to have someone I can hang with. I'm kinda tired of my job and the same ol' friends. Don't get me wrong. I love my peeps, but it's good to get out of my comfort zone and meet some new people.

"Basically, I'm tryna step up my game a little. Do some networking. A little sumthin'-sumthin'," she added.

"There's nothing wrong with that, dear," Amber interjected. "You're young and have some drive. That's important." *And you're pretty, I should add. Maybe you will hook you a good catch someday.*

"Your brother, Blaze, does he try to play the big brother? Be overprotective? Or does he let you do your own thing?" Kyle inquired.

"He tries to pull rank and tell me what to do, but I won't let him."

"You go, girl. I can tell you're a little feisty," Shayla said, noting in her mind that her brother was feisty between the sheets. "Blaze didn't tell me that. You seemed so sweet and innocent when you came to the office." She smiled. "Would you like a drink?"

"Sure, a Long Island Iced Tea."

Shayla directed the waitress who arrived at their table. "A Long Island Iced Tea and we'll take another round of strawberry daiquiris. Tell him to make sure they have some kick." The summery frozen drink was what they needed on this warm night.

After a second drink, Terra started to loosen her nerves and feel less intimidated. She'd listened more than talked to this new group of women, all mature and wealthy. They had little in common with her at this point in their lives, but all were genuinely friendly and down-to-earth. Maybe one of them had a younger brother—or older for that matter. She wouldn't be picky if she could fatten her bank account from the meager savings she'd accrued from years of working slightly above minimum wage. She'd observed the rocks on their fingers, impeccable makeup and hair, and designer dresses let alone shoes. Their table depicted a high-end fashion boutique.

The band started up with Rob Base & DJ E-Z Rock's "It Takes Two" for its new set. The same gentleman from the bar had made his way to the patio. He walked over to Terra and reached out his hand.

Terra agreed to follow him to the dance floor where they show-cased their skills. He did the two-step move while she threw down with funky steps. When the song ended, he inquired if she wanted a drink. She declined, stating she'd had enough for now and returned to the patio.

"I told you the fellas would be checkin' you out," Shayla said. "What happened, he could only hang for one song? I'm surprised you didn't stay out there forever."

"No, I guess I ended it. He tried to get me a drink." Terra sighed.

"Girl, you should've accepted it," Amber stated.

"But he'd probably think I owed him something then." Terra smiled. "I'm not trying to hook up with my *dad*." *At least not for now anyway, but hmm, if it were to come down to that, I'd go that way. Gold diggers can't always be choosy, especially since I'm tryna get on the up and up.*

"So, what do you like to do? Where do you work?" Kyle asked.

"Oh, I've been in retail since I got out of high school. That's why I'd like to do something different. Maybe college, but I'm still trying to figure out what I want to do. Right now, it's the nine-to-five thing." Terra knew exactly her goal: to snag her a rich man to offer her a luxurious lifestyle she couldn't attain unless she dealt with drug dealers. After witnessing her friends losing their lives from violence, she didn't want to follow that path. Frankly, she wouldn't be satisfied with simply diamonds and designer bags. She wanted the full life: step into a mansion, drive a luxury car and travel the world. Yes, the dealers she knew could dress her fashionably, but she'd still have to return to the modest home where she now resided.

"Your brother is a rising star," Amber suggested, nodding to Shayla.

"That's true and it's been a pleasure working with him. He's got a tour in the works." Shayla looked at Terra. "I'm sure he's planning to take you. You'll get to travel."

Terra looked down. "No, I don't believe so."

"Your brother won't let you go? You could help his manager or be his assistant," Shayla suggested.

"Actually, I'm not interested," she lied.

"Oh, I see. That's understandable. Sometimes we don't want to follow behind our siblings." Kyle's older sister had suggested she enter the fashion design world. Growing up in New York, she had been surrounded by the business, but she was determined to pursue dance. "I have a dance studio. I'd always dreamed of a place to train girls—and we do have a few young men—as I danced from age five up to twenty-one. It didn't become a reality until this year."

"And my hubby and I recently started a foundation to encourage young men to play baseball," Amber offered.

She realized that Terra was beginning to look uneasy as if she were being drilled with questions. Kyle was right to share their own lifestyles.

"Wow, you all got it going on," she said, including her knowledge of Shayla as a public relations executive. Being with this trio could obviously bring prosperity if she hung around them long enough. She could play the pretentious role for a while if she stood to gain benefits. Blaze had directed her to do more listening than talking, especially for this initial introduction. He said she had the tendency to give out too much information at times.

The familiar older gentleman entered the terrace and walked to their table. It was another break for the band, and the deejay had cranked up the music. "You ladies are having too much of a good time. Having your own little party out here. I'm gonna steal this young lady from you again." He reached out for Terra's hand, and she stood up and followed him back to the dance floor.

They danced to George Clinton's "Atomic Dog."

Hey, I could get used to this old school music and old daddy-o here. She looked closer at his expensive suit and tie, then down at his shiny gators. *Yeah, he might break me a piece off.*

The song changed to Earth, Wind and Fire's "That's the Way of the World." He pulled her closer, embracing her to slow dance.

CHAPTER 27
Kyle

K yle closed her office door and headed to the ballet class. She wanted to check out if Merlan was coming along with her lessons before leaving to meet her dad for dinner. He'd offered to treat her. This time they could focus on Merlan and discuss some suggestions on improving her life.

Merlan was at the bar and gracefully moving her arms and feet in changing positions. She noticed Kyle through the mirror and smiled. She recognized that she was dressed up for some special occasion and not in her usual casual or business attire. Kyle wore a dress and had replaced her flats with heels.

Merlan had started to blossom and release from her shell since she'd started dancing. Erick had advised Kyle that he'd noticed a turnaround and he'd attributed it to Magical Moves. He'd also mentioned that he would be willing to back her if she wanted to open a second studio, this time in his hometown D.C. instead of the suburbs. He had some investment funds set aside and he'd witnessed how dance had helped his daughter tremendously. Perhaps it would duplicate with other girls. The idea had intrigued her as she'd always envisioned a chain of studios. She doubted that Bryce would assist her in opening another one.

Kyle considered it was harmless to meet up with Erick again to discuss business and Merlan. And it didn't hurt that she'd be sitting across from some eye candy. Plus, she owed him a second chance. Their first meeting at Tropics had a rocky start; he was late and she was reeling from the effects of verbal abuse. This time she'd be more pleasant with an open mind.

Stopping at the valet parking station at the Renaissance downtown hotel, she stepped out of her car and walked through the lobby doors. She searched for the bar lounge and found Erick waiting for her. He was on time, not unlike their first bar hookup.

He stood up and greeted her. "I was having a drink, but I'd already told the hostess I'd like a table." They walked to the station where a hostess showed them to a table nestled in a private corner away from the noise of government workers and business travelers.

"Oh, this is nice," Kyle stated as he pulled out the chair and allowed her to sit.

"Ever been here?"

"No, I haven't. Lovely hotel."

They ordered their meals and drinks.

"It was kind of you to invite me out again. I stopped by the classroom to see Merlan before I left. She was dancing to Beethoven and smiled at me when she saw me in the mirror. She is such a sweetheart. If I ever have a daughter, I want her to be like her when she grows up." Suddenly, she recalled the devastating miscarriage and how Bryce had reacted. Often she thought his bitterness was still reflected through his actions toward her.

She found Erick a refreshing change from the constant bruising of her ego at home. One day, she could see herself breaking free from his tight reins. *Humph, he tried to tell me I couldn't come home after midnight.* Since then, he'd chilled out a little and realized he couldn't control her hours with the girls.

"Do you plan to have children? Some women don't want any, especially those who are focused on their careers," Erick inquired.

"Yes, I'd like to have children someday, but my clock is ticking."

"It would be rude of me to ask your age so I won't."

She laughed. "And if you did, I wouldn't tell you," she teased. "On the real, it's a personal choice. My closest friends here don't have any at this *time*; however, they all would like to be a mother." She took a fork of her shrimp stuffed with crabmeat. "Now my friends back in New York are a mix. Some settled down with babies and others are adventurous and single with no kids. Many of them from dance are still performing on Broadway and traveling. It doesn't always lend itself to parenthood."

"Merlan is truly a blessing, the reason I get up and work. I want her to have a good life. I don't want to keep repeating myself, but I can't thank you enough. I can see the change."

"It's not only me. It's the teachers at school, our dance instructors, even the classmates. I do believe in what they say, 'It takes a village to raise a child.'" She paused. "Has she ever gone for therapy?"

"No, none other than seeing her school counselor. Sometimes she acts out in class and her teachers send her there."

"That's good. I'm sure that's helpful." She sipped her martini. "This bartender is outstanding." She suddenly recalled they were to discuss a business venture. "So, tell me more about the idea for a studio in the city. This may sound crazy, but it's hard to believe a guy like you would want to invest in a studio."

"I see the effects on Merlan. It's a good thing." He looked into her eyes. "I'm sure you'd need to check with your husband—"

"Bryce…oh, yes, although he wouldn't have anything to do with a decision if I expand. He should want me to prosper. I do have to give him credit for helping me to finance Magical Moves. If it wasn't for him, it would still be an idea only."

"Well, that's true from what you're telling me. Excuse me for saying this, but if I had a trophy wife like you, I'd give her whatever she wanted…as long as I could afford it."

"Thanks, a trophy wife. Yeah, sometimes I feel like one, but not always treated like one. Ooops, I didn't mean to say that."

"No problem…not prying, but I asked you when we met at Tropics, if everything was okay?"

"I'm fine. Sometimes in relationships, marriage, whatever, it's not always what you hoped," Kyle said, her words now loosening from the alcohol.

"Nothing is always a hundred percent. You have to take the good with the bad. It can be rocky."

"Yes, but you get tired of being in a volatile situation. Then in addition to the ups and downs, I feel like I'm a puppet sometimes, like I'm being remote-controlled. I can never have peace unless I'm alone. And don't let me get started on that. *Alone.*" She harrumphed. "It's more like abandoned." She realized she was sharing more than she'd planned. Perhaps it was because she'd never told Shayla or Amber the truth about Bryce. Erick was like an open door and she'd entered. "I'm sorry, enough of this. I didn't intend to get you involved."

"I'm a listening ear. Feel free to continue, but don't if you feel uncomfortable."

"No, I think I'll stop it there. But thanks anyway for hearing me out."

Erick assessed the situation. "Let me take care of the bill and then we can head upstairs."

"Upstairs? What's upstairs?" she asked groggily. The drinks

had made her tipsy as well as drowsy. She looked at her watch. "I'd better head home. Bryce usually stays out late most weeknights."

"Are you okay to drive now? Maybe you should come up and have a cup of coffee, then head out. I wouldn't want you driving like you are now."

"No, I'd better not. I could get a coffee here, I suppose."

"Well, if you come up to my room—"

"Room?"

"Yes, I have a room here for the night. I have an early morning meeting downtown, so I figured I'd be closer in," he lied.

Kyle paused to let what he'd said register in her mind. "Okay, I gotcha. Maybe I'll go up and get myself together." She pretended that she was totally unfocused, but she was well aware of her actions. She was enjoying all of the attention that Erick was showing toward her.

When the waiter returned, he paid the check and then led her to the elevators where they headed to the twelfth floor. They entered the room and she laid her purse on a table. She slipped off her heels, replacing them with a pair of thong flip-flops from her purse and then headed to the window. It was a picturesque postcard view of the city skyline at dusk.

"Beautiful view," she said dreamily.

Erick approached her from behind and placed both of his hands on her shoulders. "Beautiful lady."

Her shoulders and heart melted. His voice was sincere and she stepped further toward the windows as he lost his grip.

"Sorry about that," he apologized.

She turned around, mesmerized by his handsome face, and reached out into his arms, planting a ravenous kiss on his lips. She rapidly wrestled out of her dress, revealing her pink floral bra and sheer panty set. She unloosened his tie and helped him unbutton his shirt. They moved to the bed for him to take off his pants.

Suddenly and gently, he removed her hands from his body. He lifted her face in his hands just as he'd done at Tropics and gazed in her eyes. "I can't, Kyle. I can't do this. You're a married woman and I respect that…and you. I didn't intend to lead you on. I never made it to the coffee pot.

"Please, put back on your dress. I'll make you coffee." He got up, buttoned his shirt back and walked toward the station. He prepared the cup of coffee and hit "brew."

When he turned around, she was stepping into her dress and smoothed it out. She walked to the mirror and tousled her hair back in place. "I apologize. I guess I got carried away. This romantic setting after a delicious dinner, it all got to me." *And the day-to-day loneliness.* She thought further about what had happened. *Or was he testing me? Seeing how far I would go or he would go? I'm not a fool. This man is as much attracted to me as I am to him. And he's using Merlan as a ploy. It's not that he doesn't want the best for her, but she provides the link. That's okay. I'm one step ahead of him.*

After drinking her coffee that he'd prepared, she perked up to leave the room. She was slightly embarrassed by her behavior, particularly since he'd rejected her.

"Please keep this between us," she requested.

"Most definitely," he agreed before giving her a hug and closing the door behind her.

He walked over to the window and looked below, ensuring that Kyle had gotten into her car safely. He spotted the valet and her tipping him before stepping into the car. He walked over and sat in the chaise. He picked up the remote and turned on the flatscreen to ESPN. After twenty minutes, he lowered the volume and picked up his cell phone from his waistband case. He dialed a number and waited for an answer.

"Hello."

"Hey, man, it's done. She was all about it. If it wasn't for me turning it down, it would've been a go." He smiled mischievously. *Your lady is* phine *and I don't understand why you don't see it. Sweeeeet, too. You're my boy, but if she'd been anybody's but yours, I damn sure would've been in those panties.* He licked his lips.

"I figured she'd be game," he said angrily.

"Man, you owe me a big favor."

"I got you, bro. Thanks." Bryce hung up the call.

CHAPTER 28
The Wives

A line of selective guests wrapped down the plank and along the walkway at the National Harbor in Prince George's County, Maryland. It included the Who's Who of the DMV, the new trend name for the District of Columbia and its Maryland and Northern Virginia suburbs. Women in summer party dresses and men in dressy casual outfits exuded style and class as they prepared to board the rented, one-hundred-fifty-foot yacht. The evening Amber had shared with Shayla, Kyle and Terra on the Southwest waterfront had given her the idea to have a birthday party on a yacht. Jaslyn had assisted in planning the soiree for 250 guests.

Amber had spent many a day on her uncle's yacht sailing on the San Francisco Bay. While attending Stanford, a college classmate, whose father was the mayor of a coastal town, had invited her on her parents' yacht where she partied and hobnobbed with the wealthy. She treasured the water and was planning to purchase a beach cottage on one of Maryland's tiny islands. It was a key reason she'd suggested to Trevor they build their home in Annapolis.

As each guest stepped aboard, they gathered on the deck and a host or hostess in all black handed them a flute of Armand de Brignac Brut Gold champagne. Terra could see that it wouldn't take much for her to be impressed. *Now that looks like top, top, top shelf,* she thought.

Accompanied by Blaze, she was laid-back knowing she had a designated driver. She observed him intensely, noting how he was a networker in a crowd. He was smooth as he mingled throughout the deck, introducing himself to partygoers. A handful of the younger set were familiar with the hip-hopper and he'd whipped out his Sharpie to autograph their napkins or tiny pieces of paper they'd pulled from their clutch bags.

Shayla had taught him well that personality was an essential key of gaining popularity. Sitting back and chilling like a block of ice would gain you haters. If you thought you were above the clouds, you needed to come back to earth and connect with your listeners and fans. Wearing a hard face also would deter others from approaching you, so it was best to adorn a friendly one where strangers would gravitate toward you. As he moved throughout the deck welcoming guests, he put her rules of thumb into operation.

Shayla eyed Blaze as he practiced. She could see his progress and his demeanor appeared more natural. Everyone was a fake at some point, but when you were in the business of seeking fans, you needed to be a fakeroo at full speed. As she watched him, her panties moistened. She realized it had been a while since the evening they'd ordered room service. She zoned in on the bulge in his black rayon slacks and up to his muscled chest peeking through his V-neck shirt.

Kyle approached her and brought her back to reality. "You always check out your clients like that?"

"What's that supposed to mean?" she asked embarrassingly.

"I'm teasing."

"Okay, that's better. Actually, I was observing how much better he's finagling with the crowd. When he first hired me, he was a little rough around the edges and sometimes kicked back. You have to be aggressive in this business and put yourself out there. I'm simply enjoying the fruits of my effort."

Any moment she expected Chad to be dropped off by a driver. They'd hired a car service, so they could get as smashed as they desired. Once he boarded, she would have to keep all eyes focused on him for a change. He would kill all opportunity of searching for eye candy, and there were plenty of Mr. Goodbars on board.

"So, did your hubby make it?" Shayla inquired. *For once?*

"You already know that answer. Except for the foundation launch, he never seems to make it," Kyle responded sadly.

"Well, mine is on this coast for a change, so he's on his way," she stated begrudgingly.

"You don't seem too happy about that." She analyzed the situation. "Oh, I got it. He'll be blocking your view." She laughed.

"Right, but it's all good. I can put on my blinders."

The sun descended and the *River Lady* pulled away to set sail on the Potomac. The brilliant glow at dusk cast a serene aura on the deck as most were on their second flute of champagne. Amber had announced that the first level was set for a buffet meal and dining, and the upper-level lounge was ready with a deejay. She'd asked for donations to the foundation in lieu of birthday gifts, and guests had dropped envelopes in a gold box throughout their arrival.

As Kyle stood in the buffet line to serve her plate, she heard a familiar voice behind her.

"You certainly look lovely this evening."

She turned around. "Erick, what are you doing here?"

"I was invited…by Amber."

She frowned and looked in the direction of the head table where Amber and Trent were seated. "Amber?"

"I heard about her party on the yacht. I've never been to an event like this on a boat, so I wanted to experience." He clutched his plate filled with food.

"I'm still trying to figure out how you know Amber?" she asked, steadily walking along the buffet and adding to her plate.

"Let's just say I know Trent, or at least, of him."

"Everyone knows Trent who is familiar with the Nationals."

"Okay, I'll be honest. I met her at your grand opening. Remember I was one of only a few guys there."

"Oh, okay, I was wondering." She wasn't totally satisfied but tired of interrogating him. He was sharply dressed and looked tantalizing. She avoided naughty thoughts and invited him to sit with her. She was the oddball tonight as her girls both had their hubbies present. He would be welcome company, despite her avoiding him since the incident in the hotel room. Besides a cordial hello when he'd picked up Merlan from dance class, she'd managed to be a stranger.

Her puzzled thoughts drifted back. *But how did he find out about the party? I'll have to ask her about this later.*

They took their plates and found a small table for two and sat.

Upstairs the deejay played Prince's "Pump It Up" in the lounge. Blaze and Terra dominated the dance floor. He gave full energy like he showcased during his performances onstage. His stamina could last nonstop for hours. After their fifth song on the floor, they left to stand along the windows overlooking the river.

"So, how you enjoying this life?" Blaze inquired.

"*Lovin'* this life. Oh, man, this *is* the life," she responded, catching her breath from the pumped-up moves.

"Now you need to find you one of these single, *available* men in this camp," he said, stressing to Terra not to latch on to anyone's man. She'd once had a reputation in the 'hood that she was everybody's woman—single, married, you name it.

He didn't want Terra to reach the same fate as her older sister who'd lost her life after dating a longtime jealous boyfriend. He'd crushed her ego so badly that during a period of weakness, she'd ended her life by committing suicide. He'd moved away as he'd claimed he couldn't reside in the area any longer. He'd lost his sweetheart and couldn't fathom staying where her memories would forever linger. It had all been a front as Toya had confided in her that her boyfriend was abusive. She'd shielded his actions from everyone except Terra who blamed him for her sister Toya's demise. Terra had also found her sister's journals, which supported the claims of abuse.

Blaze was aware that Toya had been treated with disrespect. Both he and Terra had a hard place in their hearts and vowed that a payback was in order.

"Let's go eat," he ordered and headed downstairs as she followed.

Once they were seated, Terra noticed Kyle with Erick and her mind ticked. *That's not her husband.* She noted that the two were enthralled with each other. *They're pretty cozy. She's all up in his grille. But hmmm…he looks familiar. I don't forget faces and I'm not placing his—yet.*

Kyle felt tingly that someone was staring at her. She gazed around the lounge and locked eyes with Terra. She smiled uneasily and was relieved when Shayla walked up to Blaze and Terra's table, cutting off the view and attention.

"Well, you made your way to the food," Shayla noted. Her body language read sensuality.

"Yep, we've been upstairs partying. That deejay's rockin'," Blaze responded.

"You can party *all* night," she stressed, slyly winking at him, referring to his performances in bed. "I'll have to head upstairs to get my party on, too. But not before another drink. Enjoy." She nodded toward their plates and then headed to the bar in the corner.

Chad had disappeared to make a few calls in an area where he could get a cell signal. It gave her a chance once again to check out the scenery on board—and not the river.

Amber and Trent had ensured they'd greet each guest and were making their rounds. They arrived at Blaze and Terra's table.

"Terra, are you having a good time?" She looked at Blaze. "I don't have to ask you."

"Yes, this is great."

"I'd like you to meet my husband. You may have seen him in the news or if you watch Nationals games. Terra, this is Trent."

Terra attempted to remain calm but excitedly reached out to shake the celebrity ballplayer's hand. "Yes, I've heard of you. My little brother, Torian, he's in middle school, loves to watch the games."

"Oh, he's a baseball fan, huh? You don't find that too often. We'll have to make sure we treat him to a game." He looked at Amber. "Please get his information and we'll provide him some tickets. Maybe he'd like to bring a friend."

"Definitely. He'll be excited, but maybe I'll surprise him."

"In fact, I'm not sure if you're familiar with the foundation, but I'd love to include him in some of our events. He's still young enough to start playing, if he's interested."

"That'll work."

"Well, enjoy the evening. We'd better keep pushing," he indicated to Amber.

"Nice meeting you."

"Likewise." She eyed Blaze. "Why didn't you tell me Amber was married to him? Hangin' out with pro ballers' wives. No clue." She tapped him playfully on the arm.

"I figured you'd find out 'ventually. I'm surprised Amber never mentioned it. But then again, I don't blame her for keepin' on the down low. You can never be careful enough, 'specially when you in the limelight."

"No, she's cool, I guess. From what I can tell so far, she's not the braggin' type. Or putting on airs. She's real people and I like her. All of them actually," she said sincerely. *But on the real tip, her bein' a baller's wife makes the picture even more interesting. I really may have a chance to hook me up some bank deposits.*

Upstairs, the deejay switched up to spin line dancing hits and rolled them out back to back. Guests took over the lounge with the Booty Call, Cuban Shuffle, the Wobble and Zydeco Slide.

An enormous birthday cake in the shape of a baseball glove was presented to Amber. Guests sang "Happy Birthday" and devoured the delectable dessert filled with half chocolate and half vanilla mousse.

Amber thanked those in attendance and gave kudos to the Nationals, who had a stellar record for the season. She turned and pecked Trevor on the lips. "Now, continue to enjoy! Cheers!" She raised her flute and sipped on champagne.

She was aware the foundation was beginning to be an excuse for throwing fabulous parties like this one. She was getting used to the life. Unlike Shayla and Kyle, she wasn't an entrepreneur and staying at home could create a boring existence. Focusing on the foundation was a welcome outlet, particularly when Trevor was out of town for pre-season practice in Florida and then the team's away games. Until establishing Diamond Dreams, her occupation was a career shopper. Well, it still was her to-die-for pastime.

Shayla nuzzled up to Chad on the outer deck. "Hmmm, keep me warm, baby."

He placed his arm closer around her waist, shielding her from the light breeze.

"I can't wait to get home to turn you out," Shayla teased.

"I'm feeling that. You definitely are tops in that department."

Shayla was offended and tipsy from the drinks. "What you saying? I'm lacking in other departments?" she asked, misconstruing his comment.

"Shayla, baby, I was complimenting you. Of course, that's not what I meant. Look at you. You have a thriving PR business that's catapulting your clients to the next level. You are a wonderful wife and a friend. There's a lot I can say positive about you."

"And you're a wonderful husband. Sorry, I guess I'm feeling a little sensitive with the martinis." She giggled. "Glad you hired us a driver." She repeated the words "wonderful wife" in her head. *I try to be anyway…but I can't resist being in the arms of other men. Mr. Class, Raw, Smooth Jazz. I'm trying to zero my thoughts only on you, but it ain't working.* She'd bang the lights out of him once they arrived home, but she'd certainly crave her boy toys and daytime lover. Chad could satisfy her temporarily, but she still lusted for a variety to fulfill her needs.

"I understand." He kissed her forehead. "Enjoy yourself."

"Let's go back in." She clutched his hand and led him inside to the dance floor. Bumping into Kyle, she noticed she was leaving the floor with Erick, the handsome parent. She'd be sure to query his appearance later. Obviously, Kyle had to have invited him. He certainly didn't know Amber. She smiled. *Perhaps he's taking Bryce's place. I'm tired of seeing her everywhere alone. Bryce is always a no-show...except the foundation launch party. But Kyle deserves better. She always talks about eye candy. Well, she's certainly got some to look at tonight.*

Terra and Blaze maneuvered through the crowd of glitterati. Spotting Kyle with the familiar-looking man kept creeping into her mind. She struck zero each time she attempted to determine where she'd seen him. D.C. was a small city and despite a growing transient population, if he were a native, it was a good chance they'd crossed paths.

Kyle landed on the deck, slipping there when Erick had turned his back. She didn't want to appear rude, but she was weary of him being attached to her hip. They were not a couple nor were they on a date. There was no need for them to stay together for the entire cruise. Satisfied she'd lost him, she breathed a sigh of relief. She'd already noticed an inquisitive look on Terra's face. Although Terra hadn't met Bryce, she was well aware that Erick was not her husband.

Terra was friendly, but she sensed that there was a void in her personality. It wasn't complete and genuine. Kyle would strive to be cordial but keep the networking to a minimum. Perhaps Terra was a closet vixen and soon would be throwing darts at them. Or suppose she had ulterior motives toward their wealthy husbands, she thought. Shayla simply adored her, but she could be blind at times. Her bubbly demeanor could shield her from recognizing shady traits. Sometimes Kyle regarded it was Shayla's business to be personable. After all, public relations was her forte.

Shayla spotted Kyle alone and headed in her direction. Her head was buzzing from the martinis. After all, she could drink to her delight with a hired driver. Kyle was leaning against the balcony, dazing over the water.

She walked up to stand beside her. "Hey, girl, what you thinking about so hard?"

Kyle recognized the voice and stared ahead. "Nothing. Enjoying the cruise."

"Where did your very handsome friend go? I saw you hanging out for a minute. Looked like you were having fun in there dancing. You're a *cute* couple." She giggled.

Kyle turned to face her and snapped, "We're friends, got that?"

"Okay, okay, I was playing." She took a swig from her glass. "That's what they all say," she noted, thinking of her dark behavior and her trysts with her "friends."

"Look, Shayla, don't get all up in my business and insinuate a relationship."

"Well, I can't help but notice that you're out here looking lonely. In fact, you seem that way a lot…seeing that Bryce is out of the picture so much," she stated boldly. "You hardly see his face around. Girl, if I were you, I'd check into that business of his. No man has to spend so many hours at the j-o-b that he doesn't give up time for his wifey."

"Hey, I don't hear you talking with all the days Chad spends on the West Coast. You think 'cause he's doing business out there—"

"Hey, don't be jumpin' on my man. He's right here on this cruise—with me," she rebutted, slightly raising her voice.

"Get the hell out my face," Kyle ordered, having turned belligerent. It was unusual for her as she was the cool, calm one in the bunch. Shayla had pinched her nerve and was going in for the kill.

"Who the hell you think you talkin' to?" she responded. "I can stay here as long—"

"Hey, ladies, what's going on?" Amber interrupted after noticing a catfight brewing between the two. "Like I said, ladies, we can't afford to blow our cool. I know my girls aren't going to put on a show and embarrass me at my own party." She looked at both of them, analyzing their condition. "You both could use some coffee. No more drinks, please."

"I'm sorry, Amber. I hope no one else noticed. This has been fantastic and it doesn't need to be rained on by us," Kyle stated.

Amber scoped out the surroundings. "No, I don't think anyone saw. I must have that keen second sense. We've been around each other too long. I suddenly left Trevor and looked for you."

"Well, Shayla started this mess," Kyle explained like a school-girl to a teacher.

"Yeah, she's right. I guess I started to pry too much about Bry—"

"Stop it there," Amber ordered, holding up her hand.

"Anyway, Kyle, I apologize," Shayla said with squinty eyes.

"Feeling's mutual." Kyle lifted her maxi dress, ensuring she didn't trip on it. She stepped away to blend back in with the crowd, and then head to the brew station for coffee.

CHAPTER 29
The Wives

"Your yacht party was fantastic," Shayla expressed, reclining further in her theater chair in Amber's cinema room.

"Thank you both for all you did," Amber stated, nodding at her and Kyle, also stretched out in one of the leather chairs. She was seated across from them in her favorite chaise lounge, curled up in her sweat suit. She had invited them over for a follow-up to the yacht birthday party, which had been a successful event to promote the foundation. Even though she was a clothing, shoes and jewelry junkie, she gave in and opted not to receive presents. Her love for expensive, tangible items had finally taken a backseat to donated funds. She'd thought about how birthday gifts would have padded her closets even more, but she was proud that she'd shown unselfishness. She truly didn't need anything else to call her own; it was that she was simply addicted to material goods.

"Well, all I did was check out the scenery, when Chad wasn't around. I didn't realize we had so many suave movers and shakers in the area," Shayla remarked, recalling her sneaky glimpses at the male guests.

"There was definitely a lot of that on board," Kyle agreed. "I'm still stuffed from all that food, and it's been a while since I danced so much."

"I could see you and what's your parent's name, Erick, were having a good time," Amber noted innocently.

Shayla rolled her eyes. *Oh, please don't bring up that man. That's what started the whole spat between us.*

"Did I say something wrong?" Amber asked, noticing Shayla was irritated.

"Well, Kyle's a little sensitive. I approached her on the deck and mentioned that she and Erick were enjoying the party. She thought I was alluding they were more than friends. That's not what I was implying." Shayla sighed. "But it started the damn argument."

"Amber, I didn't want to discuss it at the party or put you on the spot, but why did you invite him anyway?" Kyle asked. "He was on my trail until I had to disappear. He was choking me and I needed a breather. That's when Shayla interrupted my flow. I had finally made my dash and was chillin' on the deck. I'd zoned out everything for a minute." She sighed.

"He contacted me through the foundation site. Sent me an email and said he was proud of Trevor and me. He was a single parent raising a daughter and wanted to support the foundation. He'd also seen in the news that we were throwing a private birthday party on the yacht. Since he was aware I'd met him, he thought it was okay to be invited."

"So he could check me out." Kyle harrumphed. "I was offended 'cause I don't like people judging the situation, particularly if they're wrong." Kyle looked at Shayla. "But I will say that you're right about Bryce being a ghost. I can tell you two this, I do spend a lot of lonely nights. My pillow is my mate. And usually when he gets in, I'm exhausted. So there ain't much happenin' then, either." *And he pisses me off when it's late and he's all liquored up and wants a quickie.* She cringed at the thought of his slam-bam-thank-you-ma'ams like she were simply a piece of pussy and not his wife.

"You need to get you a little poopty to keep you company." She stroked Topaz, her Yorkie, gently.

"A lapdog would be nice, but it won't take the place of Bryce," Kyle admitted. "So, Shayla, you were absolutely correct. It's only been two years, so I'm still supposed to be on my 'honeymoon,' or at least that's what I was thinking." She smirked. "He's always at his shops, wheeling and dealing, and telling me that he'll be more available once he gets the biz running smooth.

"He takes care of all the bills and of course, he financed the studio. So the money is there."

"Okay, let me say this. You rarely stop by his shops let alone talk about them. Do you think he's backlashing at you? He feels that you don't give his shops the time of day, so he doesn't pay you or the studio much attention?" Amber asked.

"Anything's possible with him." She thought, *If they only knew how mean he can be, they would see it's plain ole evil.* She unconsciously rubbed her leg where the last bruise was finally fading from him slamming her around. "Anything…"

"I've gotta admit, Kyle, what you said stuck in my mind. Hey, I was a little crunk, but I don't ever get so wasted I can't remember." *Although that morning I woke up at Damien's and he was gone, I didn't remember everything from the night before.* She looked at Amber. "She hinted that when Chad's out on the coast, I really don't know what he's up to. Yes, he turns his real estate deals and hangs out with his plastic surgeon buddy from college." She sighed. "Sometimes it seems a little odd that he hasn't invited me out that way, since he goes on the regular. I love L.A.

"In fact, I told Passion I'm due a visit. We're connecting okay, but it would be cool to see her in person. She's still in development, so she hasn't planned a true tour yet."

She turned to Kyle and twisted her head in a roll. "So, I understood where you were coming from. I may decide to swing that way while he's there and not even alert him. Or what do y'all think, is that cool? He likes surprises and says he has a trip planned for us next year. He won't even give me a clue to what it's all about." She heard footsteps, looked in the direction of the staircase and halted her conversation.

Sonya descended the stairs and presented a platter of three plates with four cheeses, crackers and fresh fruit. She set the tray on a table and then served each of them.

"Thank you, Sonya." Amber placed Topaz on the carpet and headed to the wet bar where she washed her hands. She pulled out a chilled bottle of red wine from their massive collection and opened it. She filled the wineglasses and handed one to both Kyle and Shayla. She went back to the bar and filled one for herself.

She sat back in her chaise and placed a block of cheese with a toothpick in her mouth and munched.

"Thank you," Kyle and Shayla said in unison.

"You're welcome." Sonya, who had waited to ensure all was fine with the setup, turned and headed to ascend the staircase, Topaz following close behind her.

Shayla looked toward the stairs, giggled and then whispered, "I thought that might have been Trevor."

"Oh, no, chile, he's at an away game. Why you think I invited you over for some private girls time?" She laughed, then her facial expression turned serious. "Let me put on my psychology cap." She put her hand on her forehead. "Shayla, you should definitely plan a trip to L.A. Actually, let's *all* go. We can visit my folks upstate while we're out there."

"Yep, we're overdue for another ladies weekend. We haven't had one since the Poconos," Shayla agreed.

"I'm game…" Kyle recalled how challenging it was to convince Bryce that the Poconos trip was important. She'd lied and said it was a getaway to celebrate Amber's birthday. When the yacht party started, she'd told him it was simply part two. Her real birthday didn't exist when they'd gone to the Poconos. *He'd better not give me any static about L.A., after all the nights he disappears.*

"And now for you, Kyle," she pretended to work her brain again, placing her hand on the top of her head this time, "I'd say, hell yeah, start stopping by his repair shops. He should be proud to show you off to his employees." Amber was pleased to offer advice to her BFFs. Someday she'd thought about returning to graduate school and allow her psychology degree to benefit others. Like her closest bestie from college, Desiree, she desired her own private practice. For now, she would focus on Trevor's vision with the foundation.

"I haven't been to the three shops much. Sad to say…" Kyle suddenly thought maybe if she showed interest in Bryce's business and exuded empathy toward his long hours, he'd reciprocate and visit the studio more often. Their relationship had evolved into a business marriage, loveless, sexless, passionless. It was all about the Benjamins and bank accounts—at least for him. She was more focused on her mission to offer girls a valuable opportunity to build self-esteem, skills and talent. However, if he hadn't helped her financially, it would still be an idea in her college journal.

After a bubbly marathon of conversation and a second bottle of wine, Amber suggested they start their "Movie Night." It was what she'd planned for the evening. She slipped in *Coyote Ugly*. Next up she'd pop in *Sex in the City*. She adored the characters' wardrobes and Sarah Jessica Parker's heels. Kyle desired to see dance-oriented films like *Honey* with Jessica Alba and *Fame* with Irene Cara. Amber promised she'd choose her theme on their next Movie Night. Shayla opted for the erotica like Sharon Stone in *Basic Instinct* and Glenn Close in *Fatal Attraction*. Eventually, they'd all have their choice.

CHAPTER 30
Bryce

"Man, you were right about the new cats you brought in. They're smokin'," Bryce complimented Sam on his latest recruited car thieves. His underground chop shop was booming as they moved on up with the increase of luxury vehicles. They could get more dollars for the costly parts. The latest crew was also super quick with dismantling vehicles.

Bryce strolled proudly throughout his top repair shop where the majority of the breakdowns occurred. He was snazzily dressed on the steamy day, which prompted him to wipe perspiration from his forehead.

"I told you, bro, they're like lightnin' quick. Best in da bizness. At the top of their game." Sam smirked. "Glad to hear the boss is satisfied."

"Most definitely." He pulled up a chair in the office, away from the concert of power tools in the background. Hip-hop music on the radio played at low volume.

"They're startin' to bug me," Sam started. "Lookin' for a little mo' money. Can you up the funds?"

Bryce sighed heavily. "Okay, okay, I'll give them a little hit. We can go up a hunnid extra." He'd observed an increase in high-end cars and had also seen a rise at his other locations.

Several guys inside the shop shot glaring looks at Bryce and he reciprocated with darts in his eyes. He never had conversation with any of the thieves or workers. He left all that to Sam who barked all the orders and handled the payouts. He had to maintain his glossy image and not be associated visibly with the crooked deals. Only his longtime friends and buddies were aware that he was Jarrett and not Bryce.

Some residents of his old neighborhood where he grew up also knew him as Bryce. He had driven through his old stomping grounds, perusing the streets and blocks, which conjured up good and bad memories. He'd waved at the elderly who remembered him as a child, and snubbed the high school crew, stereotyping them as troublemakers and thugs. Once he'd transcended into the wealthy zone, he'd also transformed his demeanor. No longer the down-to-earth Jarrett, he'd started using the name Bryce, who was arrogant with an ice-cold stare.

Suddenly, all of the workers halted their tasks and gawked at the beauty of a woman who'd entered the shop. It was afterhours and the unexpected guest was shocking, especially since they were doing shady operations. The woman was dressed in a black and white halter dress and black heels. Her skin, bronzed from sunny days, complemented the outfit and the waft of perfume was intoxicating.

"Hello," she announced, still capturing their undivided attention. "I'm looking for Bryce Andrews. I'm his wife, Kyle."

A worker quickly turned off the radio blasting vulgar lyrics. They were getting ready to deepen their intensity as the beat and lyrics kept their momentum. "Bryce?" one guy asked curiously. "I think you have the wrong place. But hey, you sure are looking lovely."

"Oh, Mister Andrews?" another guy interrupted, recognizing

Jarrett's alias. He looked at the first guy with eyes that read, *Keep your mouth shut.* "Yes, he's here." *Didn't know he had such a p-h-i-n-e wife. Hmm-hmm, what I wouldn't do to have a taste of that.* He pointed in the direction of Sam's office. "Right in that office there." He smiled. "And yeah, it was nice meeting you." *And please don't ask us our names. I ain't tryin' to fake nothin'.*

"Okay, I stopped by to surprise him." She smiled and placed her finger toward her lips.

The two men nodded, indicating they understood her intentions.

Kyle sashayed toward the office. Both heads turned to observe her rear view. She stopped at the office door and knocked lightly.

Bryce jerked the door open. "Who the hell—?" He was stunned. "Kyle? What are you—"

"Doing here," she finished, emphasizing she was in his presence. "I thought I'd do a pop call and stop by to see what's going on."

He gritted, then motioned for her to take a seat. "Well, that was nice of you," he stated phonily. "You remember Sam?"

"Yes, hello."

"Hey, you decided to check us out?" He grinned mischievously. "As you can see, we be rollin' up in here...sometimes afterhours," he added, trying to cover up that illegal activity was done mainly at closing. "We have some *dedicated* employees."

"I see. I met a couple of them when I came in...although I didn't get their names." She crossed her legs and began to lose confidence and her boldness. "I thought I could show you some support. After all, this is where you seem to spend your days and nights."

Bryce expressed, "Baby, it's all for you. I told you when we got married that I was going to ensure you were gonna live large." He boasted, "I think I've followed through on my word."

"Hey, man, I'm steppin' out. Let you two have your convo. Gettin' a little personal." Sam stood up and walked toward the door. He opened it and stepped out, closing it behind him.

Bryce turned to Kyle, his facial expression turning from pleasant to sour. "Look, I understand you were lookin' out for me, stoppin' in and checkin' us out, but let this be the last time—unannounced. I ain't feelin' this...a woman interruptin' my flow."

"What do you mean, inter—"

"'Ruptin'. Yeah, that's what I said. You know *damn* well I don't 'preciate you fallin' up in here like this. Catchin' us off-guard." He smirked. "And I'm sure those hounds out there couldn't get enough." He visualized how men reacted to Kyle in their presence. She was drop-dead gorgeous and turned heads.

"Look, you're here 'cause you tryin' to show some interest," he continued. "And don't get me wrong, it's all good. It's all good. It's just that I like to keep some stuff private."

Kyle considered his comment suspicious. "Private? You don't think you're private enough? You put up a stone fence when it comes to sharing your business. So I don't pry," she said awkwardly.

She didn't expect such a reaction, but she wasn't surprised. Bryce was more like an estranged husband. No matter how hard she tried, she failed to kindle any warmth or positivity. Amber had suggested during Movie Night that she demonstrate more interest in his shops. She appreciated the advice from her friend. After getting dressed, she'd fixed a cocktail, which gave her the guts to follow Amber's direction. Otherwise, she'd never had nerve to make a pop visit. In their early relationship, she wouldn't have given it a second thought. Now, Bryce was living on the edge, agitated and aggressive.

Kyle sighed nervously. She figured once they left the office, the night would be tumultuous. She regretted that she'd visited the shop unannounced. Did he have something to hide? Or was it simply him being his usual cranky self?

Tonight's visit was her last-ditch effort to go beyond the norm to improve her marriage. She thought she'd attempt to butter him up. If this didn't work, she'd truly consider giving up the marriage. Shayla and Chad appeared solid as a couple, and Amber and Trevor were united with their foundation. She was simply showing interest in Bryce's venture, only to be chastised.

"We have a miscommunication. On the real, don't stop in anymore unless you've checked it out with me first. I ain't feelin' the fellas out there looking at you like a piece of meat," he lied, actually proud that they had admired his showpiece. "This late crew is off the chain."

"I was surprised to even see any workers. I figured I'd arrive after closing, although it's still daylight, and figured I'd find you here alone in your office. Maybe Sam would be here but it would be quiet." She smoothed her dress and leaned back, then stated coyly, "Actually, I had other intentions. I dressed this way 'cause I thought it would be nice for us to have an evening out. We rarely get the chance." She held her breath awaiting his response.

"Babe, sorry, I'mma have to take a rain check on this one." He looked at her without any remorse.

She sighed disappointedly. "Wow, I came all the way here and you're turning me down. I can't win. Let me guess, you're tired, you're busy. That's getting old." She stood up and walked to the door and opened it. She turned around and said, "See you at midnight."

She stormed away, drawing the attention of the few workers who again stopped their operation to observe her.

"Have a good evening," a guy said, tipping his hat and nodding.

"You do the same." Kyle walked ahead avoiding eye contact with anyone. *If that had been one of the boys asking him out, he would've jumped all over it. Me, I'm only a "piece of meat," as he calls it. And I'm so tired of being burned.*

Kyle lay in bed absorbing *West Side Story.* This was her comfort zone to wind down from a bitter experience. Musicals and the calming colors on the screen offered her peace of mind. It reminded her of better days when she was dancing in New York. It was another lonely night of dejection during her honeymoon years. She sulked as she zoomed back in time, remembering how Bryce was heartwarming and kind during their initial meeting and months of dating. Perhaps she'd jumped the broom in haste without discovering his true soul.

She had his routine down pat. If he ended up with his boys, whom he'd never introduced her to, only named them as Craig and Gerard, he'd slip in the house all drunk. He'd be ready for some quick action. She'd be turning to the other side giving him some back view. Tonight was not the one to have him clawing her like an animal. If he was drained, he'd shower and climb in bed with no conversation or sex on his mind. His repetitious world had become ancient.

After the film ended, she turned off the TV and drifted to sleep.

"Why the hell did you come to the shop?" Bryce yelled as he switched on the light on the nightstand. He towered over Kyle with daggering eyes.

She stirred and opened her eyes to peer at his intense look. It was more frightening than ever. She stared at his monstrous face intensely.

"Don't you *ever* do that shit again!" he growled. She noticed the swirl in his eyes that read he was in a drunken rage.

She sat up, clenching the comforter close to her neck. She was at her weakest when lying down. If she needed to, she'd make a swift dash. She eyed her cell phone on the nightstand, thinking 9-1-1 was her backup—if she could manage to pick it up.

He raised his hand as if to strike her.

She looked at him in fright. The true Freddy Krueger had arrived. *He's pushed me but never struck my face.*

His mind suddenly retraced images of his father beating his mother and hearing her horrid screams. He became enraged at the memories, realized he was repeating the cycle, and released his tension. He glared at her and then walked into the bathroom.

She sighed and was in a daze. *I thought it was anger issues, but it's beyond that. This is some scary shit. If I continue to put up with it, there could be a tragic end.* Her family and friends would never believe she was the same class leader, the lead ballerina who was revered as strong and vivacious. She had succumbed to be a victim of physical and verbal abuse. As she heard the shower water, she looked to the ceiling, closed her eyes and prayed.

When Bryce returned to the bedroom, she had quietly slipped downstairs, cell phone in hand, and landed on the den sofa. There was no way she would be sleeping any more tonight and definitely not in the same bed as Bryce.

Refreshed from the shower, he was more astute and realized his venom had caused her to leave the bedroom. He decided not to ask her to return or talk about the incidents of the night. He slid into the bed and lay down. He wasn't sure if his behavior was bad or if it was now the worst. Maybe he was bipolar as a former girlfriend had suggested. Or was he simply a clone of his past? Maybe he'd offer to take Kyle to lunch during the week—only if it fit in to his schedule. She was the trophy wife that he'd always had designs on. Gorgeous, smart, seductive and in her case, talented.

CHAPTER 31
Amber

Amber paraded around the Glitz boutique in Bethesda modeling her ensemble. Her sequined strapless dress and heels were all a show. She sashayed like she was on the runway.

"Valencia, this is adorable! Girl, you really know how to put an outfit together." She whisked back and forth. "Ladies, what do you think?" she asked Kyle and Shayla.

"Love it," they said in unison.

Amber had hired Valencia as a personal stylist. The foundation had led to her making more appearances. She needed the wow factor, with and without Trevor. She had to represent. She tossed her hair and glanced in the mirror, marveling at the look Valencia had created. The only challenge was the accessories. She preferred gold and diamonds. Valencia favored bold chunky jewelry with this outfit.

For their ladies day out, she was treating her sidekicks to a makeover. If they liked their outfits, she planned to purchase for them. Amber felt they needed a lift. Kyle appeared to be losing her vitality and she sensed a depressed mood. Fashion and styling were her forte, so she'd figured what better way to enjoy her pastime and treat her friends.

"Who wants to be next?" Amber inquired, flashing her eyes back and forth between the two.

"Me, I'm ready," Shayla volunteered eagerly. She looked at Kyle. "And so is Kyle."

Kyle was dragging. Her disposition had been sour lately. "Okay, I'll go as well."

The two followed Valencia throughout the aisles as she determined garments and shoes to complement their personalities and figures.

Valencia wore a black sheer tunic over black textured leggings. Her oversized black Chanel glasses hung low on her nose and her jet-black shiny hair bounced. She swayed as she teetered on her low-heeled strappy sandals revealing her tangerine pedicure.

"Sweetie, I have the perfect piece for you." She pulled an exotic print dress and held it up toward Shayla's skin. "This works well with your complexion." She smiled, then sauntered down another aisle before stopping in front of a mustard knit wrap dress. She looked at Kyle. "And this is simply ideal for you."

She led them to the shoe section where she identified a pair of pumps for Kyle and open-toe heeled sandals for Shayla.

"This is grand, ladies." Valencia motioned for the two to follow her into the open dressing room, without individual stalls.

"Ooh, I think that may be a little too tight. You think I can squeeze in it?" Kyle inquired with doubt and pointed at the dress in Valencia's hand.

"Honey, take it from the pros. I'll show you how to shimmy right into this number." She giggled.

"Okay, I'm with you," she agreed.

"Plus, we New York queens are known for the fashion tip." Valencia was a product of the Pratt Institute and was popular on the celebrity circuit for a host of the New York-based residents. She had hooked up with Amber when Trevor was in town for a baseball series with the Yankees. Clients willingly paid her costly fee for fashion advice.

She walked to the accessories section and picked up a chunky necklace. "I think this will look darling with this dress." She handed the piece to Kyle along with the garment and shoes. She reviewed the dress she'd selected for Shayla, then turned to the accessories. "And for you, Shayla, this is eye-catching. It'll eat up the color of the dress," she stated about a unique colorful stone necklace. She placed it around the neckline of the dress. She handed Shayla the complete outfit. "Now, ladies, follow me. It's time to get these babies on and see what we're working with," she said with flair.

They entered the open dressing room where Amber sat waiting. She had already transformed back into the clothes she'd worn to the boutique. She'd secretly asked Zodi to peruse the shop and collect certain items she'd spotted. Zodi would purchase them with a separate card and claim they were gifts. After all, Amber owned such a huge wardrobe that she rarely repeated an outfit and her friends and others likely wouldn't notice. The items on her list were all basic shades without patterns. All the psych studies had assisted her in memory and description. She'd whipped out a pen and pad and written down the items for Zodi who made a quick exit.

"Oh, I see Valencia took good care of you." Amber admired the outfits they carried into the fitting room. She circled her body and teased about the full room of mirrors. "You can't hide anything in this space."

Kyle and Shayla were used to undressing in Amber's presence during their overnight ladies weekends. Both started to remove their clothes assisted by Valencia who was helping simultaneously.

Her eyes locked on a bad and swollen bruise on Kyle's left leg. She noted another bruise on her right thigh. Valencia thought it was strange to see such marks on a woman's skin that was silky smooth.

Kyle was so elated that Amber was treating her to a new outfit. She had perked up being in the presence of fun and supportive friends. She also had become lax and forgotten that her bruises had not completely faded. She had all hopes that she could wear a swimsuit and feel at ease before the season was over. *Ooops, if she stares at me any harder, she'll burn a hole in my legs.* Presuming only Valencia had seen the bruises, evidence of an abusive past; she didn't realize that Shayla had spotted them as well. Knowing her, she would have commented. Kyle wasn't the clumsy type and did everything with poise. Shayla figured it hadn't been an accident or clash with an object that had left the imprints. However, she would not judge and leave her observations silent—at least for the moment.

Valencia pretended she hadn't noticed the bruises and simply overlooked them. She was a master of expressions. Popular among celebrities, she had learned to zone out when it came to personal issues. Her eagle eyes and ears were off-duty when it came to gossip. She couldn't name how many times gossip sites and writers had contacted her for the 4-1-1 on her client list.

As promised, she assisted Kyle to shimmy into her form-fitting dress. She did Calvin Klein proud. "Yes, my dear, this is a hot one." She walked around Kyle, examining the details of her figure. "You're wearing this dress, chile."

After Kyle and Shayla finished their transformations, they examined themselves in the wall of mirrors. Valencia then asked them to leave the dressing room and walk out for Georgia, the owner, to see them on the runway. Georgia often had fashion shows at Glitz and it was why she'd opted to have an open dressing room. It was easier for models to make quick changes and return to the audience in the store.

"You two look stunning. When's your next night out? You will ensure all eyes will be on you." She smiled, relishing the sale she'd made with her three customers within the hour. She'd already rung up bags of purchases for Zodi who'd claimed they were gifts, covering for the boss lady who would later request her to hide the dresses, shoes and jewelry. Zodi had walked to the car, placed the purchases inside of another large tote bag in the trunk and then returned inside the store.

Georgia had already summed up that Amber was a shopaholic, only exposing a limited number of purchases. She depicted Amber had an overflowing cache of expensive goods.

After Amber paid for the makeover outfits, she offered to treat the three to an early dinner at Maggiano's Little Italy. "Who said we couldn't make this a whole day's worth of girl fun?" She looked at Zodi and winked, a signal requesting her to be their designated driver. *Martinis, here we come!*

CHAPTER 32
Shayla

S hayla's libido was flaming. She couldn't get enough. Finally, on this day, she would test her biggest fantasy: sex with all three of her sides, Mr. Class, Raw and Smooth Jazz, and all within twenty-four hours.

It was Friday morning and Chad would be arriving early tomorrow on a red eye.

Kicking off her fantasy sextival, she waited in the parking lot next door to her office. Wearing dark sunglasses and dressed casually in a pale yellow tee, jeans and thong sandals, Shayla was ready for Mr. Class. She'd attempted to conceal her identity by dressing down.

Wilson pulled up in a navy company car and lowered the passenger window. "Do I know you, miss?"

"Well, I was thinking this handsome man would slam on his brakes and scoop me up," she teased. She opened the door and stepped inside.

He smiled. "Hope you don't mind. I gave my driver the day off. He's sick. So this is our limo style today without the champagne." He pulled away and headed to familiar territory, the family castle in the woods.

"No problem." She pulled off her shades.

Once they arrived at the castle, Wilson made his way into the kitchen and prepared mimosas while Shayla admired the antique furnishings of the living room. A true knight-in-shining-armor was creepy, but it was befitting to the castle décor.

After the drinks and croissants, they performed their sexual aerobics in the room named Dynasty. Shayla was aware she needed to keep on task in order to fulfill her plan. She didn't linger and the "hit it and quit it" routine worked well.

Wilson pulled into the parking lot of Joe's Diner. Shayla had lied about meeting a client for a casual lunch. He turned off the motor to walk around and open her door. She raised her hand to stop him. "Thanks, I'll get out."

She walked into the diner, then took a seat and menu, peeking above it to ensure he drove away. She looked at her watch. It was 12:50 and Blaze was to arrive by one o'clock. *Whew, close call.*

A waitress walked up and pulled straws out of her apron and placed them on the table. "Hello, I'm Emma. May I take your order? You're waiting on someone?"

"Yes, water for us both." She glanced at the menu. "I'll take a grilled cheese and fries…and for him, how about the Philly cheese-steak and fries. Everything on it."

Blaze entered and looked like a black Adonis, all buff and rippled. He spotted Shayla and walked to her table.

"Hey, babe, you're early."

"Well, I had to make sure I was on time to greet you." She removed her dark shades, batted her eyes teasingly, then placed them back on for disguise.

Suddenly, she felt a desire to freshen up for her boy toy. *Too bad I didn't bring another outfit in a tote bag.*

Never one to be seen in public with her sidepieces, she had selected the diner off the beaten track. Chances were no one would recognize her, especially since she was dressed down.

Blaze had placed his iPod in the hotel's docking station, inspired to make love to his mellow singles. He'd broken down and steered from the hip-hop to record a few ballads. He was in heaven with a publicist who was a certified sexpot and enamored with his skills.

Shayla was on her knees as he pounded her from behind. "Baby, just give me more of that elephant dick. Yeah, right there. That's the spot." He accelerated his thrusts and then flipped her over aggressively. "Hey, baby, that's why I call you Raw. You don't hold back any punches. Naw, naw."

She bit her lips, attempting to hold back cumming. "Ah, ah, ahhhhhhhhhhhh." She couldn't resist releasing a flood of her juices.

He was right behind her, ejaculating in minutes, then collapsed on top of her.

The iPod shuffled to Tyga: *"I'm all in that Virginia, I mean that vagina. Get lost in that pussy…you will never find her. Eat it like lasagna…"*

Yeah, you ate it all right, she thought, exhausted from her second go-round of the day. She was one adventure away from fulfilling the top fantasy on her bucket list.

Blaze rolled over and they both snoozed. She woke up and looked at the clock.

"How ya feelin'?" he asked groggily.

"I didn't intend to fall asleep. I've got to go." She jumped up and moved slowly to the bathroom to bathe. Unfortunately, she had to once again put back on the same clothing. *What was I thinking? A triple deal and one outfit?*

"Thought we were going for another round." He laughed.

"You wore me out and I couldn't handle that," she lied. *I'm actually getting ready for round three, my brother.* "There's always next time," she called from the bathroom.

Prepaying for hotel rooms in his name was the way to go. She had the routine down pat. They'd never entered the lobby nor elevator together, and he'd check in and get the key in his name.

Blaze had begged her to extend her stay but she didn't want to keep Damien waiting. Plus, she wasn't trying to have any of these men get attached. Despite her philandering, she was truly in love with Chad. Her issue was that her addiction surpassed any emotional relationship she had with her husband. At some point, she would have to cease her escapades and focus on her marriage, especially when they decided to start a family. That would take priority over garnishing her sex life. Chad was approaching forty, but his clock wasn't ticking at the same speed as hers. She also would welcome an addition to the household that would offer her company.

It would be heaven if Kyle were blessed after the miscarriage. Suddenly, she visualized the scene in the dressing room and her suspicious bruises. Kyle was her girl, and someday she would inquire at the "right" time. Then ideally, Amber would have a son and follow behind Trevor as a baseball star. She put her wish in the universe, closing her eyes and meditating a moment. She had put up a shield to distance herself from the long lines of passengers in the Metro station.

She'd asked Blaze to drop her at the transit stop where she was going to meet a friend for dinner. Once again, she'd lied about a meal with an imaginary person. She was going to have dinner all right. She'd already had breakfast with Wilson and lunch with Blaze. She smiled, tickled that her secretive mission was a success. After topping the day off with Damien, she would be a bad sistah, accomplishing a whirlwind lustfest.

The train pulled into the station and she boarded with a throng of downtown workers and students. She stepped onto the platform at the U Street station and headed to the escalator. She couldn't chance being seen, so she'd told Damien she'd walk the short blocks to his space. After reaching the street level, she pulled out a compact mirror and checked out her image. *I'm looking more and more like a disheveled mess.* She continued to refresh by fluffing her hair, spritzing perfume, and touching up her lipstick. Satisfied of her improved look, she placed her sunglasses back on and darted back on the street. Enjoying the sounds of the city as she headed toward Damien's, she was pleased it was gorgeous weather.

Damien, you'd better have your freaky game on. I've already been to the moon and back on a couple of rockets. Out of the three, he was the one who kept her perplexed. He was so cool and poised, she always felt he was in a photo shoot.

She arrived at his place and he buzzed her in. She walked to the bank of elevators and pushed the up button. After exiting the elevator, she turned the corner and stopped at his door. She dropped her head low when she saw a young woman in the hall. Although she felt airy and carefree in the comfort of his apartment, she couldn't risk her identity being revealed. After all, there were times when she may have to appear in the news, particularly if some of her well-known local clients needed their images boosted or salvaged.

After the woman was out of sight, she rapped on the door lightly.

Damien opened it and hugged her. "Hi, you're looking down-graded today," he stated surprisingly. He was used to seeing Shayla fashionably dressed, and the tee and jeans were a turnoff.

"Hey, thanks for the compliment," she responded sarcastically. She whipped off her sunglasses.

"Can I offer you a drink?" He asked over his shoulder, heading to the kitchen for his usual routine during her visits.

"Sounds great." She sat on the sofa and slipped off her sandals gently to ease her worn feet. She lay back on the pillow but careful not to get too comfortable. The way she was feeling, she could easily drift into a second nap. Listening to the ice in the shaker, she figured he would bring her a martini. Jazz sounds of Norman Brown spewed from the iPod and Shayla compared the taste with Blaze's playlist. *I call him Smooth Jazz like his music*, she thought.

With Damien she seemed relaxed. She always felt on the clock with Wilson as it was a morning getaway. However, he provided the mature conversation she enjoyed. He still had to make up for missing sales calls. Blaze was a piece of action, simply getting it in raw and getting out of there, bouncing between hotel rooms. But with Damien, she invaded his private spot and it was a sanctuary. His apartment was tastefully decorated depicting magazine covers, such as the home publications splayed on his coffee table. Every item was in its place and his closet was color coordinated. She was in awe about his interior design talent. Modeling was his forte, but he could easily move into styling.

He entered the living room carrying raspberry martinis garnished with orange slices.

"Hmmm. Looks delicious." She eyed the fancy martini glasses as he set both drinks on the table, then sat on the sofa. "You have exquisite taste. I guess when I've been around, we're mainly hanging out in the bedroom, so I really hadn't sat here and taken it all in."

"Thanks. I got it honestly from my mother. She had impeccable furnishings in our home, so I had a good teacher." He'd always spoken highly of his upper-class upbringing in a single-parent home and as an only child.

She sipped her martini, relishing the fruity mixture. She peeked at the wall clock and realized she needed to make her dinner snappy. She arose, delicately picked up her glass and grabbed his hand, while he picked up his glass in the other. She lured him into the bedroom.

The bed was inviting, freshly made up. They placed their glasses on the nightstand. Shayla turned around and pushed him lightly as he fell onto the bed. Ravishingly, she stripped off her clothes and then proceeded to slip off his shirt and roll down his pants.

"There's my Johnson, all perked up and ready for me." After placing a condom on him, she lowered her head, locking her jaws on his rock-hard penis. She gently licked the shaft and slurped for minutes before rising up and swinging her perky breasts in his face. He reciprocated by sucking each tenderly. It was the first time she'd actually felt any compassion from Damien. He normally was blah without feeling. Unfortunately, she'd have to make it snappy. She grabbed his rod and placed it inside her warm vagina. She wiggled teasingly and then went in for the ride. She skillfully rode him silently, slapping her pussy juices in rhythm with the beat of the jazz guitarist. She accelerated and pumped intensely, then gushed all over, cumming in sync with Damien.

Damien stopped at the curb in front of the Metro station. "Thank you for the ride." She pecked Damien lightly on the lips.

"You sure I can't drive you further than here?" he inquired. "I can drive you to Maryland."

"No, thanks anyway. I'll hop on the train to the Largo stop, then I'll catch a cab home. I'll be fine." She opened the door, stepped out, looked into the car window and smiled. "Goodnight."

"Goodnight."

She headed to the station entrance. Her body and mind were drained. *But fantasy fulfilled. Three in a day. You go, girl.* Her next mission would be to fill her Jacuzzi for a relaxing bath. She'd wake up to prepare a New Orleans-style breakfast from family recipes. Chad would welcome the homemade meal after his red-eye flight.

CHAPTER 33
Kyle

After months of rehearsals for their summer performance, Magical Moves dance students were prepped to showcase their talent at Cramton Auditorium at Howard University.

"I must say you've done a fantastic job with these young ladies and men."

She recognized the voice immediately and cringed. "Erick, I appreciate your compliments. Thank you."

"What are you doing after the show?"

"You've got me wrong. I've told you I'm not going out with you anymore. No lunches, dinners, drinks, nothing. It was a mistake to meet you at a hotel in the first place, regardless if it started in the bar."

Erick had made his way backstage during intermission, figuring it would offer the opportunity to speak to Kyle alone. After the performance, surely she would be bombarded by parents.

A young woman approached them. "Are you okay, Mrs. Andrews?"

"Oh, yes, I'm fine. Thanks," she told Tia, her stage manager, who had noticed a disturbed look on Kyle's face. She looked at Erick. "This is Merlan's dad, Erick Williams."

She nodded and shook his hand before walking away.

"Please, you're making me nervous. You're getting a little too close in my space," Kyle informed.

"Well, that's what I'm trying to do."

"Okay, this is getting out of hand. I really don't want to make a scene and call security. We're really not supposed to have folks back here unless they're with the show." She sighed. "Please show some respect for all of us and take your seat. Merlan would be upset if she knew her dad was back here out of control." The students had congregated in the Green Room until the performance resumed.

"Okay, Merlan, Merlan. I'll do it for Merlan." He turned and walked off the stage area.

Whew. What's up with him? He went from nice guy to a maniac. I'm not feeling him and sorry I misled him. Damn, I never should have stepped foot in that room. He's acting ridiculous.

Obsessed. Erick had become obsessed with Kyle. His childhood associate, Jarrett, who now went by the name Bryce, had asked him to entice her to see if she'd fall for it. He was simply a decoy and had complied as a favor. The neighborhood cohorts had a bond and had pledged as children to always have each other's backs.

Bryce had a reputation as a con artist and a skilled one. He wanted to test her faithfulness and detect if perhaps his marriage was on shaky ground, Erick had thought. Actually luring her to his hotel room was unimaginable. Erick realized he would never have taken it that far. He was too jealous to ever have anyone tempt his own mate. When Kyle fell for it and they were inches away from a sexual encounter, it was hard for him to resist. He was glad that he'd abruptly halted them from going further.

His two meetings with Kyle and the drop-bys at her office were now a hazardous sign. He was falling in love with his friend's wife. What had started as a simple experiment had grown into a massive crush. Merlan mentioned her frequently and adored her. This didn't help divert his thoughts from the growing desire he felt for Kyle. Now their friendly outings were history, and she was rejecting all conversation except about business.

CHAPTER 34
Terra

Work it, girl, Terra thought as she posed in changing positions in front of her full-length mirror on the back of her bedroom door. *Impress* was the word of the day. Too bad Gram wasn't home to experience how she'd puckered up for her blind date. Her savings had come in handy to purchase a new dress and heels for the special occasion. The black taffeta dress with a flirty hemline showcased her figure, and her open-toe Tory Burch heels highlighted her pedicure. She moved in closer to scrutinize her new makeup to ensure it was flawlessly applied.

Amber and Zodi had gone outfit hunting with her after she'd requested their assistance. Amber was the fashionista and Zodi was in her age range, so she'd ensure Amber didn't select anything that read "old maid."

She spritzed on J-Lo's Glow. Gram had always told her to look your best whenever you had high hopes of clinching a prize-winning mate. She'd be proud to witness her granddaughter had heeded her advice, shedding her jeans and tee routine for a more sophisticated image. First impressions were lasting ones.

Shayla had grown to be like the big sister, Toya, that she'd lost to suicide. She and Toya didn't hold the same taste or personality, but both had been supportive. She had to give Blaze props for insisting he introduce them. Maybe some doors would open to the upscale lifestyle she coveted.

Shayla was due to arrive at any moment to whisk her away to the restaurant where the two would hook up with Chad and one of his business associates, Lamont, a fellow realtor. Lamont was twenty-six and had a decent portfolio. He was considered one of the rising stars in the D.C. market and was starting to pocket some cash.

Shayla had asked Chad to be aware of possible dates for Terra. Hell, she didn't want to be on the prowl for any candidates. She would've considered them for her own stash.

It would be Terra's second time in Chad's presence after meeting him at Amber's yacht party. Shayla didn't invite strangers to her home and preferred to conduct business at her office or public locations.

Terra peeked out the front window to look out for Shayla's BMW convertible. On such a warm evening, she expected her to have the top down. Hopefully, it wouldn't wild out her hair. She went to the first-floor bedroom and found one of her grandmother Elaine's scarves. The last thing she needed was to arrive looking like a scarecrow. She placed the scarf in her clutch bag as she walked back to the window.

After a few minutes, Shayla pulled up. Before she could call or text her, she opened the door and exited. Her new shoes clicked on the pavement as she walked to the convertible and hopped in. It was a romantic evening and she hoped that she and Lamont would hit it off.

Terra was mesmerized with Lamont, a fine specimen with mocha skin, about six feet and medium build with light-brown eyes. He was likewise satisfied and initially found her attractive. She had a killer body and looks that were easy on the eyes.

"I'll take Bacardi Limon and Coke," she told the waiter.

"Chocolate martini for me," Shayla ordered.

"We'll both take Hennessy and Coke," Chad requested, nodding toward Lamont.

When he returned for the meal orders, Shayla and Terra decided on the sea scallops and sesame salmon. Chad ordered prawns in sauce while Lamont requested tuna steak.

Terra checked out the romantic setting and glared at Lamont over the candlelight. The stone walls, hardwood floors and white tablecloths added to the historic ambience at Tarragon.

"So, tell me a little about yourself," Lamont asked Terra.

"Well, I'm D.C. born and raised. I've been here my whole life. I've worked in fashion," she responded, sounding nebulous about her work history in retail. She didn't think it was anything incorrect about her background, but she was hoping to make an impression that it was more extensive than in reality.

"Wonderful." He didn't want to pry any further. Perhaps he'd gather more later. "Where did you go to school?"

"I graduated from McKinley Tech," she stated, alerting him that she was without an advance degree. "I had always hoped to attend college—and it's never too late—so I'm thinking of going online. I didn't get the opportunity and had to get to work full time."

"Oh, I see. I'm from Philly. I believe that's why Chad and I clicked the way we did. Homeboys." He looked at Chad.

"That's right. We connected right away," he agreed.

"I'm a Temple alum and came to D.C. to start a business and ended up in the real estate arena. I've been on the grind selling houses, multiunit buildings and commercial property. And of course, since the city is booming with the renovation of buildings into condos, things are on the uptick."

"You're right, Lamont. And I'm grateful that Chad is planning to spend more time here because the possibilities are endless." Shayla looked at Chad and smiled. "Plus, I'm hoping we can start a family someday."

"That's a long ways out for me. I want to ensure I'm stable—financially and personally." Lamont ate a forkful of his entrée.

"Sure, no rush on that. Chad is pushing the big four-oh and I won't say what I'm pushing, but I don't have decades to play with." She giggled.

"So, what's everyone up to this weekend?" Shayla interjected, noting that the baby conversation was making everyone uneasy.

"I'll probably check out a wine festival in Virginia," Lamont responded.

"I'm planning to go to a Chuck Brown tribute at the Howard Theatre. A lot of bands are performing."

"That's classic for D.C. Go-go music and he was the king. I love that song *Go-Go Swing*." Lamont sipped his drink. "We had the Philly Sound."

"Yes, that was our classic," Chad agreed.

"And down in New Orleans, or N'awlins, we had zydeco, but the most famous were the Neville Brothers," Shayla shared. "It's interesting how music was generated in different areas of the country."

Lamont asked Terra, "Are you always this quiet?"

"It depends. I'm enjoying the conversation." Gram had always told her sometimes it was better to listen than speak. You could figure out how your cards should roll by first observing.

Terra had toned down her manner considerably since she'd started socializing with Shayla, Kyle and Amber. Her co-workers had teased her, trying to figure out if she were the same person they'd known for years. Her few friends thought she was dissing them by turning down invitations to their hangouts. She was transitioning because she was seeking another way of life outside of her comfort zone. She was hobnobbing with folks from another level—not to say they were "better" than her clique, but they could open doors to new opportunities.

Shayla cleared her throat. Perhaps Terra was uncomfortable joining in the conversation or maybe it was simply a hidden side she had never seen. Terra as the bubbly talkaholic had not shown up for dinner. Whenever they were alone, she was all for discussion. Then she was aware that Lamont was all eyes and ears, so maybe it was a strain to be herself. Sometimes during a first date, and in this case, a blind one, you wanted to be on your A-game. He was definitely top shelf, so Terra likely was trying to be at her best.

They'd all finished their meals. Shayla suggested she and Terra go to the ladies' room. They grabbed their purses and rose from the table, then walked away. Shayla's lemon wrap dress accentuated all curves as she strode. Lamont turned to watch Terra from the rear.

"Hmm, hmmm. Thanks for the invite, bro. She's a fine sister," Lamont told Chad.

"Hey, it's my wife's doing and her idea. Apparently, her big brother—who's a rising star, by the way—is Shayla's client. He approached her about helping out lil' sis who's been going through some things and needed a change of scenery. So they hooked up." He sipped his cocktail and motioned for the waiter to serve another round. "Man, if you're looking for more about her, you're on your own. I know very little."

"I hear you, and believe me, I plan to check her out. So far, I like what I'm feeling."

Inside the ladies' room, Shayla and Terra freshened up. "Hey, girl, do I detect a match?" Shayla fluffed out her hair in the mirror.

"I'm about speechless. Definitely."

"Good. You two look great together." She smiled. "I sense that you're a little quiet 'cause you're feeling him out. Trying to be on your p's and q's. Honey, I know how it is working on making that lasting impression. Humph, I'd never met him, but I told Chad don't be bringing any rotten candy. So, I was pleasantly surprised. Well, Chad has good taste anyway, so I wasn't *totally* surprised."

"He's got it goin' on, for sure."

"And hey, I never pegged you to be a gold digger, *butttt* a little money never hurts," she said, the tipsy effects now beginning to surface.

"It helps, but it's not my focus," Terra lied. *I can't wait to dig into those pockets and start dressing like you and your girls. It's about time I catch me a brotha with some gold. But I hope he has some golden dick as well and can throw down in that department.* "Gram always said, 'If it's meant to be, it will be.' Marrying in to money, that is."

"No one's trying to get married yet. This is your first damn date."

"And I thank you for setting it up. I'm cool with it." She gazed in the mirror to double-check her image.

"Good. I'm sure they're wondering what's taking us so long. Let's roll."

"You figured we got lost, hon'?" Shayla inquired, sitting in her chair.

Terra returned to her seat and smiled seductively at Lamont.

"No, we realize going to the ladies' room can turn into an adventure." Chad smiled. "We've been having our own convo on what's up with real estate."

The waiter had cleared the table and brought out the dessert menus.

"Care for dessert?" Chad asked, handing Shayla and Terra menus.

They perused them and both decided on chocolate brûlée. Chad and Lamont ordered key lime pie once the waiter returned.

After the desserts arrived, they were stuffed but still enjoyed the tasty homemade creations.

"Hmmm, I love me some chocolate," Shayla teased. *And chocolate men, too. Yummmmy.*

"Yes, this is so good." Terra eyed Lamont. "I don't eat sweets too much."

Trying to keep that knockout figure of yours. "Neither do I, but I figured I'd indulge since I'm with special company." He leaned in closer to speak in a lower tone. "So, what's it looking like? We going to hook up again in the *near* future?"

Terra blushed. "You don't have to ask me twice."

"So, please," he pulled out a card and handed it to her, "call me and I'll save your number in my phone."

"Okay, I'll call now." She pulled out her cell and dialed the number on the card. She slipped the card into her purse. "Thank you." She placed another forkful of chocolate in her mouth.

Lamont pulled out his vibrating cell from his waistband, and locked in her number. "Thanks."

CHAPTER 35
Amber

I t was the seventh inning, and Trevor Trent was at bat with two players on base in the Washington Nationals game against the Atlanta Braves. The pitcher was throwing balls at ninety miles per hour and after two strikes, Trevor whacked a ball into the stands to the cheers and thrills of the fans. He batted in two runners from first and third bases, and brought up the rear to score three on his home run.

This was a fantastic feat on this special game when forty boys from his Diamond Dreams Foundation were watching the game live. The foundation had provided tickets to the group from D.C. and its suburbs. It was their first Major League Baseball game. They'd only seen professionals in action on the tube. Their hero, Trevor, had demonstrated that baseball was a viable sport in which any one of them could achieve success.

Next week, another group would head north to Camden Yards in Baltimore to view the Orioles versus the Yankees.

Trevor and Amber were pleased that so many of the parents were enthusiastic about their sons participating in the field trips. An overwhelming number of them had volunteered to chaperone the youth, ages six to sixteen.

After the Nationals beat the Braves 6-4, the crew posed for a professional photographer before security led them to an under-ground tunnel to greet Trevor and team members. Amber, dressed in a team cap and jersey with Trevor's number, proudly joined in the photo shoot along with the youth and Trevor.

A sportscaster approached the foundation group and reported live from the scene. She asked several of the youth to comment and capped off her interview with Amber.

Funds continued to pour in for the Diamond Dreams account. Donations had escalated to an all-time high, and each time media were involved, there was steady growth. She and Trevor appeared on this month's cover of *Washingtonian* magazine, increasing awareness in other communities. African-American males were gaining appreciation for the sport.

Trevor and Amber snuggled in the comfort of their bed. They'd toasted with their wineglasses celebrating the Nats' victory and its superb season record.

She was drained physically from the field trip and supervising the energetic youth on their first foundation outing. She looked over at Trevor lovingly as he lay beside her on his back peacefully, his head propped with down pillows. He was such a positive role model, a champion on the field and off. She figured she'd give him a nightcap and slid under the covers to seduce him to sleep. Her jaws and tongue weren't tired.

Zodi rang the bell at 9 a.m. to kick off another shopping spree with Amber. The number of fashion extravaganzas was now off the Richter scale. She'd never expressed her opinion to her boss. After Amber's last splurge session, she'd made her routine stop at Jaslyn's to stash away the purchases.

Zodi expressed ultimate silence when it came to Amber. And

when Jaslyn attempted to squeeze out information to get inside Amber's head, Zodi remained mum. In her own head, she was becoming concerned with the frequency of Amber's shopping and the kind of dollars she was dropping on excessive items. Yes, she was married to a pro athlete and could afford the world, but Zodi was aware that it could be affecting her mental health. She'd searched online to see if there was a condition and discovered obsessive-compulsive disorder. She had pegged that her boss, whom she adored, was suffering from it.

Zodi rang the bell again, admiring the lovely flowers in the front yard along the stone walkway. Shayla opened the door.

"Hi, Zodi." She motioned for her to enter. "I thought I'd surprise you this morning with a great breakfast." She walked toward the sunroom. "That's why I suggested you come a little earlier than usual. I had Sonya whip up some goodies."

The brilliant sunlight exposed a buffet table of mini wheat pancakes, scrambled egg whites, turkey bacon and home fries. A pitcher of mimosas and a pot of herbal tea completed the display.

"This looks like it's from a food magazine." Zodi picked up a plate and served, then Amber followed.

After enjoying Sonya's scrumptious meal, they left for White Flint mall in Bethesda, Maryland.

Zodi carried the twenty dresses that Amber had selected to the counter. She followed Amber who had nine tops and four pants. She'd already made one trip to the car to drop off eight pairs of designer shoes in her trunk to add to her massive collection. When they reached the cashier, they took turns placing the selections on the counter.

Amber enjoyed shopping online, but it was something about

stores' ambience that gave her the ultimate rush. She enjoyed being in the mix.

After Zodi dropped the dresses, she walked away and perused
the aisles. It was sickening to stick around to see how much Amber
would be dropping in a couple of hours. She whizzed through the
store like a tornado, disrupting all in its path. It was a blessing
that Trevor didn't accompany her on shopping trips. He never
would have the patience. Often Amber would offer to buy her a
new garment, but today she hadn't suggested she pick out any
pieces. It was all good. She had a cool wardrobe and never wanted
to emulate her boss' over-the-top mentality, whether she could
afford it or not.

"Could you please try again? I'm sure this is an error," Amber
requested.

"Okay, miss, I will definitely swipe your card, but it's being
declined," the sales clerk stated.

Zodi's ears perked up when she heard the word *declined* and immediately presumed that Amber had overdrawn an account if it
was a debit card. She glanced inconspicuously at the unfolding
scene at the register. Amber was laid-back, but she could be a hot
tamale when necessary. The sales lady had better not be in error.

After several attempts, Amber was embarrassed and didn't want
to make a scene, drawing even more attention to the decline status.
She often wore sunglasses to shield her identity, and she certainly
didn't want any of the D.C. gossipmongers to notice the shopping
mishap. She could see the headlines: *Nats Star's Wife Overspends
in Excessive Shopping Spree.* It would be too fluffy news for local
papers, but it certainly would be a target for the tabloids.

She looked over to find Zodi in the nearby aisle and waved for
her to come over. Zodi arrived at the counter.

"It looks like I overdid it. I don't understand as I oversee this account." She looked at the garments. "Help me decide what I should put back. I can't get it all today."

Zodi selected the wares to purchase. Amber never wanted to make those kinds of decisions. It was tough as she loved everything. Turning away fashions was a no-no. She selected various items and pushed the others aside.

"It's a mystery how I didn't have enough to pay for everything." *I can't believe I'd go over. It's not that it's a bottomless account. But I thought I did better keeping track. I've been shopping more than normal lately, but…hmmm. I will check it out when I get home.*

The ride home was quiet. Amber was stumped but didn't want to use her Smartphone to check her accounts in front of Zodi. She preferred to do so in privacy on her laptop. It was her sole account where Trevor funneled spending "change" for her personal shopping and household goods. Apparently, she had spent excessively without scrutinizing. His accountant handled his major records.

When they buzzed through the gate, Zodi texted Jaslyn to alert her that she would reach her home shortly along the winding road. Once again, she'd bring in Amber's purchases until she had a chance to sneak them into her own home.

After stopping at Jaslyn's, Zodi dropped Amber off who entered with one bag with a few purchases. Trevor wasn't home, but she always felt a tinge of guilt if she had more than several new items.

With her bag hung over her arm, she headed to the refrigerator and grabbed a cold bottle of water. She walked out of the kitchen and up the stairs. She opened the door to her office and plopped down on the swivel chair. She turned on the laptop and waited for it to load, then went online to check her account.

She took a swig of her water as she started to sweat. Nervously, she scrolled the pages of her account, noting that she had run through the funds like a reckless storm. Trevor's accountant deposited a lump sum quarterly, and it had always been more than enough to accommodate her spending habits. This time she had exceeded all expectations.

As she examined the account line by line, she noticed that most of her purchases were on fashions—for her. What did all of this portray? Was she addicted even more than she realized to shopping? What would she ever do with all of the material things she had acquired?

She sighed, then prayed that this enlightening scenario might help her improve her out-of-control spending. For the first time, she realized it could truly be a dangerous fixation. For years, she had trivialized her love for shopping, considering it as fun and frivolous. But perhaps, it was something deeper. A short bank account may have been a wakeup call.

"Hi, Shayla. How are ya?" Amber asked after dialing her cell phone.

"I'm good, and how about you?" Shayla was prepping for a lust-filled night with her hubby. She'd soaked in her Jacuzzi, given herself a pedicure and was wearing the latest addition to her lingerie collection. Chad would be arriving home late after a closing appointment on a pricey home on D.C.'s Gold Coast. "How was your weekend?"

"Fine," she said blandly. She had relived her debit card rejection scene like a video in repeat mode. She zoomed back to the purpose of her call. "Have you thought about when you'd like to go to L.A.? Remember we discussed you going out there to check on Chad?"

"Yeah, girl, don't I remember." Shayla had vowed she'd join Chad on one of his business trips on the West Coast. She'd recalled that Amber, during their recent movie night, had suggested she make a pop visit as she'd advised Kyle to stop by Bryce's shop. Unlike Kyle's, her surprise drop-by would be a 3,000-mile one, and she doubted she could pull it off easily. "Well, he's here in town now," she said coyly, rubbing scented lotion on her arms and legs while cradling the phone to her ear.

"I'm asking because I want to go to the coast to visit my parents. I haven't seen them in a while," she noted. "I'm thinking we could fly out together, hang in L.A. for a while, and then I'd go on to Oakland. You could stay in L.A. with Chad."

"Hey, sounds like a plan. I'll check his calendar and see when he's out there next." She toyed with the thought. "It'll also give me a chance to meet up with Passion. I keep telling her that I plan to see her in action, or at least in person, out there."

"How's she doing anyway? I heard her song on the radio the other day."

"She's working on her video. Things are on the up and up. No negative press. For a minute she was hanging out with a bad boy, and I convinced her he would hurt her image."

"Now that was a good thing."

"Yeah, she's a youngun and we have to look out for the babies," she stated of the twenty-year-old. "The label folks are cool, but sometimes you need someone on the outside looking in," Shayla advised. "Plus, she's the first client from L.A. that Chad brought to New Visions. I feel like I need to take extra care."

"Tell me about it," Amber agreed. "Well, let me know when you have some solid dates and we can book our flights. As long as it's not during the playoffs, I'm good," she added, anticipating the Nationals would continue their winning season.

CHAPTER 36
Shayla and Amber

"May I get you ladies something to drink?" The flight attendant smiled gracefully.

"Yes, I'll take Chardonnay." Shayla maneuvered in her seat, adjusting her seatbelt.

"A rum and diet Coke, please," Amber requested.

The flight attendant in first class returned with their drinks as passengers continued to board the jet headed to L.A.

When Amber had called to suggest they travel together, Shayla didn't hesitate to make plans. Amber had decided that she needed a reprieve from her environment. It would be hard for her to resist shopping in La-La Land, especially after Trevor's accountant, Ian, had replenished her funds. It was considerably less, but she dared not question the amount. She didn't want to draw any attention to the depleted bank account. Perhaps Ian had alerted Trevor of her outlandish splurging, and he'd downsized.

Since she had a little something-something to work with, she'd sneak in a few outings while in L.A. for a few days. Then she would head to Oakland to visit with her family. She couldn't wait to hook up her with best friend from college, Desiree.

Shayla and Amber enjoyed the scenic ride through the streets of L.A. en route to the Beverly Wilshire Hotel. Chad had hired a limo service to drive them from the airport. She had wanted to surprise him, but that seemed impossible. She had considered showing up at Charles' home. He was Chad's bachelor cousin who was his host during his L.A. visits.

After checking in, they walked to Scarpetta for an Italian lunch inside the Montage Beverly Hills Hotel. Spaghetti and chicken parmesan had them ready to take a nap combined with the long flight and time difference.

"This is such a beautiful hotel and you never know who you'll run in to in this area," Shayla commented after arriving back at their hotel. It was her first visit to L.A. and she was excited to be among celebrities. "I see why Chad makes this his second home."

"Yep, Chad knows what he's doing hanging out here in this gorgeous weather." She pushed the button for the elevator.

Shayla looked at her watch. "He plans to take us to dinner after his meetings. Says he'll be here with a driver by seven." The elevator stopped and they stepped on to head to the seventh floor. After arriving, they headed to their separate rooms down the hall from each other.

"Well, happy snoozing," Shayla stated, opening the door to the room. "Got to keep up with our beauty rest." She smiled at Amber.

"I definitely will." She placed in the key card and entered.

Amber was restless and batted her eyes. She forced herself to stay awake with the flat-screen on high volume. She noted it had been an hour and figured Shayla was a sleeping beauty. She walked to the window and gazed at the famous Rodeo Drive street sign. This was the wrong location for a shopaholic considering recovery. She looked over at the clock. It was now four o'clock and she was tempted to disappear to window shop.

Rodeo Drive is calling my name. Shayla won't suspect anything. She

*wouldn't think I'd have energy to step out before dinner. We are both
exhausted from the flight.*

She freshened up in the bathroom, reapplying her makeup and
washing lightly, then spritzing on perfume. She'd shower when
she returned.

Amber relished the warmth of the sunlight as she strolled along
the shopper's paradise perusing the windows and noting luxurious
items for her list. Now is when she would miss Zodi to help her
select what to purchase plus help her carry bags.

She had become spoiled as she'd never had a personal assistant.
When she'd hung out in L.A. with Desiree and hobnobbed with
the wealthy, she was on her own. Instead of shopping in Beverly
Hills, she was a fixture at the resale shops in West Hollywood.
She never dreamed she'd someday be able to afford the price tags
of this famous row of high-end boutiques. Her life had made a
huge turnaround after meeting Trevor.

An hour had passed and she'd enjoyed traipsing throughout the
designer stores. She'd gotten her rush for the day, her fashion
high. She returned to the hotel and slipped quietly into her room.
She'd need every bit of the two hours to prepare for the night.
Shayla would be well rested and ecstatic to see her hubby.

Chad had invited Dr. Pierce Collins. She definitely appreciated
the chance to meet him in case she ever decided to have surgery.
She'd heard so much about him from Shayla, how he'd hooked
up Chad with various clients. She was satisfied with her reflection
in the mirror. So was Trevor and that's all that mattered. She flipped
on the TV to ESPN to check on the team's score. Hopefully, they
had continued their winning streak. She truly wished Trevor could
have met her in Oakland, but she was accustomed to him often
being unavailable during the season.

Chad strolled into the lobby to await Shayla and Amber. Dressed in a tan suit with tie, he swallowed his uneasy feeling to adjust to the unusual circumstance. It was rare for Shayla to be in town. He was accustomed to riding solo. He adored his wife, but sometimes she was over the top, drawing unnecessary attention. Overall, he missed her bubbly personality and bedroom skills. He'd suggested they meet in the lobby or they may not make it to dinner.

The elevator doors opened and Shayla and Amber stepped off. Shayla was stunning in her ensemble that the stylist Valencia had selected for her during their ladies day out. Amber was equally as sharp with a black dress. Both were flaunting their cleavage and walked gracefully with confidence toward Chad.

"Don't you ladies look lovely," Chad stated and embraced Shayla, then kissed her lightly on the lips. "And baby, you are gorgeous tonight." He gazed at her total look. "I missed you."

"Missed you, too." Shayla locked her arm into his. He escorted her to the front door while Amber followed alongside them.

Outside he helped them enter the backseat of a black Mercedes with a driver.

"Pierce is waiting for us at MR CHOW," he said, sliding into the front seat. "Thought you ladies might want some Chinese."

"I'm glad it's a light dinner. We had Italian for lunch," Shayla noted.

"And I had planned to go to the gym," Amber stated. "Maybe tomorrow." *But walking on Rodeo Drive was physical and mental exercise.*

The driver headed onto Wilshire Boulevard to the popular Beverly Hills tradition. When they arrived at the restaurant, Pierce was waiting at a table and sipping on water with a slice of lemon. He stood up as he noticed them approaching.

"Greetings." He hugged Shayla gently, then reached his hand out to Amber.

"Amber Trent."

"Pleasure. I'm Pierce Collins."

The four sat at the table.

"I'm a fan of your husband's and a fan of the Nats unless they're playing the Dodgers or the A's," Pierce teased.

"That makes two of us. In fact, my home is Oakland and I'm heading there in a few days," Amber noted.

"And you met Trevor—" he started.

"Here in L.A. at a game after-party." She smiled. "That was some party."

Pierce turned to Shayla. "I've heard a lot of good things about your business."

"It's coming along. My client base is building. Thanks to people like you for the referrals, including Passion. It looks like she's heading to the top."

"Passion?" he asked, caught off-guard. Chad eyed Pierce with a "watch what you say" look. "Oh, yes, Passion…the singer." He sighed silently. "Well, honestly, I haven't followed her, but I'm glad to hear her career is off to a great start."

"And it's no problem regarding my referral of Passion," Pierce lied. "That's why we're here. Chad and I are all about networking. One hand washes the other. I enjoy what I do, but after I remove the surgical gloves, I'm searching for a new means to occupy my time."

Amber noticed his ring finger was bare. "I'm not prying, but I see you must be a single man." She thought about her little sister, Autumn, who was on the hunt for a prestigious bachelor.

"I'm not ready to settle down—yet," he stated. Pierce's past had included clients who attempted to break the client-customer relationship and seduce him, and elderly women who were enamored with their young, charming doctor. Some desperately sought surgery thinking they would be transformed into a beauty queen, and others thought that plastic surgery was magical and synonymous with snagging a husband or maintaining the current one.

Pierce inquired if a variety of dishes from Sky, Land and Sea were fine to order for the family style restaurant along with red wine. All agreed.

"I finally took the time to stop in to see how L.A.'s treating Chad. It's his second home now," Shayla stated.

"I've been asking Chad when you were planning to visit. He's out here all the time these days. Our clients are dedicated and recommend us to others, so we've been building our base for years."

"As I told her, I'm securing more and more properties in D.C., which is a hot seller's and buyer's market." Chad was proud of his career opportunities.

Shayla looked at Amber and cleared her throat, hoping the men wouldn't dominate the conversation about real estate and plastic surgery. "I'm looking forward to my visit. Chad's going to show me around." She reached over and stroked his hand on top of the table. "Aren't you, sweetie?"

"Most definitely. Anywhere you want to go, I'm game."

"You can be my tour guide. And I promised Passion we'd get together at some point."

"Yes, I'd love to meet her if you hook up before I go to Oakland."

"Passion keeps a busy schedule," Chad interjected. "She's a hard one to catch."

"Well, I'm sure she'll make time to see me," Shayla stated. "Camilla has already reached out to her and she's waiting for her to return her call. I was hoping to see her perform."

"She's been in the studio lately, working on her CD," Chad advised.

"I'm aware. In fact, we're working on a campaign in conjunction with the label to kick off her tour and debut CD."

"Have you thought about her and Blaze touring together? Your youngest artists?" Amber inquired.

"Oh, no, not a good idea." *Hell naw, they might hook up. I can't let my boy toy be touring with a hot star like Passion. No doubt I'd turn my back and they'd be getting it in.* "I don't believe in my clients meshing, and they'd definitely be in each other's arms before long. Seeing they are both young and hot," she offered. "It wouldn't be a good look," she added mindlessly, not offering an explanation. Envy was beneath her facial expression, but she dared not let it surface.

"You're right. I've never met this Blaze guy, but it doesn't mean they're a good fit," Chad commented. "Plus, I'd like to see her with one of these seasoned celebrities, not a rising star," he stressed, secretly overprotective of Passion.

Hmmm, why does he care so much about Passion's love life? "Whoever she dates, she needs to keep a clean image 'cause the paparazzi will be on her." Shayla was irked and felt that he was overstepping his boundaries, offering advice for Passion. *Your ages are worlds apart, so what would you know about what a young woman needs? You need to focus on what you do best—real estate.*

CHAPTER 37
Terra

Cutz Salon and Spa was packed with teens getting braids, the grown and sexy waiting to get their weaves and mothers getting perms, while others were embracing their natural hair. Terra desired a brand-new style to complement her fresh makeover. She had her first solo date with Lamont and she needed to be on point.

The upscale salon was blanketed with sunlight and large plants. The ultra-modern shop with stainless steel framed mirrors and a burnt-orange and pecan porcelain floor with pale bronze walls offered a calming ambience.

If it ain't broke, don't fix, Terra had thought, when she'd decided to return to her favorite shop and not to try a new one. She doubted she could afford the salons that Amber, Kyle and Shayla frequented. It was enough of a challenge to squeeze money from her budget to afford today's visit.

She strutted to the rear area past a row of clientele.

"Well, hello, lady, look at you," said her stylist, Dillard. "Coming up in here like you off the runway," he complimented.

"Hi, thanks." Terra sat in one of the colorful cushioned seats. She was dressed in a cute dress with a cutout back and wedge sandals.

"And right on time I might add." He smiled. "I'm finishing up and will be with you shortly." He nodded in the direction of a small refrigerator. "Help yourself to a drink."

Terra stood up and walked over to select a Diet Coke. She returned to the seat facing Dillard's station.

"And I see you watching that figure of yours," he blurted, sharing her business with the patrons.

Terra smiled and opened her soda. She took a sip and then picked up an *Essence* magazine from a side table. She flipped through the pages until Dillard completed his client's hair.

After a ten-minute wait, the customer's blunt blow-dried bob was bouncy and lustrous with a high sheen as she walked toward the front. Terra put down the magazine, picked up her bottle, then crossed over and sat in Dillard's styling chair. Dillard was always close to being on time. It had been a while since she'd stepped in his shop. Lately, she couldn't afford the luxury of a hair appointment. It was one of the setbacks after dropping the neighborhood guys from her roster. They'd frequently help her when she desired to bling-bling.

"What's new?" he inquired as he draped a jacket over her dress. "You rockin' that outfit. Love it."

"Thanks."

Dillard was making his own fashion statement in a long-sleeved, crisp, button-down white shirt with jeans. His Mohawk haircut and oversized black frame glasses made him look flawless. "You kinda quiet today. It's so not you. Plus, how long has it been? At least a year since you been here. Honey, I know you have plenty to scoop."

"Well, I'd like a new style. Maybe cut it all off. A pixie. You think that'll work for me?"

Dillard swiveled her chair around to face him. He observed her features, shape of her face and head. "Hmm…definitely. Don't worry, hon, I'll fix ya up. It'll be gorgeous, frame your face." He motioned for her to sit at the shampoo bowl. After washing her hair, he lightly dried it with a towel. Then she returned to his stylist chair where he used the blow-dryer with comb attachment. He whipped out scissors and proceeded to cut. "So, what it be? I can tell something's amidst with ya. You never this mousy. I feel like you holdin' out on me."

"Well—"

"Look, what goes on in Cutz stays in Cutz. You feel me? So, go on and dish." He continued to snip slowly and meticulously.

"I met this cool dude on a blind date. I've been hanging with some new ladies, a little older than me, and let's just say they got it going on."

"Oh, a new beau. I could see it in your eyes." He laughed.

"Not—but I got that vibe."

"I admit you got intuition though." She peeked in the mirror. "I like it so far."

"You're gonna *love* it." He clipped more hair, holding the scissors delicately. "Tell me more about this newbie."

"He's in real estate and a few years older than me."

"Oh, sounds like he's got some pockets. Okay, I'm convinced he's a keeper." He caught her eyes in the mirror and winked.

"And I have my first real date with him tonight. So I figured why not change my look? One of my new associates and her husband turned me on to him."

"I see…"

Terra was being cautious not to share too much 4-1-1 with Dillard as the whole shop would eventually know let alone all of D.C. Dillard was sweet, but he was a gossip guru. If he discovered she was networking with a PR entrepreneur, a pro baller's wife and a dance studio owner, he'd attempt to maneuver in to their clique.

He was always on the hunt for socialite friends. This was all fresh to her, so she didn't want anything to ruin her opportunity. And his gift of gab could truly put a dent in her mission.

Dillard completed her cut and turned her to face the mirror. "So, how do you like?"

"I love it," she said excitedly.

He swiveled her chair, then handed her a hand-held mirror. She took it and gazed at the back of her hair in the wall mirror's reflection.

"Love it." She was pleased with the cut and how it was shaped along her neck.

"I told you that you'd adore it." He admired his work as if it were a masterpiece.

She was forever grateful to Blaze for suggesting she step outside of her comfort zone. He would be proud to see her now.

"So, sweetie, I hear there's a lot going on in your 'hood."

"Bet there is and you know more than I do."

"The 'round-the-way girls been keepin' me informed." He leaned in closer. "Ya hear that old-timer Wilburn got that teen girl—and pardon, no disrespect to her, so I won't mention her name—knocked up?"

"*Wilburn?* I'm not surprised," she said with disgust. "He gives me the creeps."

"Everybody… well, word is he's not tryin' to go down for jailbait, so mum's the word. So her baby daddy's *anonymous*."

"Humph. If it's supposed to be quiet, that's a joke," she remarked sarcastically. "I see there's enough loose lips chatting it up."

"Mmm…you know I always have some good dish for ya. And yo' girl, Tasha—"

"Correction. Not my girl. I don't associate with her anymore. So please disconnect me from that ratchet hussy."

"Ooops…okaaaay. Miss Tasha, or Miss *Ratchet*, was your gurl, but that's history."

"Yep, that deal is over." Once again, Terra wouldn't reveal too much information in fear that her business would be prime time. Tasha had backstabbed her by dating the same guy she was interested in. She'd found out from a mutual contact. "No thanks."

"I hear she's the queen bee at the club. Doing her thang working that stripper pole. She got it goin' on. Hear her performance is bootylicious, honey."

"Oh, well, that's cool. Nothin' wrong with that. I wish her well and I'm sure she's pulling in a strap of cash."

"And get this, you remember that dude Jarrett, uh, last name… oops, I hate to even bring up his name."

"Bastard. What's up with that punk?" she inquired. Jarrett was the former boyfriend of her late sister and the well-documented reason she'd committed suicide. He'd physically and verbally abused her and when she passed, her journals indicated it was over the love she had for Jarrett. She didn't see that their relationship would ever be improved. She'd taken out a restraining order against him and feared for her life.

"Well, you sure, 'cause I ain't tryin' to bring back any bad memories," he stated, overanxious to share news and pretending he'd hold back if she requested.

"I can't stand the sound of his name."

"Yes, your poor dear sister. May the Lord rest her soul."

"R-I-P, Toya." Terra recalled the torturous relationship between Jarrett and her older sister. She'd sworn she'd never accept any abuse from anyone.

"Well, dear, the devil in disguise actually had some luck, quiet as it is kept."

"What you mean 'luck'? Someone put a beatin' on him or

somethin'?" *That's what I call luck in his case*, Terra thought with extreme resentment for Jarrett.

"Noooo, I have to give you the four-one-one. I'm kinda surprised you hadn't heard." He heightened with surprise. "Well, Jarrett, is tryin' to keep it on the down-low, but he hit the lottery for some mils. He never came forward to show his identity, but his peeps were aware. Heard he gave a few of his boys a little sumthin'-sumthin' to keep 'em cool."

"Say what? Lottery for millions? I'll be damned, that son of a bitch."

"Yes, darling, for millions. And I hear he's perpetrating out in the 'burbs." He leaned in. "Even better, I understand he's even taken on an alias. Got himself a new name, now that he's outta the city and hanging in Maryland."

"So what's his fake-ass name? *Stupid?*"

"No, chile, it's Bryce like in rice."

She almost choked. "Bryce?" She frowned. "I've heard of a Bryce, but I know it's not the same one. This one has a good head on his shoulders and has it goin' on. Entrepreneur and all that jazz. The Jarrett aka Bryce *we* know ain't hardly a businessman. Plus, I've been hanging with his wife."

"Now you beat me to it. That's what I was gettin' ready to tell ya. He jumped the broom a while back. It could be a coincidence, though. As ya said, old Jarrett was never business material, so I hear ya. I doubt it's the same *Bryyyce* that's married to ya new associate."

"No, it wouldn't be him. Wifey is laid-back, classy, has her own dance studio that Bryce helped to finance." She frowned. "Hell, either way, you say the sucker hit the jackpot," she continued. "He owed a lot of that to Sis, considering she was the one who put up with his shit all those years. Makes no damn sense."

Terra was spellbound about the news, finding it unbelievable that a coldhearted soul like Jarrett would strike it rich overnight. Now he was living large while her mistreated sister lay six feet under. *Life's not fair.* "I figured he'd scrambled out of dodge to get the hell away from here. Had no idea his pockets are lined. Wherever he is, he's living a lie and I feel sorry for his wife. She doesn't have a clue about his past. I wonder if the monster has come out yet."

"Yeah, how about that? Well, we'll have to pray for wifey. Again, I crossed paths with one of his boys from back in the day. Apparently, they still tight, and he told me brothaman is rollin'."

"Well, he'd better not cross my path," she said sourly. Her bitterness seeped from her face.

She could take Dillard in doses. During each visit, he'd lay out the latest news from his loyal gossip artists. With the news of Jarrett, she'd had her share.

"And Mother Geraldine, she's still lettin' that no-good grandson of hers use her place for illegal activities. You name it, numbers, drugs, after-hours, whatever. She's all about the cash."

"Look, Dillard, I appreciate you lettin' me know what's up, but I've heard enough. It's amazing how I can live right in the neighborhood and be blind to all this stuff around me."

She pulled out her wallet and paid Dillard, adding a sizable tip. She'd ensured she'd set aside enough to pay for her new 'do. Now she needed to impress her new man.

"Why, thank you, sweetie." He accepted the bills.

Terra checked out her new image in the mirror and smiled. "Dillard, you hooked me up."

"Glad you like it, sweetie."

"I looove it." She lightly touched her new cut.

"Don't forget the referrals." Dillard winked.

"I got you."

Terra walked past the customers and headed toward the door, accepting compliments on her hair. She exited the salon feeling brand-new. Sometimes you needed a fresh start, not only with appearance but with your circle of friends, she thought.

Now she would have her second chance at securing her coveted prize, Lamont.

CHAPTER 38
Kyle

S itting in her kitchen, her favorite room in her house, Kyle thought about how she had missed the ladies' trip to the West Coast. Life was tough living with a control freak like Bryce. *Why couldn't I be married to someone like Chad or Trevor? Shayla and Amber are so lucky to have understanding and supportive husbands. I can't do any right with this monster I'm stuck with.*

She thought about how she'd never experienced such brutal disrespect. Her parents in New York were in their own world, presuming she was in marital bliss with Bryce and living the good life. Her luxurious home and dance studio represented she had arrived. She definitely didn't want to share the truth with them and especially not her brothers. They'd be on Interstate 95 South in a flash prepared to kick some ass. She and her sister weren't close and for now, she would keep up the pretense that all was fair in love.

She sipped on her iced green tea and ate a forkful of her spinach salad with cherry tomatoes, feta cheese, raisins and pecans. She had taken the day off at the studio simply to relax. She missed Shayla and Amber, who had both called and texted her to check on her. She'd told them she couldn't go to L.A. as originally planned. She needed to hang tight to oversee the studio. It was far from the truth. Bryce already was not trustworthy and her hanging on the coast would've conjured up all kinds of insecurities and false accusations. He was nearly impossible to deal with and she was still reeling from his over-the-top reaction to her stopping by the shop.

She was never a weakling. It was confusing that she had lost a tough image and hadn't stood up to Bryce. Was it because he initially assisted her with making her dream a reality? Was it that he provided her a wealthy existence? She was slowly discovering that the grass may not always be greener in financial paradise.

Her cell phone vibrated. She checked the caller ID. It was Erick. *He really doesn't accept no, does he? I attempted to stress to him at the performance that it stops here. I made a mistake going to the hotel room that night, and thankfully, I didn't go all the way with him. If he's this obsessed now, if I'd slept with him, he'd be hysterical.* After a handful of rings, his call went to voicemail.

CHAPTER 39
Shayla

Christening the suite at the Beverly Wilshire Hotel, Shayla and Chad had bounced off the walls with their sexcapade. They lay on their hotel bed exhilarated. Shayla missed her hubby despite that she was getting polished on the regular back home by her crew.

"Chad, that made my night. I needed that workout." She laughed. "After those two meals today, I'd better be working out." She kissed him lightly on the cheek. She looked at the clock: it was 1:10 a.m. "Plus, it's like ten o'clock to my body, still on East Coast time. Maybe that explains the energy. But, whew, I missed you, too."

The warm Jacuzzi bath they'd shared left her refreshed and she was eager for another round. She refrained as his body language read he needed a break.

He turned to face her. "It's not about the sex, Shayla." He looked over at her deeply in her eyes. "I truly love you. Sure I miss when we're not together, but it's more than the bedroom. I don't think I tell you enough how much I do love you. I'm proud of New Visions and how you've taken it to another level—"

"Thanks, but I have you to thank for a lot of that," she interrupted, stroking his cheek. "You've referred me to many clients."

"True but you still have to make it happen. A referral is simply that, a referral. You are good at taking it from there," the Wharton School of Business graduate advised. Chad had been asked to give speeches at his alma mater as well as historically black colleges and universities. He was considering it to supplement his income, especially if the market crashed again. Either way he wanted to give back to the community and would eventually arrange activities on his schedule.

"It's also been a learning experience and that's with everything. Sometimes you have to wing it."

"True again, but you are great at winging it."

"I'm looking forward to meeting up with Passion again tomorrow."

"Likewise for her."

"So what fancy restaurant are we going to in La-La Land? She's got that air about her that she only wants the finest. I'm schooling her that that's all good, but she needs to ensure she also has that down-to-earth appeal. Particularly she's young, and she doesn't want to turn off any fans. Ruin her reputation in a heartbeat if she comes off arrogant."

"Actually, we're meeting in private. No fancy restaurant or public venue." He stretched his legs and twisted to face the ceiling. "I asked one of my clients—you'll love her—Isabella Moore, to allow us to meet at her estate in Malibu. It's a fantastic home, and I thought it would be more intimate. If that's okay with you…"

"Okaaay, it's fine with me. You know her better than me; at least it seems from a personal perspective."

"Yes, I'd say we bonded cool. I tried to look out for her since she's your client and I introduced you two." He sighed. "Plus, the paparazzi can be vicious. She has to be careful about where she goes. She's new on the scene and gaining popularity, but she tries to avoid that type of publicity."

"I've told her that when she finishes her CD, I'll be setting up some interviews. Get her name and face out there to those who are unfamiliar. But that's all positive publicity."

"Yep, she doesn't want to be seen in her bikini on the beach or going to clubs, you name it," Chad stated with a protective tone. "I don't think that's a good image—at least for now. She's too fresh on the scene."

"She's young, though, so she also doesn't want to appear as an old-fashioned fuddy-duddy."

"I'll leave that female stuff up to you and Darla. How she dresses," he said, referring to her female A&R rep at the label. "From what I've seen and heard, she has to keep the wolves off her."

"Don't we all?"

He frowned. "Say what?"

Oops, did I really say that? "Nothing. I'm not sure what I was talking about," she lied. *But yes, all of us ladies have to keep the wolves, bears and lions off.* Suddenly, she felt sad. Her husband had expressed his love and nothing about him had ever read infidelity. She'd slipped her tongue to indicate that men desired her openly. In fact, it was the other way around. "In general, most women have men finding them attractive," she added, her best attempt to clean up her statement.

"That's true, especially when they are as lovely as you." He kissed her on the lips.

"Thank you, my love."

She closed her eyes and pretended to drift asleep.

Connecting with Passion was high on Shayla's agenda during her L.A. visit. Chad had rented a special vehicle for the weekend to zip through the streets of L.A. Occasionally, he relished a luxury sports car to wheel around the city and up the coastline. In lieu of hiring a chauffeur, he was ready to take over the driver's seat. Isabella lived in Malibu and the scenic drive along the Pacific Ocean would offer Shayla a grand view of what the sunshine city had to offer.

The valet driver pulled the shiny red car up to the Beverly Wilshire Hotel. Chad opened the door for Shayla, wearing an orange rayon sundress, and then closed the door. Amber, dressed in a lime dress, hopped in the backseat. He walked around the car and jumped in, then pulled his sunglasses from his pocket and slipped them on.

Chad maneuvered the ride west along Wilshire Boulevard and then headed north toward Sunset. He turned on the boulevard and continued west to the Pacific, coasting and swerving on the route past famous Hollywood haunts and estates. After arriving at Route 1, he headed north toward Malibu. The ocean beckoned as they cruised in sync with the waves. Shayla was mellow after a few glasses of Chardonnay in their hotel room.

He exited and headed uphill to a private community, arriving at a gate with a white mansion peeking through. He rang the buzzer at the gate and announced his arrival. Isabella opened the gate and he drove through and pulled into the circular driveway.

Chad parked the car and looked at his watch. There was no sign of Passion's limo. He had stressed she be on time and was certain she'd arrive momentarily. He walked around to open the door for Shayla, who stepped out regally. She felt as if she'd arrived at a queen's palace, but nothing had topped the castle. The two walked to the large wooden door of the stucco mansion. Before Chad had a chance to knock, a tiny woman about five feet tall opened the door.

Dressed in a Japanese kimono and wearing her silver hair in a bun neatly positioned with chopsticks, Isabella smiled. The seventy-six-year-old placed pecks on each of Chad's cheeks, and then extended her hand to Shayla.

"I'm Isabella."

"Shayla, nice meeting you." She turned to Amber. "And this is my longtime friend, Amber. We traveled together from the East Coast."

"Hello, thanks for welcoming us into your home," Amber stated graciously.

Isabella shook Amber's hand and then motioned for them to enter. The estate was graced with colorful abstract artwork on the walls and floor-to-ceiling windows. Tall plants were placed throughout the living room. A black Pomeranian was at her heels, following her every step as she led them to a massive room facing the ocean.

She turned around as she walked, peeking over the rim of her chained reading glasses. "And this, of course, is the lady of the house, Princess," she noted, referring to her devoted pet.

Once they reached the den, they all sat in oversized, fluffy chairs. Isabella reminded Shayla of a flashback in time: her outfit, her demeanor was straight out of the sixties. Had she ever left?

"Chad, it's good to see you again. And Shayla, it's great to make the connection." She pushed a button on the side of the chair.

"Yes, Ms. Moore?" a woman's voice answered through an intercom.

"Please bring us some white wine and some of your delicious, fresh-baked cookies," Isabella requested. "Prepare for five and thank you."

"Yes, my pleasure."

Passion joined them and strolled in wearing dark straight-leg jeans, a sheer black blouse and black stilettos. Her large gold hoop earrings dangled as she strutted. She reached out and gave

Isabella a big hug, then approached Chad, who stood up to hug her and kiss her lightly on the cheek. She walked to Shayla and pecked her cheek.

"Welcome to La-La Land," Passion directed to Shayla. "I'm ecstatic you finally made it. I believed ya when ya said we'd meet up next on the West Coast."

Shayla cringed. *You*, not *ya*, Passion… "I told you I'd be heading this way. It was only a matter of time. I kept my promise."

"That's what's up," Passion remarked.

"And this is Amber. You've heard me speak about her."

Passion walked over and shook Amber's hand. "Nice meeting you."

"The same, Passion."

Passion sauntered across the room and sat in a loveseat.

"Would anyone care for tea and not wine? I can have Marcy put on a kettle," Isabella inquired, her patchwork quilt nestled over her chair.

Shayla looked at Chad. "Wine is fine." She looked through the windows at the vast landscape of the picturesque Pacific. "You have a gorgeous view of the ocean. I'd be so caught up in it that I doubt I'd ever get anything done."

"Actually, it can work the reverse. It inspires me. The paintings that you see are mine."

"How beautiful. Chad didn't tell me you were an artist," she complimented.

"I've been painting since I was a teen. I grew up in Hollywood and cherished all of the artists. I used to go to Venice Beach and watch the artists paint on the boardwalk. It's legendary."

"Well, thanks for offering us your lovely home." Shayla continued to gaze around the room and out of the window.

"You are quite welcome." Isabella adored Chad and was always eager to provide his every need. "I'd travel to the depths of the earth for my dear goddaughter," she vowed.

"Goddaughter?" Shayla inquired. "I didn't realize—"

"Chad didn't tell you—"

"Not yet...I like surprises, remember?"

Marcy arrived and served the cookies and wine.

"Thank you," Isabella announced.

Shayla bit a piece of an oatmeal pecan cookie. "These are hmmm." She turned to Passion and smiled. "It's good to see you face-to-face again. Sometimes I'm tired of the emails and texts, but that's what we thrive on these days."

"You can count me out. I'm not a bit interested in learning. Give me a phone and some fancy stationery," Isabella interjected.

"So, how are the studio sessions going? I can't wait for the CD, so we can move full speed ahead. I'm lining up the interviews," Shayla stated.

"Yeah, it's supposed to drop soon. Darla at Redstone is keeping me informed. Meanwhile, I'm doing what I do best. I'm ready for the game plan." She smoothed out her jeans. "And my stylist is working on my show outfits. I told her she's gotta make them sexy."

Amber nodded. "Yes, young lady, you must roll out sexy." She smiled. "Look, don't start me talking about clothes and shoes. But I'm glad to hear you're fashion-conscious." She looked at her pricey-looking heels. "I love those." She was such a shoe fanatic she was aware of the designer.

"Thanks. I try to rock the finest."

Chad interjected, "Remember to be mild sometimes and show a conservative side. It doesn't matter what your stylist says. No one said in order to be successful, you have to always show a lot of skin."

Passion eyed Chad with pursed lips.

"Hey, dear, if you've got it, there isn't anything wrong with flaunting it," Shayla offered. To Passion's defense, she had advised her to avoid a granny look and embrace her youthfulness. *There he goes again, trying to regulate her. They don't have anything in common.* "Please, let me show her the ropes."

"Believe me, if Mrs. Benson is helping me, no worries. I can see for myself that she's got it going *onnn*. Old enough to be my moms and she's holding it *down*." Passion laughed, tickled she could take sides with Shayla.

"Okay, Shayla, I'm not up to debating." He sighed. "We're proud of her success. So let's keep it that way."

"Congratulations are in order, so let's toast." Isabella lifted her wineglass and the others followed. Passion held up her glass of Diet Coke. "Cheers to continuous success on and off the red carpet."

They all clinked their glasses and then sipped from them.

"Passion, you're heading to the top, so get ready." Shayla was pleasant, pumping up her client's ego so she wouldn't get sidetracked. "You have a level head, and don't let anyone dumb you down."

"That's what I tell her about the men in her life. Stay focused and don't be blinded by the users and wannabes," Chad added.

Passion looked at Chad. "I need to speak with you, please." She stood up and walked comfortably down a long hall to a room for privacy. She wasn't considered a guest at Isabella's.

"Sure." Chad arose. "Excuse us." He followed Passion toward the rear.

Shayla and Amber continued to familiarize themselves with Isabella. They were enamored with the eccentric woman and her fabulous home. She shared her interesting tales of behind-the-scenes Hollywood drama and that she'd once worked as a gossip columnist for a Tinseltown paper. She'd hobnobbed with the elite and later met her deceased husband, who was a well-known director of B movies. Their original home was lost in one of Malibu's well-known mudslides and she'd lost irreplaceable belongings.

Shayla became curious why Chad and Passion were harbored for the length of time. She was so enthralled with Isabella's lifetime that she initially hadn't noticed that a half-hour had passed. Not that she was keeping track. It was Amber's last night in town and they'd planned to wrap up her stay with a bang. She looked at her watch.

Amber caught her drift. "Isabella, may I use your restroom?"

"Sure. Let me show you where to go." She started to stand up.

"Oh, no, I'll find it. Please, stay and relax." She smiled. Amber had noticed that Isabella had become slightly tipsy.

"Well, you have a choice. Go to the left or the right." She reached out for Princess and propped her on her lap. The dog had been lying beside her owner's favorite chair, her usual hangout. She stroked the dog gently.

Amber stood up and left Shayla and Isabella to continue their conversation, although Shayla was ready to cut it. She'd come to Malibu to spend time with her client, but now Chad had her holed up someplace. Her patience was waning and she was prepared to interrupt once Amber returned.

Amber was curious about Isabella's home and was eager to see more of the property while she headed to the bathroom. She decided to head to the left and walked down a hall. She stopped in her tracks to hear a strained conversation between Chad and Passion. She could recognize tension in their voices and crept closer toward a room with a door slightly ajar.

"I'm so tired of you trying to rule me. I'll be twenty-one this year and you still giving me orders. And it's embarrassing in front of Mrs. Benson, your *wife*, and Amber. She keeps telling you to let her handle my act. That's why I hired her. Help build up her portfolio, as you called it. So I don't need you telling me how to dress or what kinda men to hook up with."

"Look, Passion, I love you…"

Amber, who had wandered as close as possible without being noticed, cringed. A chill resonated throughout her body as she froze. *Love?*

"Dad, yeah, you love me, but you gotta understand. I've got to become my own woman. You're off-the-chart overprotective and every move I make, you constantly on me like a hawk. No disrespect, Dad, but it's gotta stop…"

Amber's heart dropped to her feet. *Dad? Daddd? Whoa!!…Shayla can't possibly know. Maybe she's calling him that 'cause he's like a father.* She attempted to rationalize that perhaps it wasn't what it appeared, but her gut told her that the tone when Passion spoke "Dad" was real. *Shayla wants to have a child with Chad and always says they truly want to experience parenthood. He's already a parent…with an adult child.*

She quickly backed up gingerly and entered the bathroom, closing the door softly. Later, she exited and sauntered to the room where Isabella and Shayla awaited.

"We were hoping you found it okay," Isabella commented as Amber sat. Her face looked like she'd seen a vampire and Shayla noticed her change in disposition.

"You ladies want something else? I wonder what's keeping Chad and Passion. Looks like their chat turned into a conference." *But that's rather rude seeing that these ladies came a long way.*

"No, thank you. You've been a gracious hostess." Shayla sighed. "I presume Chad and Passion—"

"Sorry, ladies." Chad suddenly appeared in the room. Passion followed and stood beside him. "We ended up into a deep discussion and apologize. No intention to be rude."

Passion remained silent.

"Well," Shayla looked at her watch, "I'd love to stay longer and enjoy this view, but we'd better go. Amber's flying out tomorrow and we need to have our girls' night." She smiled.

"I remember those days. I used to frequent all the popular spots to find juicy topics for my column, you know." Isabella giggled. "In fact, it was always best to follow the females because they had a lot of fellas on their trails. And of course, women love to gossip."

"We plan to hang out." She looked at Chad. "Thanks to a wonderful hubby who understands I treasure my 'me' time."

"I have studio time this evening, so I need to head out," Passion exclaimed. "I 'preciate the hookup."

"Likewise and we will be in touch about the marketing plan," Shayla noted.

On the drive back to the hotel, the mood was uneasy and silence was golden. Shayla was curious about the lengthy period Chad was with Passion and why it was necessary for her to request they step aside. The word "Dad" kept ringing in Amber's head. And Chad seemed disturbed about what may have transpired. It was obviously a turnaround in atmosphere during their return trip from Malibu.

After valet parking, the trio entered the hotel and took the elevator to their rooms. Amber and Shayla decided to allow three hours before they'd hit the nightlife scene.

The uptempo music streaming throughout Escapade in Santa Monica gave an adrenaline rush. The chocolate martinis were tantalizing. Amber and Shayla were constantly on the dance floor, their wedding rings sparkling in the low-light lounge. The party atmosphere was at its peak as the deejay played constant old school and new school hits.

When they finally gave their heels a break, appetizers were ordered. Their plan was to hit one or two more recommended venues. As the martinis took effect and their stomachs became overly stuffed, they doubted their mission would become reality. The fun-filled night was a reprieve from how their afternoon had ended with tension.

Amber sipped the last drop of her drink. Her brain was dizzying about the father-daughter revelation. Whenever they'd settled at their table in between dance time, she was tempted to bring up the 4-1-1 with Shayla. Every time, her heart suggested she talk about the matter, her mind told her to reject the idea. Then she'd hear Trevor's advice in her head to stay out of others' business. But this was her girl, and she was compelled. Trevor, being in the limelight, was shrewd about not spreading gossip or personal news. He'd cautioned her not to get caught up in drama. Their reputation was always at stake and their life was seen through a magnifying glass. He had witnessed how a snippet of talk could evolve into a whirlwind of misinformation.

"You okay? How about another martini?" Shayla inquired.

"Oh, I'm fine." Amber snapped out of her trancelike state.

"You were going zombie on me over there."

"I guess I was in deep thought."

"Aww, about…"

"Oh, nothing…," Amber lied. *It's something all right, but I can't bring myself to share with you—at this time.*

It was as if the deejay realized it was time to spin one of Shayla's favorite throwback songs, the SOS Band's "Take Your Time." She pulled Amber to follow her to the floor where they started dancing. Then two twenty-something men squeezed through the crowd and landed in place to party with them. The floor was packed again.

Amber felt she was saved from the possibility of spilling the news. The longer she sat with Shayla, who was picking up her strange vibe, the more likely she would open the floodgates about Passion.

Their dance partners kept them on their toes as they partied with the old school Kool & the Gang's "Hollywood Swinging." The title was in sync with the scene as the rhythm of the night blended with the celebrity set.

CHAPTER 40
Kyle

Walking along the pier at Solomons Island, Kyle reminisced about her early days with Bryce. Although they had been married less than two years, it seemed it was worlds ago when their lifestyle was simple and at peace. Now she was living in a rocky marriage, and her escape to the small island in Calvert County, Maryland was an opportunity to seek solitude.

She always found the water a peaceful coexistence. Whether it was a visit to Coney Island during childhood or a weekend journey to visit her college friend's summer house at Martha's Vineyard, Kyle sought serenity by the shore.

Shayla and Amber were surely enjoying California and it would have been ideal for their trio of friendship if she had joined them. She had found herself in a precarious position as a tinge of jealousy resonated throughout her household when she'd mentioned traveling for a ladies weekend. Bryce had acted as if the Poconos retreat was a privilege.

Bryce was busy acting out a role as king of the castle while she was the servant maid, she thought. Doubtful that she would see three years of marriage, Kyle searched for the truth and the solution for her mental anguish.

She reenacted in her mind the series of abusive scenes with Bryce. It was like she was on punishment and was forbidden to share the realities of her life. Edging closer to revealing her destruction, she pondered if she were comfortable enough to tell Shayla and Amber. They'd fight back and ensure that Bryce would have to suffer. When the next ladies day or night rolled around, she would expose everything that she had swept under the table. After all, they were her girls and if she couldn't be for real with them, with whom could she share her misery?

She found a bench and sat to watch passersby. The waves calmed her senses and all she needed was a glass of wine. Maybe she'd step into one of the restaurant bars on the island before heading home.

After an hour, the light breeze caught her off-guard and she batted her eyes, attempting to avoid dozing. Suddenly, her cell phone vibrated.

Kyle looked at the text. It was Erick: *Checking in to make sure u r ok.*

Arghh, she thought. *I can't believe he's still not getting the message. I've tried to be firm and be nicey-nicey me, but this man is turning into a stalker. I love little Merlan, but her dad is going insane.* She hesitated to respond. Believing that she was a mentor for Merlan, she thought it was appropriate to reply.

She texted, *I'm ok. Thanks for checking.* It was only politeness as she didn't give a damn what he thought.

Erick's intentions were actually faithful. Bryce's reputation was harsh and old friends like him were well aware of how he rolled: below the belt. He was an unlikable bastard who was a female's nightmare. Since high school, Bryce had been viewed as the one who constantly changed girlfriends like his razor blades. Now that he'd used Erick as a decoy and Kyle had fallen directly into his trap, Bryce was like a madman on a battery pack. He could switch the script dangerously.

Erick was concerned about Kyle's safety and despite her dissing him on the regular, he felt obliged to reach out to her. She was constantly in his thoughts and Merlan adored her. He was aware of Bryce's past and how he'd abused the women in his life, relished seeing them fail and controlled their moves.

Although he'd agreed to be a pawn in Bryce's game, he had started to develop feelings for Kyle. He was now on a guilt trip. It was all he could do to hold back telling her the truth about "Bryce," her husband, the ultimate fake master. The man with the phony name was not the Howard University graduate he purported to be to those unfamiliar with him. His alleged business forte was an illegal racket fronted by his repair shop venture. He was a popular dude from around the way who'd won millions in the lottery and struck it rich—not the prosperous businessman. After the winning ticket, Bryce had one mission: clinching a trophy wife.

And in Erick's eyes, Kyle was all of that. And yes, he was falling in love with his friend's wife.

Kyle arose from the bench and decided to head home. Her idea to stop off for a glass of wine was shattered when the text from Erick had thrown her off course. He simply didn't get her drift. *A lovely daughter and a loony dad*, she thought. It was later than planned, so she figured it was best to head home. She didn't know which side of Bryce would be showing up tonight.

CHAPTER 41
Amber

Family was a priority, but Amber couldn't wait to meet up with Desiree, her BFF from Stanford. Sometimes she regretted that she hadn't followed the same path by pursuing an advanced degree and advising others about their lives.

Her parents had rolled out the bells and whistles for her arrival. Despite her being married to a baller, they still would go on spoiled overload when their oldest daughter visited. Amber's privileged roots signaled the need to keep up with her current lifestyle. Having their own share of wealth, they had their private cook to prepare Amber's favorite meal of oven fried chicken, stir-fry zucchini, mango rice and apple raisin Caesar salad along with homemade wheat rolls.

No matter how determined she was to focus on family at the dinner table, her mind kept reverting back to overhearing the conversation between Passion and Chad.

"Amber, I can see you're doing well. Trevor's keeping you looking good," Duncan Reid remarked. Her father was proud that his oldest had married into wealth. She could continue the family tradition, although he couldn't compete with her husband's millions. He dreamed that his youngest daughter, Autumn, would also find a partner to cater to her exquisite taste. He was growing weary of dishing out change for her top-model looks.

Yes, he does enable me to shop and shop more, even though it's off the

Richter Scale at this point. "Thanks, Dad." Amber recognized that her contributions to Gucci and Chanel and Versace were enormous.

"And your foundation, we are sooo proud of what you and Trevor are doing to help our youth. That's what it's all about. Helping others less fortunate and in your case, introducing them to a positive experience." Her mother, Juanita, sipped from her wineglass and smiled. "I agree with Duncan that you look like the epitome of success." She looked at Autumn. "Both of you do," she complimented, urged to recognize her other daughter.

"Well, I had great role models," Amber complimented.

Duncan and Juanita Reid were patrons of the arts in the Oakland community and had trained their daughters to be self-less by donating their time and fortune to others in need.

"Someday you'll be a role model with your *own* children, in addition to the foundation kids."

"Mom, please don't go there right now. Trevor and I will start a family when we feel it's the right time," Amber responded.

Autumn cleared her throat. Her parents were awesome, but sometimes they brought up subjects at an awkward moment. They were beginning to pressure her into marriage and finding the ideal mate. It all translated into them being eager to have grandchildren.

They seldom united as a family since they were on opposite coasts, but if Trevor was playing the Oakland A's, Amber made a point to be at her hometown stadium.

Amber walked up to the suite of Desiree Winston in the plush office building in downtown San Francisco. She grinned when she saw the placard outside of the door. Proudly, she entered and approached the front desk assistant. She placed her finger to her lips to announce it was to be a surprise. Desiree was aware that Amber was in town, but she had no idea which day she would stop by her office.

"Hi, I'm Amber, Dr. Winston's best friend from college."

The assistant nodded and smiled. She looked at the calendar.

"I don't have an appointment as I wanted to surprise her."

The assistant motioned for Amber to walk toward Desiree's office. Amber continued toward the door and knocked.

"Come in," Desiree announced.

Amber pushed the door open slowly. "Hello, *Doctor* Winston."

Desiree jumped up from her desk when she saw Amber and rushed toward her, closing the door. They hugged excitedly, then pushed back.

"Hey, girl!" Desiree shrieked and then caught her breath. "You trying to give me a heart attack. Why didn't you tell me when you were stopping by?"

"Hey, you know me with the surprises." She looked around the office. "You on the up and up," she complimented. "Look at this place. I'm scared of you," she added, flattering her friend from college.

The posh suite featured textured wallpaper, mustard and chocolate leather chairs, and floor-to-ceiling art. A loveseat and chaise lounge situated in a corner beckoned.

"Your office is gorgeous and this is exciting to see how you're living. You deserve every bit of it."

Amber recollected how Desiree was raised in poverty and had worked several jobs to supplement her college scholarship. She was praised for being the first in her family to attend college. In contrast, Amber was from a privileged household and from a family with generations of the college-educated. Ecstatic her friend had accomplished success, she walked toward the picture window.

The Golden Gate Bridge and the city skyline created a post-card image. Amber smiled as she recalled sharing with Shayla and Kyle her rendezvous along the rocks below the bridge.

"I thought we were going to hook up at Jaleo's," Desiree remarked. "You were going to give me a heads-up when you got in town. I was going to make special plans."

Amber turned around. "It's all good. Girl, whenever, wherever I see you, it's fine with me. Look, I need to speak with you on business terms first. *Personal* business. Then we can go for our alcohol session," Amber teased, then walked to the desk chair across from Desiree. She sat on the comfy chair. "How much are you charging me?"

"Amber, what are you talking about?" Desiree queried. "You should know better. The answer is zero, zip dollars." She rested her hands on her desk and intertwined her fingers. "Spill the beans.

"I don't want to drill you or question you like a patient," Desiree advised.

"But I want you to. You don't understand, girl, I'm come to my senses that I need some help." Amber sighed.

Desiree sat back at her desk and changed her demeanor. "Okay, Amber, this sounds serious…but I can't imagine. You're not around here to hear how people talk about how lucky you are to snag a pro baseball player," she stated, referring to Bay Area residents and former classmates.

"I'm sure some of them are haters."

"Of course, they're always haters on the planet."

"I don't give them any play either. They can hate forever for all I care."

"You're looking well."

"My dad said the same. Then they ended up jumping on that baby thing. I'll have a child when I'm ready…although that little clock is tick-tocking."

"You and me both. But I'm still in no rush until I find the right connection."

"Desiree, if you never get married, I'll understand. It's not for everyone. *Puh-leese.*"

"Amber, what's on your mind? For you to stop at the office and not ask me to meet you at Jaleo's, there's something going on." Desiree attempted to read her mind through eye contact. "I always have your back, so please, I'm listening."

Amber looked down and twiddled her fingers, then looked up. "Desiree, I've concluded that I'm over the top."

"Over the top? As in…?"

"I can't get enough of the stores. Or online. I always have to be buying. I don't care if it's a YSL dress or Prada sandals or a Tory Burch bag or a Tracy Reese shower curtain, you name it.

"When it comes to buying for me, I'm ashamed to say, Desiree, I have *no* guilt." She added, "When buying for others, I think I can cool down. Not that I'm selfish, but I'm not as enthusiastic."

"You need self-control, Amber. You always were a clothes buff, and I see later, *shoes*—"

"Don't say the word. *Shoes?* Huh, I'm swimming in shoes." Amber leaned in on the cherrywood desk. "I have a closet for shoes. It's actually a *room*." She shook her head. "But shoes are not the worst. It's okay for a woman to have a lot of shoes."

"I agree, Amber, if they take over your life, it can lead to other issues."

"I'm obsessed, possessed, whatever you want to call it."

"Amber, when did you recognize that you have a challenge?"

"Well, one day I was with Zodi for my usual shopping spree. I went to buy some clothes I didn't need, got to the register and my account was short. My shopping had been so intense that I didn't realize I'd drained the account. So it was a wakeup call."

"What does Trevor think of your shopping mentality?"

"Desiree, he doesn't have a clue how much I truly own. He sees what I bring into our home, but he has no idea I stash a bunch of stuff at my neighbor Jaslyn's house."

She became quiet. "You hide some of your purchases?"

"Do I? I'm not kidding. I have to keep it on the down low or Trevor would go off." Amber sighed. "He doesn't mind spending money—he's providing it for me—but he would die if he found out I bought so much. So I take a limited amount of my purchases home. And then sometimes I even hide them around the house.

"I was never more embarrassed when my card was declined, girl. That was the turning point. I've never surpassed my limit."

"You must learn self-control and I can work with you on that." Desiree smiled. "I'm pleased that you were able to come in and share your life with me."

She was certain her best college friend would have outpoured with a drink in her hand, but it was something uplifting about Amber confiding to her in her office, a professional atmosphere. They could always hang out at the bars. She was pleased that her graduate degrees were more than paper. Even with close friends or colleagues, sitting behind her desk in her private office dishing out advice provided a rush.

"I appreciate your ear. Desiree, this particular account is the one Trevor sets up for me to shop. Once it was depleted, it was so bad that I contemplated going in my foundation account and taking some of those funds to feed my habit."

"No, Amber, don't go there, friend. You want to destroy your wonderful marriage? Then that would be cinch the deal. Trevor wouldn't have any of that. You tamper with what he's passionate about? You need to show restraint.

"I'm proud that the two of you are helping young men. Don't yield to the temptation. Keep those funds isolated and designated to the cause.

"And what can you possibly do with all of the material goods?" Desiree continued. "I love them, too, don't get me wrong, but enough is enough. And when you start thinking about going out of your comfort zone and delving into other sources for money, that's a problem."

Amber had an epiphany. "Now that I'm describing everything, I feel like I sound greedy, and I act like I have a bottomless bank account. That's why I wanted to see you face-to-face. We go way back, and you wouldn't give me any BS advice."

"Right, I need to save you and your marriage, so pump your brakes. When you get back to D.C., analyze what you need to hold on to and donate the rest."

"You're so right, Desiree. I appreciate your advice." She sighed. "My friends Shayla and Kyle don't have an idea how bad my shopping addiction is…I never shared the truth."

"There's nothing wrong with sharing, especially if it helps you to grab the issue."

"I'm tired of holding back."

"I recommend you opening up. You're always telling me how close you are to them."

"You're right. I'm going to confide in them when I get home," she promised.

"Great. Now, you ready to hit Jaleo's for some cosmos?"

"Definitely. I need a drink, and I hope my favorite bartender is around." Amber smiled. "And during this short minute, you've convinced me to go back to school. I'd like to be like you when I grow up."

"Girl…now I'm off my official session I can talk the way I want." She laughed. "I've been telling you to return, and nowadays, you don't have to sit in the classroom. Take the classes online.

"I'm telling you, Amber, you were always cut out to be a therapist. And hey, get this, you could even incorporate it with your foundation. They're a lot of young men out there who need guidance."

"You're right. I see it all the time when we have the boys, or rather young men, at our events and on field trips. Some of them need direction." Amber started feeling more and more guilt about her overspending. Some of it could be channeled to help others. Sure, she was investing in the future of youth with non-tangible benefits. On the flip side, she could provide material goods to those less fortunate.

"Okay, *Doctor* Trent. Let's get out of here so we can toast to your future as a therapist."

Amber arose, amazed it had taken only an hour to change her life around. A simple visit to a longtime friend had opened her eyes and her mind.

CHAPTER 42
Terra

Soaking in the tub, Terra relaxed and then fretted that she'd better not frizz up her hair, although she had it wrapped sufficiently not to sweat.

Grandmother Elaine was like a recording when she'd stepped into the house after leaving Cutz. She had continuously complimented her new hairdo.

After taking two hours to immerse herself in a makeover frenzy, Terra finally was satisfied with her first-date presentation. She had to bring on her A-game. Tonight was her first and possibly only chance to snag her a trophy man, she thought. She'd obviously impressed Lamont on the blind date; now she needed to step it up a notch.

A little black, spaghetti-strapped dress with an open back enhanced her sculpted figure. A dainty gold necklace and small cubic zirconia studs complemented her simple look. She desired to play down her usual flashy style so not to turn off Lamont. She'd figured he was all about the low-key and moderate type.

She opened her bedroom door and crept into the hallway. She could hear her thirteen-year-old brother, Torian, upstairs playing video games. She peeked around the doorway to the living room to check on Elaine. She had drifted to sleep in her worn-out but comfy La-Z-Boy chair while *Jeopardy* was watching her from the floor-model TV. Terra looked at her watch. Her friend, Donnie, would be picking her up shortly to drop her off at the restaurant for her date. Lamont had offered to drive her, but she felt it would interfere with her plan. She had described being from an advantageous background and had grown up in the upscale neighborhoods where he sold real estate. If he picked her up from home, he'd likely come inside and then Gram's storytelling would reveal her lies. She didn't want to take any chances, so she'd asked her childhood buddy to drive her. Donnie was a cool platonic friend who was willing to assist her in any way.

She hadn't told her grandmother about Lamont as she would surely pry and offer her unwanted advice. Every relationship was always viewed under a microscope with Gram offering life lessons about men.

Terra clutched her petite bag and gazed at her stilettos. If she tipped lightly, perhaps she wouldn't awake Gram. She definitely wasn't leaving out the back door and dashing through the back alley.

She started across the hardwood floor lightly and headed toward the front door.

"Gurl, I thought you were still gettin' ready."

Terra cringed and stopped in her tracks. She turned around. "Gram, I thought you were sleep, and I was tryin' not to wake ya."

Elaine grabbed the remote and turned down the TV. She adjusted her chair to allow her feet to reach the floor. "Humph, I see why. Where you goin' in that sheet ya got on? I know you ain't callin' that a dress. What I tell ya 'bout showin' all your goodies?"

"Gram, I'm twenty-five and I wish you'd stop tellin' me how to dress."

"Okay, okay, I'm not tryin' to hear about ya on the news. You be careful out there."

Terra turned to peep out of the window through the sheer curtains. She spotted Donnie's car in front of the house. She turned around to Elaine. "Well, I've got to go—"

"You must have a date tonight wearin' that thing—" She scooted to the end of the chair. "Maybe I'd better check out who you hangin' out wit'—"

"Gram, I'm fine." She sighed. "He's here now," she lied, "and I'd rather you not. Please."

"Okay, as long as he's picking you up. You know what I tell you 'bout those men when they can't be comin' to your house. That's the gentleman thing to do." She pushed back in her chair and turned the TV volume up. "Well, have a good time and be safe."

"Thanks, Gram. See ya in the mornin'." She opened the door and walked to the car as she envisioned her life was about to change forever.

Lamont was dressed in one of the finest suits in his wardrobe. The taupe jacket and slacks were complemented by a light turquoise tie. His tie-up shoes were highly glossed and his fresh haircut completed his smooth appearance. He admired his vision in the mirror.

It had been a while since he'd felt this way from a first meeting. The blind date was titillating and he was eager to see Terra again. Always one to impress and clean up nice, he was aware that women often regarded a fashion statement as high as good looks. He never desired to appear vain, so he intended to dumb down his ego. Terra seemed sincere and interested in him as a person, not only his bank deposits. He couldn't pinpoint what it was about her, but he adored her from top to bottom. He sensed that she could be a little rough around the edges, but that was all good as he liked a challenge. He didn't desire a mirror of himself.

Lamont was teased in high school for his nerdy image and then laughed all the way to the bank when he reached the top rung of the ladder. As with Chad, real estate had opened doors to a comfortable lifestyle.

Reluctantly, he had agreed to allow Terra to meet him at Lolita. He'd offered to pick her up but she appeared elusive each time he inquired about her residence. Surely, Chad never would introduce him to anyone married, so what was there to hide? He had put it all on the back burner and would broach the subject later. Perhaps next time Terra wouldn't hesitate to accept his offer of a ride. After all, he enjoyed driving with beauty in the passenger seat.

He pulled up to valet parking in front of Lolita, handed the attendant his keys and then walked inside the plush restaurant.

Wise choice, he thought. *I'm trying to impress Miss Terra.*

He had arrived prior to their scheduled time and had made reservations. The waiter escorted him to a table in a corner with low lighting and privacy.

When Terra entered promptly, she captured his attention. "Hello."

"Well, hello. You look stunning." He stood and kissed her lightly on the cheek before pulling out her chair. Normally, the chivalrous move would die after he became acquainted. For now, it was crucial to be a gentleman…unless it was between the sheets.

"I hope you like this place. It's received rave reviews and I thought I'd try it." He walked around and sat on his chair.

After eating and sharing a bottle of wine, Lamont invited Terra to sit beside him on the leather booth. She obliged, cozying up to him now that she was relaxed.

"Let's check out the dessert menu." He picked up the card the waiter had left for them to view. "Hmm…what about sharing the chocolate bundt cake with vanilla ice cream?"

"Sounds great. I'm game."

Suddenly, Lamont shed his gentlemanly persona. He reached over and touched the top of her dress and fondled her in the vagina area. Her spot became soggy as she excitedly tingled. He teasingly continued as she giggled despite the waiter delivering their cake with two spoons.

"I can see you are a lot of fun."

"Yep, you haven't seen a thing yet." He smiled.

Terra and Lamont bustled through the door of his fifteenth-floor condo overlooking the Potomac. She barely had a chance to comment on his posh décor as they immediately started stripping off each other's clothes. Lamont put aside thoughts that his best suit was at risk for damage. His hunger sex pangs overpowered caring about the clothes. Terra helped him pulled her dress over her head to reveal lacy thongs and a strapless push-up bra.

She gaped as she saw he was strapped and rock-hard. Pulling out a condom quickly from her dainty purse, she helped him put on the sleeve. After wrestling their way into the bedroom, they climbed atop and devoured each other fast and hard. The passionless session left them both breathless.

I get tired of Gram's advice, but she's right about one thing: make sure you pussy-whip them the first time around. And I think I just did. She looked over and Lamont was in another place.

CHAPTER 43
Shayla

Reclined in her window seat, Shayla looked over at Chad next to the aisle. A weird feeling overtook her. The cross-country flight was a breeze for Chad who was accustomed to the journey on the red eye. She wondered why he had insisted on meeting with Passion earlier in the day. She was uninvited and didn't query as she'd seen her twice during her visit. Their relationship was to maintain strictly business, however, she sensed that Chad's connection had developed to another level.

He appeared overly concerned about Passion's every move, her attire, her attitude, her associates. She'd ruled out that they were intimately involved. Her keen affair radar hadn't detected any activity. Despite feeling slight jealousy, she didn't reveal her curiosity. There would be a proper time to inquire and it wasn't on the long flight ahead.

She pulled her iPod from her purse and plugged in the headphones. She closed her eyes and envisioned Blaze's buff body. She would check Chad's schedule and manage to sneak away for her usual sexual tryst. She planned to show off her latest addition from Victoria's Secret. Chad barely noticed her lingerie and at least the younger man would comment on her new wares.

Blaze decided to change up their meeting place and this time, he'd selected an outdoor venue, as he had described it. Shayla was slightly disappointed since her little lingerie show would be in the dark. She'd conjured up a lie and told Chad that she was hooking up with Kyle to check on her status. She truly needed to scope out her activities as Kyle was down that she and Amber had left her to hold down the D.C. front alone. She hadn't seemed like herself in months.

In reality, she'd tend to that concern another day. Tonight was her chance to get away with Blaze and her pussy was on fire. It was overdue for a workout after being back in town for a few days.

Chad had an evening appointment, so she acted on the opportunity. She drove to a central meeting place at dusk and hopped in Blaze's car, leaving hers parked in an empty lot. She was pleasantly surprised to see his tight shirt and bulge in his pants. They kissed passionately before he drove off.

Blaze entered Rock Creek Parkway and drove a few miles before exiting into a lot. He jumped out and pulled a blanket from his trunk and a sheet.

Shayla opened her door and stepped out. She looked up at the full moon and smiled. *My young hero is sooo creative, although it's not exactly new. But I love him being spontaneous!* She followed him as he grabbed her hand while carrying the blanket and sheet in the other. They arrived at a picnic bench where he set up the top like a bed.

He's going to bang the shit out of me out here in these woods! I love it! She felt like a kid sneaking into the candy jar while her mom wasn't looking. She enjoyed the idea of sexing it up while drivers rode along the parkway a short distance away. She suddenly had a voyeuristic rush.

After she seductively undressed, he laid her gently across the thick blanket and climbed on top of her. He stroked her gently as she gripped his back, her juices flowing steady.

The Blackbyrds' "Rock Creek Park" rang in her head: *Doing it in the park, doing it after the dark, oh, yeah, Rock Creek Park...* She doubted Blaze was familiar with the 1975 anthem about the outdoor D.C. institution. *He's all about music, so he likely knows the song. If not, let him consider this park idea is his original.* She smiled as all gushed out and she was satisfied under the moon.

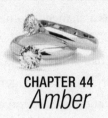

CHAPTER 44
Amber

Oakland had been an eye-opening experience during Amber's visit. She had arrived back home and Trevor had planned a whirlwind pamper weekend.

The day centered on the conveniences of home. He ensured full relaxation where she could bathe and enjoy the luxury without leaving outside of their door. It started with a personal massage followed by a mani and pedi and ended with an exquisite meal by their chef, Sonya. After their late-night lovefest, the following morning included brunch at a waterside restaurant and then a private yacht outing on the Chesapeake Bay with two other couples.

Amber opened the door to her shoe room she called "Heel Heaven." She gawked at all the rows from floor to ceiling. She held three boxes to be added to her collection, all designer brands that she'd purchased in the Bay area. She laid them on a table to place on the shelves at a later time. She sat on her black leather chair and felt the sunlight stream through her window. It was like paradise.

She reminisced about the revelation with Desiree. Her best college friend had triggered a fresh attitude about her shopping addiction. It was no longer viewed as frivolous and fun; it was a harmful habit. She would come clean with Trevor, and the girls, and inform them she was a changed woman—the only part she'd refuse to let go would be shoes. She smiled at the thought.

And then there was Chad and Passion, another revelation that had evolved during her West Coast getaway. The father and daughter appeared to be at odds. She stored the family connection in the back of her mind. Someday if it never came to fruition, she might give Shayla the scoop. Trevor would reprimand her for sharing personal news with her friend. He would think it was Chad's place, not hers, to confess that he was a parent. Her loyalty was with Shayla, but at the same time, she didn't want to crush her feelings. For now, she'd put it aside until she figured out how to handle it. She also valued their friendship and didn't want to rattle the status.

CHAPTER 45
Kyle

Loneliness had become a tradition at the Andrews household. Kyle and Bryce were growing further and further apart. The verbal abuse combined with the physical was a constant strain on Kyle. She had reached the peak of withstanding the abuse.

Charmed by Erick, she realized that despite her resistance, she actually was enamored by him. She avoided him as she didn't want to succumb to temptation and have an affair. Her body craved some attention and if it didn't receive any soon, she would think about Erick's constant flattery. Each time she considered hooking up with him, she'd shudder at the thought of Bryce finding out. She could take the risk, but she was petrified. It would be best to end the marriage rather than cheat, she'd concluded.

It was after midnight and as usual, when Bryce arrived, he'd be bitter. The scenario played in her head as it was the same.

The classic black-and-white movies were her bedmates. She lay peacefully watching *The Postman Always Rings Twice* and eventually fell asleep.

After about an hour, the room lit up. "Wake the fuck up, bitch!" Bryce yelled angrily.

Groggily, Kyle awoke, rubbed her eyes and sat up against her pillow.

"Who do you think you are?"

"What's up with you? I'm lying here sleep and you come in here acting crazy."

"Get up," he ordered, standing over her.

Eerily, she zoned in on his eyes, which usually told the story. She could see he had been drinking and surmised that he'd hung out with some of the shop buddies.

When he was drunk, his violent behavior was more intense.

"You're a big-ass liar," he charged.

"What—"

Bam. Bryce slapped her on the face near her lips.

She gripped it in shock. He slapped again and this time striking her hand.

"Owww…" She pulled her hand away and cringed. The pain from her cheek, lip and hand resonated throughout her body.

"You've been in touch with Erick."

"Erick? How do you know Erick? He's one of my students' dads." She placed her other hand toward her cheek and noticed blood. Her lip was cut and bleeding. *I can't believe this crazy bastard. Erick?*

"Erick is one of my boys from waaaayyy back in the day."

Kyle gasped.

"Yeah, right, and you been fuckin' with him."

"I have not—"

"The hell you ain't. I know all about it." He looked at her with rage in his eyes. He'd held back from confronting her with his knowledge. "You were about to give him some ass until he stopped you. He wasn't planning on going all the way."

"Wait a minute."

"You can't lie. I set it all up," he said proudly about his scheme using Erick as a decoy. "He's my boy and I told him to see how far you would go. Humph, and he said you were all about it. I was tryin' to find out how so-called faithful you are as a wifey. I found out you ain't shit."

Kyle was in awe. *He set me up and I fell right in his trap. And here I thought Erick was cool and was interested in me simply because…not that Bryce was behind the ploy to reel me in.*

"Why you goin' silent on me? Nothin' to say, right? I'm not as dumb as you think I am." He grunted. "When I found out from Erick that Merlan was one of your students, I figured he was the ideal candidate. And you fell for him. How many other dads been hittin' on you? Maybe some of them been all the way, gettin' it in while I'm at the shop."

He reached down and grabbed Kyle on the neck with both hands. "How many dads? Answer me. How many dads you been fuckin' with?"

His grip became tighter and she could hardly breathe. She kicked her feet under the covers, struggling to get away. Her light complexion started turning pink and Bryce let go of his grip, realizing he could have choked her to death. Disgusted, he walked away and left the bedroom. He headed downstairs to the kitchen for a cold glass of water.

Kyle held her neck and collapsed backward on her pillow. Tears streamed down her face as she was in extreme disbelief. *I've got to leave this bastard. And I've got to tell my girls the real deal.* She looked at the clock and it was 2:17 a.m. She was terrified to fall asleep. Even though Amber and Shayla were likely asleep, she was compelled to text them.

She listened for any sign of Bryce's presence. She'd heard his steps descending the stairs but hadn't heard him return upstairs. She picked up her cell phone from the end table.

She did a group text: *If anything happens to me, look no further than my roommate.* She deleted the message from her history. Sighing, she placed the phone back on the table. She arose and walked into the bathroom and looked in the mirror.

A bruise and bloody lip screamed back. Along with the red eyes, it was a portrait of an abused woman. She rubbed her temple, experiencing a physical and mental meltdown. Praying silently for strength, she closed her eyes. She turned on the cold water and reached into the cabinet for some cotton balls and hydrogen peroxide. She cleaned up her face and then washed it before turning back to bed with a cotton square held to her lip.

Bryce was still downstairs and she figured he'd sleep either on the sofa or in one of the guest bedrooms. He wouldn't dare lay his body down next to hers after the beatdown. Then again, he had a lot of nerve. She placed her head on the pillow and planned to stay awake. She zoomed in on the TV. The original *Psycho* with Tony Perkins was now playing. How ironic, she thought. *Psycho.*

CHAPTER 46
Terra

S tanding over the kitchen sink, Terra washed chicken breasts and placed them in a colander. She'd already cut up raw veggies and placed them in a glass dish. It was the first time she was preparing a meal for Lamont, and here she was at his condo, attempting to show off her non-cooking skills.

Grandma Elaine also had schooled her with the old adage that the way to win a man's heart was through the kitchen. She already had Lamont on lock in the sex department, as Gram also had advised, and had fulfilled his fantasies. He was adventurous and when he shed his professional exterior, he was explosive. Terra didn't want to kid herself; he was as much in lust with her as she was with him.

It was a month in to their relationship, and she was on track to put her plan in action. Determined to rock an engagement ring within a specific time frame, she steadily schemed toward that goal.

She laughed to herself about how she'd memorized the recipe for the chicken casserole. The idea was to pretend this was her specialty dish that Gram had shared and that she'd created it on numerous occasions, including all the holidays. She was tickled that she was an accomplished pathological liar.

Lamont was bright and book smart; however, she deemed him slow when it came to street smart. He could easily be fooled and she was pleased with how the game was playing out. She had observed that he was gullible and easily manipulated. She planned to sucker him right to the courthouse to repeat wedding vows.

She continued to prepare the casserole, then popped it in the oven. It would be ready in an hour. A bottle of wine was chilling and she'd set up his glass table for their cozy meal in his combined living room-dining room.

Lamont reclined and watched the evening national news. He made a point to be aware of the happenings in the world. He especially focused on the real estate market, mortgage trends and finance. He anticipated a scrumptious dinner and was anxious to witness Terra's kitchen skills. They'd gone out on numerous dinner dates and he'd simply waited to see when she would finally suggest she cook them a meal. She'd bragged about the casserole and he couldn't wait to sample it.

Terra entered the living room and climbed alongside him, squeezing into the chaise lounge.

"Won't be much longer, babe. I put my foot it in and I'm sure you'll enjoy." She kissed him on the lips lightly. "I only make this dish for special people in my life," she lied.

"I thought you made it on holidays—"

"Yes, and those people are special," she responded, defending her statement and hoping he would drop the cooking conversation. She stroked his chest. "But, not as special as you."

"This is delicious. So, *mami*, you got it going on in the kitchen, too." He placed a chunk of the chicken dish in his mouth, savoring every chew. He picked up his wineglass and sipped. "I'm truly a blessed man."

"Thank you, Lamont. And I'm a blessed woman." She smiled, pleased that the casserole had turned out well on her first try.

"And I must thank Gram for teaching you." He paused. "Say, when am I going to meet Gram? She has such a lovely granddaughter and surely, she's a charmer as well." Lamont had continued to make attempts to visit their home, but Terra always denied access and discouraged him.

"Gram really doesn't like strangers at our house. She's paranoid. Always watching soaps, game shows and the news. Even with the alarm, she's got us bolted in like a fort." Terra was proud that she appeared convincing despite her habitual lies. Elaine had actually invited Lamont to the home, and Terra was elusive, stating that he had such a busy schedule. Yet Gram realized he wasn't too busy to fit Terra on his weekly calendar.

"Okay, got it. I certainly don't want to make her feel uncomfortable. I guess when the time is right, I'll meet her."

Not if I can help it. "True," she stated uneasily. The way Gram chatted, Lamont would discover all the fakeness in an hour flat. Sometimes Gram never knew when to stop.

Terra already had created a persona of growing up in an affluent neighborhood in Northwest. After her parents' untimely deaths, she'd moved in with Gram. She'd fabricated that she'd planned to attend American University and major in art. She'd stated that she had plans to travel abroad to continue her studies, but once she landed a job working with the curator at a local art gallery, she remained in town. She had enjoyed adding more and more to her Pinocchio web of lies.

Terra glided seductively out of the bathroom. Clad in skimpy lingerie, she pranced across the room where Lamont lay waiting in his boxers. Strutting in her stilettos, she went to the dresser, pulled out her iPod from her purse, then placed it on the docking station. She had it already set to queue up the specific song. She turned it on to the sensual vocals of Sade's "Love is Stronger Than Pride" to perform her best stripper routine. Unsnapping the bra and facing him, she jiggled her breasts, grabbing each one underneath and moving them up and down teasingly. Lamont could see the rear view reflected in his dresser mirror that faced his bed. Then she turned toward the mirror and revealed her curvy hips and removed her thong, giving him a wide-angle view of one of her best assets. She did a booty shake and puckered her lips at him through the mirror's reflection.

Lamont enjoyed his private showing and was thrilled with Terra's teasing. His rock was simply waiting for her to join him in bed. She continued her gyrating and kicked her legs in the air to show dynamic balance in her heels. Stroking her arms and legs, she appeared as if she were auditioning as a prime dancer for an erotic video.

He relished how the evening was about to end and couldn't wait to devour her following her tantalizing act. After the song ended, she headed toward the bed to continue pussy whipping. Of course, Babyface's "Whip Appeal" would play next.

CHAPTER 47
Passion

"It's Real" had hit no. 1 on *Billboard*'s hip-hop chart, and Passion was reeling with excitement. Seated on a barstool in the Green Room, she was surrounded by stylists who were prepping her hair and makeup. She had arrived in D.C. on the previous night for her first-ever press conference.

Having taken Shayla's advice that she appear in D.C. with a wealth of political and celebrity figures, Passion anticipated a major positive response. She adored her L.A. hometown but was compelled to kick off in the capital city. However, she would plan her tour with a West Coast start.

"You look fantastic," commented Alexa, Passion's thirty-year-old assistant, who helped during her travels. She looked at her watch and clutched her cell. "Okay, ladies, we need to wrap it up. It's almost show time."

Passion stood, dressed in a low-cut, long-sleeved shirt tied at the waist. Her low-rise jeans accentuated her abs. Her large gold hoop earrings accented her face and her new Mohawk haircut framed it.

"You all set?" Alexa asked.

"As much as I plan to be." Passion smirked. "It's weird, but I'm a little nervous."

"Oh, don't be. You've got it goin' on, so you'll be fine," Alexa suggested. "You may as well get used to it. Once you reach that top spot, it's all over, gurl. You need to put your face out there so folks will know it to go along with the name."

"Right, I've heard it over and over from Shayla."

"She is out there in the front row, grinning it up for the cameras. She's already done some mugging and I'm sure the paparazzi will want to take photos of the two of you."

Passion left the room followed by an entourage headed by Alexa. She walked to the reserved room at the Hamilton Crowne Plaza and adjusted the mike at the podium. "Good evening, everyone. I'm ecstatic to be in D.C., giving a shout-out to President Obama, Howard U., the college crew. 'It's Real' has brought me here. As you're aware, it hit number one last week."

The crowd cheered and applauded as flashes bounced off Passion. She looked down and observed Shayla and Chad on the first row and smiled.

"When I was little, I always liked performing. In fact, I hear I would dance around the house and sing in the tub. It continued and then when it came time for high school, I went to a school for the arts. When I decided to pursue the talent I was told I had, I decided it was best to stay in my hometown of L.A. I was winning talent shows in the city and then the county.

"I want to give props to Ed Salmon for the lyrics and Jazzy Guru for creating the beats for my top seller. I want to thank my label, Redstone, for signing me, for seeing my vision. Thank you to my publicist, Shayla Benson of New Visions. Many props for your direction." She nodded to Shayla and smiled. "And another shout-out to my other publicist, Darla, at Redstone." She nodded at her on the first row of the audience. "Both of you keep me focused. And of course my assistant, Alexa, who keeps me on my toes." She turned toward Alexa, who gave her a thumbs-up.

"I'm excited about my debut CD and my upcoming tour. I

promise I will sell out the venues. Thank you, everyone, for show-ing your support.

"But there is one person in particular whom I need to thank. This person has been by my side and supportive from day one. This person has offered encouragement and pushed me to be-lieve in myself and my talent. This person has remained in the dark by choice, but I'm over eighteen now, an adult, and I feel I need to recognize him. All these years I've had to hold back, keep hush, be on the down low, whatever you may call it.

"I'd like to thank my number one supporter, my dad, my father… Chad Benson." She looked down at Chad and opened her hand toward him.

The audience applauded.

Chad's mouth popped open and he melted with embarrassment. He was in shock.

Shayla's eyes bugged out and she looked over at Chad in dismay. She was speechless.

Chad bent his head down and whispered out of the corner of his mouth, "I can explain."

"You'd better," she whispered angrily. Then she smiled to cover up her resentful expression. As a publicity guru, she was well aware of the face being the gateway to the truth.

They both looked up at Passion as she continued. "You see, I only have my dad to thank. I'm told I lost my mom during her childbirth. I unfortunately never had the opportunity to see her or get to know her.

"But I understand she was a star, an actress who was famous. When I got old enough, my grandmother, Isabella…"

Shayla turned to Chad and pouted. *Isabella, her grandmother? I thought she was one of your clients and she bought her mansion from you? You're a big liar.*

"Oops, I've been forbidden to call her 'grandmother,' but was instructed to call her '*godmother*,'" Passion continued. "Now that I'm an adult and it's been revealed to me about why I couldn't call her Grandma, I plan to start calling her that.

"It's been so tough not being able to recognize my dad or my grandma all these years. Pretending they were either strangers or folks with no relation to me.

"As for Mom...no disrespect to her, either, may she rest in peace. But word is she was married to a man who wasn't my dad. So, it was all a cover-up. And 'cause she was in the limelight, it was pushed under the rug. They couldn't let Hollywood know that she was expecting a baby outside her marriage. It would've ruined her career.

"But I'm here to tell you, I love my mom, and I love you, *Grandma* Isabella, if you're watching this on TV. Thank you, but I couldn't keep this in the dark any longer." She looked at Chad. "And I love you, Dad."

Passion released her pent-up emotions. She felt a ton of weight instantly lift. After years of pretense, she was relieved to finally share the truth. She turned her eyes toward her father and now recognized stepmother, Shayla. She could see bitterness in her eyes. As a female, Passion was aware that a revelation such as this would be shocking to another woman. Dad had begged her not to come out with their relationship. She was prepared to tell Shayla the day she and Amber had visited with them at Isabella's. She and Chad had left the room to discuss the situation in private. Chad won the debate, but she'd decided privately after the visit that she would come forward in the future.

When the press conference was created, she figured it was the moment to speak out and the whole world would find out at the same time. Despite opening up, she still would not reveal her mother's identity. Isabella was not her grandmother's real name and using Passion as a stage name was ideal to keep her identity on the down low.

Passion realized that Shayla would be devastated once she discovered. Passion had grown to adore Shayla as her publicist. She wanted her to be aware that their bond was more than on a business level. There was a deeper connection. She was her stepmother.

Chad sat and twiddled his thumbs. He couldn't look Shayla in the eyes at this point. He'd lived with the lie that he wanted them to experience first-time parenthood—together.

Passion strutted off the stage after glancing at Chad and Shayla. She'd have to deal with them later at her CD release party.

Shayla was torn about attending the party, but she pulled the professional move and not the personal one. Since she'd had a major role in planning the event, she felt obligated to show her face. It was be the ultimate test in publicity where she had to mask her true feelings and show a fake image. Her mind drifted to Kyle and Amber. They surely were in awe as they had planned to watch the live press conference on TV.

The press was unaware when Passion announced her father to the world that Shayla was unaware she had a stepdaughter. Shayla was a master actress and she appeared that she wasn't surprised. After a festive night of dancing and drinking, Chad and Shayla headed out. Chad had avoided Passion except for photo ops. He was scheduled to do the toast and did so gracefully. He'd kept his distance as he had to simmer down his anger. Passion realized that her decision might backfire and cause a strain in their marriage. She loved them both, but she felt justified to open up after a lifetime of silence.

Chad and Shayla drove their separate cars to Gavin's and pulled up for valet parking. She was proud of the release party's success and the favorable response from listeners and industry execs. Her grins were planted on her face for snap after snap from cameras. Now she would face the hard cold truth.

On the ride over, Chad had received a text from Pierce. His doctor friend had seen the press conference. *I see the ish hit the fan. Hang in there.* He needed some man talk, but for now, he'd need to break it all down for Shayla. He'd never intended for his fatherhood to come to light in this fashion. Actually, he didn't know if he ever planned to share with Shayla. He'd continue to be the behind-the-scenes dad. Passion had pulled a fast one on him—for the world to see—and he was pissed. *I'm glad she didn't identify her mom.*

"What can I get you to drink?" a waitress asked.

"Drink, I need a bottle. No, I'll take a Ciroc and Coke." Shayla felt like a zombie.

"And I'll take a scotch straight up, please." He looked Shayla in the eyes.

"You've got a lot of fuckin' explaining to do." Resentment filled her face.

"Well, first, I owe you an apology." He reached across the table to hold her hands, and she pulled them away, placing them on her lap. "Okaaay, I understand you are crushed. I'm sorry that you had to find out this way." He shook his head. "I didn't mean to hurt you, Shayla. I love you and always will. I try to show you in every way. But this time, I failed…I made a huge mistake."

"And here I am representing your *daughter.* Publicist, humph. No wonder she so easily hired me—"

"Look, don't dumb yourself down. She would've hired you either way."

"Yeah, right, and for the record, I'm never dumbing down. I'm aware of my skills, but I surely didn't need you to find me clients—especially your daughter."

The waitress returned with their drinks. "Are you ready to order?"

"Only drinks. Thanks." Shayla was visually bitter.

The waitress politely picked up their menus. "Thanks." She walked away, recognizing the negativity.

"All this time you were frontin' going back and forth to L.A. for real estate investments."

"That's true. I have a number of them there as you are aware."

"But that wasn't the only reason you were out there so much."

"I'll admit that Passion was an influence. I had to keep check on her, and she was my responsibility until she turned eighteen. I couldn't leave her hanging and once she got into the music biz, she needed my guidance. I suggested she hire you for professional help. And in a way, I may have been overprotective."

Shayla recalled how Chad was always concerned about Passion's lifestyle, from her outfits to her associates. It was all making sense why he smothered her. After her L.A. visit, she almost wondered if they were having an affair, he seemed so enamored with her.

"So, I'm waiting to hear about this mystery mom of hers. You haven't mentioned her name—"

"And I won't. I promised her—even from the hospital as I was there during the birth—that I'd never divulge that information. Neither will Passion, and it wasn't me who told her. It was her grandmother, Isabella."

"Hmmm, this is all so screwed up. So, this woman you were having an affair with, whatever happened to her husband?"

"He actually disappeared off the planet after she passed. Before going into labor, she confided that he wasn't the father. He freaked out and was never heard from again. Dunno where he is decades later. And frankly, I don't give a damn." He sighed. "I was young and immature. I'd gone to California with some classmates from undergrad. We had a wild night where we hung out in Hollywood bars. I ended up hooking up with her for a one-night stand. I had no idea she was a star...in fact, I wouldn't have thought she'd have been hanging out in that spot. And she wasn't wearing her ring."

"And you couldn't tell me this, especially before we got married? Plenty of men have children, but let their fiancées know about it. All you had to do was tell me about Passion.

"You could've shared that with me. Even told me the whole story that you needed to keep it on the low because of the mother's identity, the affair, everything. Instead, you've been stringing me along acting like when and if we have a child, it would be your first. Now this doesn't make a damn bit of sense."

"Well, again, my apologies. I never thought it would come out and especially in this way." He sipped his drink. "I'm presuming that all the secretive pressure sent Passion off the edge. In fact, remember when we were holed up at Isabella's? Sorry that we were missing so long. She was trying to convince me to tell you at that moment. I finally got her to agree to keep our secret forever. She's young, so she was on a different page.

"Shayla, I can truly say that she adores you and I believe she was also motivated because she likes you as a mother figure, not only as a publicist."

With that, Shayla started visualizing the situation in a new light. She desired to have a child; she was actually a stepmom. She thought the world of Passion, having worked with her for a while on her career, but she also liked her as a person, a young woman. Perhaps she needed to take the mature outlook and plan to grow an even greater bond. Passion had grown up without a mother and was forced to hide her identity. That was a lot to handle.

On the drive home, Chad was relieved and felt like he was floating on air. He was free now that all had come to light. He followed behind Shayla to ensure her drive home was safe. Before leaving the restaurant, they had embraced. He loved her and felt blessed to have a wife who was understanding of his skeletons.

His cell phone vibrated. He looked at the caller ID. It was Isabella calling from Malibu.

He picked up. "Hello."

"Hi, dear, I saw all the floodgates open at the conference. I hope you are still in one piece. I encouraged you many times to reveal the truth to your wife—even if it was only to her. Now the world knows," Isabella stated in motherly fashion.

"Isabella, I'm hanging in there. It was a shocker for sure. I've accepted that my dishonesty backfired and I'm not bitter at Passion anymore. She was carrying a heavy load." He sighed. "And thank you for your support. Of course, still no one is aware of Passion's mom. And as I promised Gen—ah, her, at her bedside, I would never reveal that she was the mother."

"Well, mum's the word, dear. So, how did Shayla take the news?

She seemed so fond of Passion when she was here. She also had discussed having a child someday. She and her little friend, what's her name?"

"Amber."

"Yes, Amber, she's adorable. Very fashionable and perky." She cleared her throat. "The two both mentioned their desire to be mothers."

"That's just it. I believe I read Shayla correctly. She appeared to have accepted the whole stepmother thing, despite my dishonesty, the bitterness, embarrassment, you name it."

"I'll pray for you both, dear."

Chad noticed an incoming call. It was Pierce.

"Isabella, I need to take this call. Thanks for checking on me. I'll be in touch."

He clicked over. "Hello."

"Hey, man, I was spellbound."

"You? It was real, but hey, I'm dealing with it, Pierce."

"I was watching her, excited about her top single and new CD, and then bang, she spilled all of that information."

"It was a shocker and there I was sitting next to Shayla," he stressed.

"I feel for you. How is that going?"

"Well, Shayla and I just left Gavin's. We went there for drinks after the release party. That went well, by the way. In fact, I'm trailing her home now. Making sure she gets there okay."

"After all these years of hiding the facts, how did she react?"

"At first, she was a mix between going off on me and being extremely angry and silent. Then after we relaxed with our drinks, she mellowed and appeared to have accepted it.

"Nothing will change as far as me being her father. It is what it is.

I'm sorry, though, that it turned out this way. Shayla was devastated."

"Well, buddy, I wish you the best. Let me know if there is *anything* I can do on this end. I have your back. And, I'm looking forward to that game of golf you promised me on your next visit."

"You got it. Bye." Chad hung up the phone. Now in future visits to the coast, he wouldn't have to hide his visits were two-fold: networking with business investments and checking on his daughter.

He was proud of her musical accomplishments and what she'd achieved since observing her talents during childhood.

The following afternoon, Amber decided to reach out to Shayla. She and Kyle were stunned about the news of Passion. She didn't want to call in the morning, figuring she needed a breather. She'd called Kyle and dialed Shayla to make a three-way call.

Shayla noticed the caller ID and started not to answer Amber's call. It was now or never because her friends would blow up her phone until they got a response.

"Hi, girl," she answered.

"Hi, it's two of us on the line. Kyle's here."

"Hi, Kyle."

"Hello. We realized you must have had a rough night."

"That press conference was truly eye-opening," Amber expressed. "We're checking up on you, lady."

"I appreciate it. You both always have my back. Yes, it was a struggle, but I survived."

"All this time you've been planning a child with Chad and he was already a parent," Amber stated.

"I had no clue. We went out for drinks and he explained everything." She placed her hand over the receiver and listened to hear if Chad were around. "Think the coast is clear, but I'll have to share with you later," she said in a lower tone.

"We understand, and we have nothing but time," Kyle interjected.

"We won't keep you on the phone," Amber stated. "I'm sure you need to relax and rest your mind. We're sorry that you had to find out about Passion this way. And to think, you've been representing her all this time."

"At least you always said you liked working with her," Kyle added.

"Yes. I've enjoyed it," Shayla agreed.

"Well, we'll talk later and let us know when you have some time. We can hook up for our girls' night…or day. Bye, ladies."

"Bye, Amber." Shayla sighed and clicked the phone off. She'd need a whole day to share the experience.

"Bye and take care." Kyle hung up.

Amber looked at the cell before placing it on the table. Her thoughts drifted to the visit at Isabella's and overhearing Passion call Chad "Dad." She was extremely tempted to tell Shayla, but was pleased she didn't, listening to Trevor's request not to become involved in personal business of others. A tinge of guilt appeared, but she rubbed it off, thinking that it was best Shayla had found out from Passion. She figured Chad may never have told her the truth.

CHAPTER 48
Terra

"You back so soon?" Dillard inquired as he shampooed and then rinsed Terra's hair. "It took you a whole year, now you back in a month."

"Yeah, I got to keep it on the regular nowadays."

"Oh, that date musta gotten you hooked."

"I got *him* hooked." Terra laughed while rearing her head back into the bowl.

"All right now." Dillard squeezed conditioner on her hair, placed a dry towel around her neck, and then gently pulled her up forward. He placed a plastic cap on her head and motioned for her to walk toward the hooded dryer. He zoomed in on her figure. "I can see you holdin' it down. Looks like you might be spendin' time in the gym."

Terra smiled mischievously as she sat in the chair and pulled the dryer over her head. "Humph, been working out in the *bed*." She smiled.

Dillard responded playfully, "I bet you have, honey." He walked to the dryer and turned it on, then returned to his chair and flipped through a magazine.

While under the dryer, Terra thought about how Dillard loved to dish. She had her own gossip to share today. Surely, he'd seen Passion's press conference. He was the king of radar and it was rare for any celebrity news, or neighborhood news, to get past his ears or eyes. She decided she would be mum. As soon as he discovered Shayla was her mentor and one of her new associates, he'd drill her. Then again, it was her husband who had introduced her to Lamont. *No way*, she thought, *I ain't goin' there*.

The dryer stopped, Terra pushed the hood up and walked back to the chair.

Dillard stood, motioning for her to return to the shampoo bowl. "Well, you bein' mighty private, hon. Tell me 'bout this new man in ya life." He pried as he rinsed out the conditioner, then started combing her hair.

"What can I say? He's everything and got it goin' on. In fact, he's the one who gave me the duckets for my hair. Likes me to look good *all* the time."

"Ain't nothin' wrong with that." Dillard cleared his throat. "Dearie, I got some mo' news for ya about that—I hate to say his name…"

"Jarrett…you said he's goin' by the name Bryce nowadays. The bastard. What's he done now? Don't tell me he's won the lottery again."

"Oh, no, nothin' like that. But I hear he's spinnin' that cash and makin' some dough."

She moved back to the stylist chair. He turned on the blow-dryer and quickly dried her short hairstyle.

"I can't stand his ass, so I don't wanna hear how he's doin' good."

Dillard leaned in. "But, honey, you may want to listen up. I can see by your body language that you got a vengeance. He's not doin' good; he's up to no good."

"Like what?"

"Word is—and my sources are quite reliable—that he's in the car business and I don't mean selling cars or repairing them. He's got a car theft ring goin' on and selling illegal parts." He raised his hand. "And believe me, that's all I know. I'm not privy to any mo' info other than he's frontin' a legitimate biz, but got dirty-after-dark stuff goin' on."

"Humph. Well, thanks for the tip. I can get my boys to check it out." She observed her fresh hairstyle in the mirror admiringly. "Dillard, you put your foot in it again."

"Why thank you, lovely. Anytime. And good luck with gettin' deep down to the nitty-gritty," he teased dramatically while bobbing his head. "Take care, sweetie."

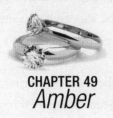

CHAPTER 49
Amber

"Good afternoon, Jaslyn. And how are you doing on this beautiful day?" Amber inquired as she gazed out of her sunroom window.

"Hi, Amber. I'm well and getting ready to go for a quick walk. Want to join me?" Jaslyn paced back and forth. She was dressed in an oversized T-shirt, leggings and tennis shoes. Her iPod headphones swung around her neck. "Sometimes the home gym isn't enough and you need fresh air."

"True and today is gorgeous," she agreed. "I wanted to alert you that I'm expecting—"

"A package, right?"

"Not this time. Actually, it's an envelope coming through the mail."

"Oh, okaaayyy. I'm so used to the delivery trucks and all your goodies."

"Girl, I appreciate it and I promise I will get by there soon to empty your house."

"Listen, Zodi and I keep hearing you say that," she teased. "We've given up on you." She laughed. "And don't get me wrong, she's not disrespecting you. She's a gem."

"Yes, she is, and I don't know what I'd do without her." Amber sipped her wineglass. She paused. "I'm expecting it to arrive by today. Call me when the mail's delivered and I'll stop by. Trevor has an away game. Maybe we can have dinner—at your place."

"Look at you, inviting yourself. I don't plan to cook a thing today."

"Well, we can go out then. I'll be waiting on your call and enjoy your walk. My lazy ass needs to be with you."

"Thanks. We'll talk soon." Jaslyn hung up. *An envelope? Hmm, that's odd. I wonder why she simply didn't have it sent to her own house. I'm used to the packages and understand that deal. But I do think she needs to come clean with Trevor about her shopaholic ways.*

After her walk, Jaslyn checked her mailbox. She flipped through the envelopes and found one addressed to Amber's attention. *Hmm, this must be it.* The envelope had a California postmark and she figured it was likely from one of Amber's relatives. She opened the door, entered and placed the stack of mail on her kitchen table. She grabbed a bottle of water from the refrigerator and gulped. She pulled out her cell phone from her sweats pocket and called Amber.

"Hello."

"Hi, your mail arrived."

"Great. I'll be right over." Amber made a quick dash to Jaslyn's and walked past a few houses, getting in her exercise. The sprawling estates were five acres apart. When she arrived, she was in such a rush that she didn't enter. Jaslyn handed her the envelope at the door.

"Thank you." She turned away and headed back to her home.

She sat on a barstool where a bottle of wine was chilled in a bucket and poured another glass. The sounds of Jill Scott filtered through the speakers. Hopefully, her mood would be uplifted once she opened the mail. She sipped her glass and then tore the envelope. She closed her eyes and smiled, thanking her prayers were answered. She pulled out a cashier's check for $50,000. She sighed and promised herself that she would never cross the line again.

Her greediness and shopping addiction had caused her to dabble in her foundation's account. That was strictly a no-no. She was petrified that Trevor would discover the missing funds. He trusted her to oversee the account and she had betrayed him.

Although she'd visited Desiree and confided about her spending habits, including an idea to use her foundation's funds for personal shopping, she didn't share the awful truth. She actually had stolen from her own foundation account for youth to satisfy her own overindulgence. Sadly, it was a reality check that it had come to this.

After speaking with Desiree, the wakeup call made her determined to change her habit and confess to Trevor—but not before she could replace the funds. Desiree had strongly advised her not to be tempted to borrow from the foundation. But it was too late. It was already bad enough that she couldn't control her personal banking account. It had hit rock bottom again and that's when she'd decided to sneak the funds from the foundation.

Whew, she thought. *Now I can replace the money without anyone being aware I had "borrowed" the money. And what do I have to show for it? Simply material things that I don't need.*

Although she and her sister, Autumn, were not close, the visit was one time she'd decided to confide in her. Autumn had told her many times about her friend Venice who was a professional gambler. She was a Vegas native who had grown up in a family of gamblers and once she was legally able to step inside casinos, she excelled on the slots and gaming tables. She later spent her time between the Bay Area casinos, where Autumn met her, and Vegas.

Amber had convinced Autumn to inquire with Venice about gambling on her behalf. She'd taken a chunk of the funds to purchase personal goods. She would provide $25,000 to invest in gambling in hopes that Venice could double it. Then she could replace the $50,000 she'd borrowed from the foundation. Venice figured Amber was married to a pro baller and if anything fell through, he would be of financial assistance. Venice had great respect for Autumn and had Googled Trevor's net worth. She'd figured why not take a gamble and help out her best friend's sister?

Amber's head dizzied as she thought about the harsh reality of her problem. She would work with Zodi to plan on purging out her closets as well as her hideaways, particularly at Jaslyn's. The effects of the wine increased the intensity of her realization.

She picked up her cell and texted Autumn: *Thanks, sis. I owe you a big one. Please tell Venice she's awesome and she's got skills.*

You're welcome, Autumn texted. *Next time you can sell all your stuff.*

You are so right. I could simply sell my belongings…except my shoes. LOL

Hmmm….

Please tell Venice I can't thank her enough. See ya.

Amber arose and walked the stairs to her shoe room. She had a special hiding place where she kept important documents. She slid the check inside a box and covered it with other boxes inside the closet. *Autumn gave me a great idea. I could sell half of my wardrobe if I ever get in a jam again.*

Amber kept her word and invited Jaslyn and Zodi for dinner that evening at Georgia Brown's downtown. It was her treat. She appreciated how they both had helped with covering up the extremeness of her addiction. She was certain they'd be elated for her new self-control. She'd ask them to help once she had a plan of action to purge.

CHAPTER 50
Shayla

C had and Shayla had several lovemaking sessions following the revelation about Passion. Shayla failed to be satisfied. Part of it was her mind was still focused on the false pretenses. She was unable to fully let go during their passionate encounters. Her nymph sense had kicked in and she craved one of her boy toys.

It was Wilson during the morning, Damien during the day or Blaze at night. Since it was afternoon hours, she picked up her cell phone and dialed Damien, who was listed as Diane in her contacts.

"Hey, what's on your agenda today? Longggg time, no see you." She smiled seductively as if he could see her through the phone.

"Well, you have a permanent spot on my calendar whenever we both are free. I don't have any photo shoots today."

Shayla glanced at the clock in her bedroom. It was a lazy morning but she was prepped to tussle with the handsome Damien. "See you in two hours."

"Whew, it's hot out there today. Think you could throw something to grill on the sidewalk," she said about the ninety-degree heat.

"I'll fix a good one to cool you down." Damien went to the kitchen to prepare his usual specialty cocktails.

Shayla relaxed and sunk into the living room sofa. Admiring his décor and noticing he had made some recent changes, her eyes zoomed to a portrait of a man. The framed photo sat prominently on a corner table. *He's good-looking. Hmm, must be a model, too.* It hit her suddenly as she recognized the man in the photo. *Wait, that's the same picture I saw in the bathroom that day, when I looked in the counter under the sink. It was turned over and I wondered why it was there, apparently stashed away, hidden perhaps.*

Damien returned with the drinks, strawberry mojitos. He set the glasses on the coffee table and sat beside her.

Shayla picked up her drink and tasted it. "Hmmm, this is delicious."

"Thank you." He noticed she suddenly seemed uncomfortable and not her usual seductive self. "Is everything okay?"

"No, it's not okay." She set her drink on the table. "Who is the guy in that photo over there?" She nodded toward the framed picture.

Damien tried to brush off the sudden shock he felt inside. "Oh, that's one of my model friends," he lied.

"No way. I don't believe you," she snapped. "I saw that picture in your bathroom cabinet the time you left me and I was looking for pain medicine. The frame was flipped over. I didn't think much of it at the time. Who knows why folks stash pictures?"

"Look, you don't have to believe me, but he is a model friend. We often have shoots together." *Well, he is a model and a friend, so I'm not lying about that. I enjoy getting it in with him as much as I do you.*

"My mind tells me that's not the truth. You haven't been straight up with me," she charged. "If you were a down-low brother, all you had to do was tell me." She arose. "I don't have to deal with this. I apologize if I'm wrong, but my intuition is usually on point." She picked up her drink and pretended to take a sip, then she tossed it on him. "You, bastard, who the hell do you think you are?"

He arose, wiping the liquid from his shirt, and followed her to the door.

She turned toward him, noting that his tan shirt was now a pinkish red. "Lose my number." She opened the door, walked out and slammed it behind her.

During the drive home, Shayla was hysterical. Her world seemed to be crumbling. First, it was Passion and now Damien. All the drama and craziness. *Guess that's what I deserve. Can't keep my panties on. Even though I can't seem to get enough, I have a good man at home. And Damien, it looks like I've been in the dark once again. These men need to be straight up and let me decide if I can handle what they're hiding.*

CHAPTER 51
Terra

"Well, Donnie, I got him hooked," Terra announced proudly as she strutted throughout the living room of her buddy's apartment. Donnie was her "go-to" man, her ace boon coon, her adviser. Blaze played a similar role, but his status was more of a big brother to Terra. And for Shayla and her crew, he was her fake birth brother.

Since Blaze's career had taken off, Terra had found him to be increasingly aloof. He hadn't checked in with her in a while. If he was acting brand-new on her, she would reciprocate and not give him any attention. If it wasn't for him, she would've never met Shayla, and without that introduction, she would've never been so blessed to hook up with her trophy man, Lamont.

"Hooked, huh? I see you beamin'. You lookin' good, girl, slimmin' down I might add. Guess he's keepin' you happy. Look at ya, drippin' in diamonds and shit." Donnie observed her blinging jewelry and designer wear from his sofa view.

"Yeah, babe, he gives me whatever I want. Although I ain't tryin' to come up greedy 'cause he'd recognize where I was comin' from. He's smart, ya know. And he's a hell of a realtor. Look, I can't keep up with him. Always on the move. But that's all good. As long as he's taking care of *moi*, I'm fine."

"And you are that, *phine*," he complimented, leaning further in the sofa to check her out. *I wouldn't mind gettin' some of that myself. But naw, baby girl is strictly platonic. Friends for life.*

Donnie had a harem of women and surrounded himself with beauty. He disregarded his fleeting thought.

Terra had worked and arrived home to change her clothes. She'd made a habit of calling in sick since she'd started hanging with the crew, including Lamont. Her retail job had always been a blessing and she was able to supplement the household income with Gram's fixed monthly check. She wasn't planning on giving it up yet. Anything could happen between her and Lamont.

Terra stopped walking back and forth and sat in a chair across from him. She crossed her legs and smirked. "All is going smoothly. Now, I need to put my plan into action." She settled in the chair. "It's been about a few months and I told myself to give it half a year, then go for it."

"What you mean, Terra?"

"Time to put some bling on it, baby," she said, proudly holding up her ring finger. "I've been totally in to Mr. Lamont." She smiled. "And he's been totally in to me," she bragged.

"Hol' up, you don't know that for sho."

"Oh, I'm sure," she said confidently, batting her eyes teasingly.

"Hey, I can believe that. You on top of things."

"Here's the deal. I realize I owe you the world, babe, for all you've done for me. Good lookin' out, gave me money on the side when times were hard, helped Gram when she needed it. You've been my rock." She paused. "I always said if I *ever* came into some cash flow that I'd hook you up."

"I gotcha." Donnie nodded, his eyes bulging with excitement. "I 'preciate it."

"No problem, Donnie. You've always been there for me, so vice versa, babe." She smiled. "Gram loves you, and she always asks about you. When you picked me up for that first real date with Lamont, she thought it was him. I had to tell her it was 'cause she always sayin' my date should be pickin' me up."

He laughed. "Oh, for real? That's cool, though. She thought I was him."

"I haven't introduced them yet. Gram will be so much up in my bizness. And if she finds out he's got some cash, she'll really be tellin' me what to do."

"I like Gram. She's always been cool and straight with me."

She uncrossed her legs and scooted toward him. "But hey, it won't be long before she sees me flossin' some cute clothes and wheelin' some luxe."

"Cool." Donnie's cell phone vibrated. He looked at it. "'Scuse me a sec." He arose and walked into the kitchen. "Yeah, man, what's up?"

"Hey, I think they startin' to zone in on us, man." It was Sam, the manager at Bryce's main repair shop.

"How so?"

"There was a suspicious-looking chick here this evening, and she made a comment about one of the cars. Said it looked familiar. Man, I stopped breathing."

"Man, you prolly paranoid. How could she even put two and two together? She wouldn't know what kinda operation was goin' down."

"Yeah, maybe I'm overreacting. You could be right." Sam sighed. "Anyway, you still on for tomorrow? You think you and your boys can handle the job?"

"Hey, we always at the gate, ready to go."

"Cool. Check you then." Donnie hung up the phone and walked back into the living room, then eased into the sofa.

"Everythin' okay?" Terra asked, sensing something was amidst.

"Yep, all is good."

Terra twisted her face and looked at Donnie suspiciously. She questioned the caller he'd spoken with in private. The two were so tight she thought it was odd that he'd walked out of the room.

"What's the deal? You psychic or sumthin'? I didn't want to get into this. You hate to hear his name, but Jarrett's got a racket goin' down. Ya heard? That call was pertainin' to his bizness."

"Funny you said that 'cause one of my sources told me he was frontin'…and successfully, I might add."

"Yeah, I realize he's not ya boy and there's no love."

"The son of a bitch made Toya take her life. Threatenin' her, dissin' her. It was some kinda brutal. I don't ev'r wanna see that bastard again…unless it's ta hurt his ass.

"He's got nerve perpetratin' a fraud, puttin' himself in the lime-light. Heard he's got some megabucks, too."

"Oh, he's got some all right. Mega mega. But, whoa, Terra, hol' up. He's keepin' some folks on the up and up wit' his new bizness." *Including me.* Donnie was aware of her hatred for Jarrett. He didn't want to divulge he was doing side work for his racket—not yet. His "repair shop" was keeping his pockets lined. She'd consider his connection with Jarrett as the ultimate betrayal.

"What goes up must come down." She sneered. "I hear he's taken it to another level. Got a fake-me-out business but then pretending he's someone else with his wifey."

"Yep, goes by the name Bryce and hear he lives in the 'burbs with his wife, someone like Kayle…no, Kyle. Yeah, that's her name, Kyle."

"Kyle?… Bryce?" She frowned. "That's the name of one of the sistahs I'm hanging out wit'…and she's called her hubby by the name Bryce. It's gotta be the same folks." She paused. "That's the same thing Dillard, my hairstylist, was tryin' to tell me. We didn't think there was any way it was the same person 'cause Jarrett wasn't the brightest bulb in the lamp."

"Hey, it doesn't take a smart one to win the lottery, either. It's all about luck."

"Yeah, Dillard told me that he hit it big and won millions."

"So, let me get this straight. You're sayin' you think you're hanging with his wife?"

"Apparently, she truly believes her Jarrett is *Bryce*." *Hey, but not for long, Kyle. I'm gonna give you the 4-1-1 on that no-good knuckle-head. First, I gotta find out more about his so-called bizness.* "So, what kind of bizness is this fool runnin'?"

"Well, uh, I ain't got a clue," he lied, then felt badly and cleaned it up. "Actually, I think it's somethin' to do with cars." Donnie frowned. "Look, how did we get on Jarrett anyway? He don't deserve the time of day, the way he treated ya sis."

"Got that right."

Moments ago, he was talking to Sam and making plans for his next assignment to steal luxury cars. He didn't brag on his car theft career and he'd rather have another means of income. For now, it simply paid the bills.

CHAPTER 52
The Wives

The colorful chaise lounges encircling the pool beckoned. Amber had invited the girls to her home for a party. She was already certain Shayla would be concerned about her hair and likely wouldn't allow a drop of water to touch her perm. Kyle likely would swim. Her natural waves wouldn't be affected. She was the athletic one in the bunch, although Shayla was the epitome of a grown-up cheerleader.

Sonya had decorated the patio with bright paper lanterns and the table with summer-themed glasses and plates. A palm plant served as a centerpiece.

Besides the usual fanfare and girl talk, this get-together would be eye-opening, Amber had decided.

After Kyle and Shayla arrived and were comfortable in their chairs, sipping on margaritas specially concocted by Sonya and tasting her homemade appetizers, Amber relaxed, surrounded by her East Coast friends. She missed Desiree and wished she could be in her presence.

"Ladies, we've been hooking up like this for a while and always have a blast."

They laughed, agreeing with Amber.

"This time it's a special occasion. I've been dealing with an issue for some time, and I decided to share something with you."

Kyle's eyes widened and Shayla stopped drinking and leaned in.

"I love clothes, shoes, jewelry, you name it, and I've been on a serious binge for years. You cannot imagine how bad of a habit I have with shopping."

"Girl, we are aware you are a shopaholic, or rather a shoeaholic." Shayla laughed.

"Seriously, it's truly an issue."

Kyle smiled. "Amber, I realized it was during your foundation launch event."

"How so?"

"When I went upstairs to get your brochures—your heels were killing you—I walked in the wrong direction. I discovered your shoe room—"

"You did? That's my palace," Amber said dreamily. "Girl, you played that off. You didn't mention you'd discovered my Heel Heaven. That's what I call it."

"No, why bother? That's your thing and not for me to intrude. It was by accident. I figured if you'd ever wanted Shayla or me to see it, you'd have shown it to us."

"It's not that. I kept it secret. Trevor teases me but otherwise, he thinks I'm obsessive." She sighed and sipped her drink. "Well, I am. So much so that I overbuy constantly. I have been getting Zodi to hide stuff for me, as well as Jaslyn. It's so bad that I have a major stash at Jaslyn's."

Shayla and Kyle looked at each other and then turned their attention back to Amber.

"Yes, it's been over the top. It was so bad that I thought about tampering with the foundation account," she shared, attempting to get their reaction.

"Oh, no, honey, don't go there," Shayla advised.

"Right, that would kill your marriage. That is Trevor's passion," Kyle added.

"Well, I thought about it," she lied, aware that she had borrowed from the account to suit her shopping frenzies. "But after going home and having a therapy session with Desiree at her office, it was on. I had a problem. It wasn't the cutesy shopping sprees anymore. I'm going to purge my closets—and Jaslyn's place—and donate a bunch of my stuff. It may be difficult to part with some of it, but it must be done."

"That's wonderful, Amber. I'm proud of you." Shayla smiled.

"Thanks."

"I'm sure it was a hard decision," Kyle stated.

"It was a wakeup call when I went to Cali. One thing, though; I'm not giving up my shoes." She shook her head. "I'll stop buying so many of them."

"Does Trevor know about your decision?"

"No, I plan to tell him but not everything. He'd think I was crazy if he knew I was hiding stuff at Jaslyn's and making Zodi my accomplice." She paused. "Also, after recognizing my addiction and seeing Desiree in action behind her desk, I've decided to pursue my master's and go further so I can start my own practice as a therapist."

"Cheers." Shayla held up her glass. "That's great."

"Yes, it's awesome," Kyle complimented.

"Thanks. It was karma and maybe the true reason I went to Cali."

"Trevor will be proud of you," Shayla suggested.

"I'm proud of me. Ladies, I never realized the addiction was that insane."

"No, 'insane' isn't the word. Let's say it was mind-blowing or over-the-top," Kyle offered.

Shayla sipped her margarita. "Well, now that we're having a confessions night…I have some zombies in my closet, too."

Kyle and Amber leaned in attentively.

"I've been having an affair," Shayla admitted.

"You don't say." Amber was stunned. "I've always admired you and Chad's relationship as it reminds me of ours. Both he and Trevor are frequently out of town."

Kyle remained quiet and thought about her near fling with Erick at the hotel. She was on the verge of an affair, or at least a one-night stand.

"It takes a strong woman, mind and body, to maintain when her husband is absent frequently," Amber said, relating to the experience.

"Amber, that sounds sweet the way you describe it. Actually, it's more of an addiction, as you stated about your clothes and shoes." She paused. "It gets worse. It's not an affair; it's *affairs*."

As if on cue, Sonya entered the patio with another pitcher with a mixture of freshly made strawberry daiquiri. She walked to refill each of their glasses with her new concoction and exited. Next she planned to serve mango mojitos.

Close call, Shayla thought as she picked up her refreshed glass and sipped. She didn't want to share her personal life with Sonya. "I repeat, *affairs*. I can't help it. I'm a self-confessed nympho. I never stopped to think about it this way, though. Now that I'm actually discussing it, I realize that's the deal.

"It's not that Chad can't hold it down in the bedroom. He's a skilled lover, and of course, I love him and we have an emotional connection." She sighed. "I can't seem to get enough…"

"So, who are these affairs?" Amber inquired.

"Honey, you may not be ready for this, but one is my client… Blaze, the hip-hop artist."

"Oh, he's a cutie. I'm not judging or encouraging. I'm just saying," Amber added.

"Humph, and believe me, he knows it. I don't do the client thing, but I haven't been able to resist him. I created a nickname for him—I have one for all of them—"

"*All?*" Amber inquired, but then toned down. "Well, you did say 'affairs' as in more than one." Amber's interest was piqued.

"Blaze's name is Raw."

"Oops, and I'm sure it's what it sounds like," Kyle stated.

"Yes," Shayla agreed. "He's got that bad-boy swag. That's what I like about him. He's younger and turns me inside out." Her body tingled from remembering her hotel trysts with the young star.

"Then there's Wilson. He's an older gentleman whom I call Mr. Class. He takes me to exotic locations and is a wine connoisseur. He's turned me on to some wonderful flavors."

Amber stared in disbelief. Shayla hadn't given any clues about her infidelity except during their visit to the Poconos. The dots were connecting now. She realized when Shayla had disappeared that night and returned later, she was likely with a man, perhaps the hunk she'd spotted in the lobby. She'd seen them eyeing each other earlier and heard when Shayla quietly reentered their villa during the wee hours. She figured then she hadn't been hanging out alone.

"Then there's Damien," Shayla continued. "He's the youngest, a print and runway model with interior design skills."

"Oh, he sounds interesting," Kyle interjected.

"Yes, he is, or rather *was*. He was a little boy toy for me." Shayla scowled. "I called him Smooth Jazz. He was suave like I nicknamed him. He was always moving around, never still when it came to his lifestyle. He's cool and laid-back." She paused, then said bitterly, "He truly was a smooth operator. I discovered the other week that he's riding both sides of the fence, or at least I believe so."

"For real?" Kyle inquired. "How'd you get to that conclusion?"

"Well, he's the only one where I went to his place. He has a condo in D.C. so I was all up in his environment. During one visit, I was in his bathroom cabinet looking for some pain medicine and noticed a framed portrait of a guy. It was placed face-down. I found it strange that a photo of a good-looking man was stashed under the cabinet, but I didn't think much of it.

"When I went back recently," she continued, "he'd gone into the kitchen to make us some drinks—oh, that's another skill, he's a mixologist—I was on the sofa and looked over and saw this same man in the picture frame. My antenna immediately went up so I inquired about him. He told me it was simply a model friend and I definitely didn't buy in to it. He did a hell of a job trying to convince me it wasn't someone whom he was involved with, but I didn't budge. I immediately got the vibe after seeing where the photo was placed prominently, in a corner and alone."

"How long did you go toe to toe with him?" Kyle inquired.

"It was quick. I got the hell up out of there. He was trying to persuade me to stay, but I wasn't having it. Whew!" Shayla shook her head.

"So are you still involved with the other two guys?" Amber asked.

"I still crave Wilson and Blaze; they're opposites. That's what makes them special to me. I'm experiencing both of their two worlds."

Kyle and Amber reclined and had listened intently as Shayla described her trio of men.

"Getting back to Damien, I don't get it. He could've told you he swings both sides," Kyle stated.

"Definitely, and let me decide if that mattered. And yes, I'm not even looking back on that one. He's out of my life."

"Well, girl, excuse me for asking, but you are ensuring they wear a sleeve, right?" Amber insisted.

"You bet your life on that one. No raw here. Keep them in my purse like my lip gloss."

"Now that you're opening up to us, what are you going to do? Continue the lifestyle and take the risk of Chad finding out? Have you considered the consequences?" Amber continued the round of questions, realizing she was gearing up to be a therapist. It was time to fulfill her dream.

"Honestly, Amber, I hadn't thought about any of that. I need to go home and let it all soak in and see what my next move should be. Until now, it truly never dawned on me that it was a psychological issue, and of course, sexual addiction."

"I'm not only saying this because of my psychology background, but you could use some therapy," Amber offered graciously. "Desiree told me she has a few patients via Skype. Maybe you could consider her. She's my girl and all, but she's more than a fee collector. She cares about her patients. You would feel comfortable with her. Of course there are many options out here locally if you prefer. But I would suggest you share with someone other than us."

"Amber, I'm going to take your advice, and thank you, sister."

"You're welcome, Shayla, and I wish you the best, girlfriend."

"Thanks." She reclined back in her chaise and sipped on her drink. "Confessions, confessions."

"Right, whoever thought it would turn into this type of ladies session?" Amber was feeding off the evening as if it were a support group.

Kyle looked down at her daiquiri she held in her hand and sipped. She looked up and eyed Shayla and Amber. "Well, I also have something to share, and this is really difficult for me." She set her glass on the side table. "I realized recently that I needed to tell you a side of my life that I've kept to myself."

Shayla and Amber listened in suspense and could determine by her tone it was critical.

"I've only been with Bryce a short time and at first, he was so kind and sweet and adorable. Then it got worse, especially after he opened his business. He's always gone and arriving home late at night. He's bitter all the time and aggressive. He blames it on the shops."

"Yes, it can be a challenge as an entrepreneur," Amber interjected.

"And then he seems so secretive, like he doesn't want me to stop by his shops. Amber, you remember you suggested Shayla and I go support our men by surprising them? Well, I did, and was he an asshole that night. He was outrageously angry about it, like I'd invaded his privacy or something."

"Wow." Amber was amazed.

"Let me get to the bottom line. I'm abused, ladies, physically *and* mentally. You never realize how horrible it is until you experience it."

Amber and Shayla were in awe and gasped.

Kyle pulled off her sarong as it was turning dusk. She revealed her latest bruise on her leg. "Notice how I keep my legs covered a lot lately? I'd love to wear more dresses and shorts."

"Aw, Kyle." Amber glanced over at her leg and could see the mark in contrast to her lighter skin. "That's terrible. I wish you had reached out to us."

Inspecting the bruise, Shayla's mind raced back to the pamper day Amber had planned with stylist Valencia. She'd noticed bruises on Kyle's thighs in the dressing room and had disregarded them. She never inquired and pretended she hadn't noticed. Now she felt badly.

"Both of you are like sisters to me. I hadn't told a soul, but I'm glad I feel comfortable enough to share. Actually, it's bad regardless of the nature, but this last time it was the worst. He came in late and slapped me so hard. That's why you didn't see or hear from me for a week.

"He was a madman so enraged. I realized then it was time to open up to you. I'm tired of being a little church mouse and taking his abuse."

"We're sorry that you held all this inside. You didn't have to deal with this alone." Shayla offered her empathy. "And from this point, you won't be struggling solo. We will help you get through this."

"I'm devastated. When you get married, you take those vows for life and hope that it's forever. I had a short dating period, but now I see I should've taken more time."

"And sometimes, it still doesn't show the other side of a person," Amber added. "Sometimes you may never learn the real deal."

"Here I thought I was going for the educated, sensitive, mature type. It was all a façade. I never imagined I'd be sitting here sharing a tale of abuse." Kyle started crying and picked up a napkin from the end table to wipe her tears. "I was extremely torn, but after speaking to you, I've made my decision. I've got to go. I don't deserve to be treated like dirt. It's broken down my self-esteem."

"Isn't that usually the objective?" Shayla suggested.

"Well, it worked. Kyle, the ballerina with grace, the jazz dancer with strength. He managed to break it all down. The abuse crushed my confidence," she said sadly.

"Yes, you must build it back up. You have pride. You're living your dream with the studio," Amber stated, delighted about her accomplishments. "Well, dear, please be safe. I can understand now why you sent the text alerting us if anything ever happened to you, to look no further than your 'roommate.' I didn't decode it correctly. We all have our spats and disagreements, but I never imagined you'd be in true danger with Bryce."

"There have been some scary moments. The only things that help to relax me are the old black-and-white movies. Usually, they're my best friends at night. I fall asleep with them."

"Sweetie, we feel badly about what you're going through. Please, call us anytime," Shayla offered.

"Thanks, it's such a relief that you are aware of what's going on in my life." Kyle paused. "Years ago, I read the article in *Essence*. I can relate to it now, but I found it unbelievable. It was about the domestic violence issue in Prince George's and how it was swept under the table," she shared. "Women living in luxury but bruised behind mansion doors. Truly sad and now I'm one of those victims."

Amber looked in her eyes. "Kyle, it's urgent you decide how to handle your situation. It's nothing to put on the back burner. It could keep brewing and stewing and then explode. After consulting an attorney and a therapist, it would be ideal to join a support group." She hoped that she hadn't bombarded her. "I didn't intend to throw all of this at you at one time. It's a serious issue."

"No, it's fine. I appreciate your and Shayla's advice and value your opinions." Kyle forced a slight smile. "This ladies evening has turned into true confessions and it's been extremely helpful. Thanks for listening." Her facial expression turned sour.

"I do have one more thing that I've kept inside. The miscarriage was so disappointing, I went to Tortola for a mental break." She looked down and then back up. "The truth is I did lose the baby to a miscarriage. But it wasn't natural. It was forced. Bryce knocked me down at the top of the staircase. I almost slipped down the stairs, but I caught my balance. Fortunately, I survived from major injuries, but sadly, not the baby."

"Aww." Amber gasped, then stood and walked toward Kyle, who arose. She reached out and hugged Kyle. "That's awful. Bryce is truly...a bastard."

Shayla arose and headed in their direction. She placed her arms around both of them for a group hug. "God don't like ugly. Bryce will reap what he sows," she stated, reaching back to childhood expressions from her Christian grandmother in New Orleans.

Sonya arrived with her finale and poured fresh glasses of her mango mojitos. She handed one to each of them.

"Thanks, we needed this," Amber stated. *Wow, it's been an eye-opening night.* "Cheers, ladies, to our new sisterhood."

They held up their glasses, toasted with clinking them and sampled the refreshing drinks.

Sonya walked away, sensing from their mood that her cocktails had offered comfort along with the conversation.

CHAPTER 53
Terra

S itting in the corner booth of the café, Terra looked at her watch and then toward the entrance. Surely, Roland would be in any moment. She sipped her tea while waiting.

Shortly, he walked through the door and scouted the room before noticing her location. He walked toward her table with a confident swag. After he approached, the five-five, dark-skinned twenty-two-year-old sat across from Terra.

"Hey, Roland, it's been a minute." Terra laughed. "You lookin' well, baby."

"Thank you, and likewise."

A waitress arrived. After perusing their menus, Terra ordered an omelette and wheat toast, while Roland requested a short stack of pancakes, turkey bacon and hash browns.

Roland was curious why his longtime friend from around the way had summoned him to the café. "Well, shoot, what's up?"

"You still doin' the detective thing, right?"

He laughed. "Detective, if you wanna call it that. But yes, you could call it investigatin'."

"I need a favor," Terra spoke seriously.

"You want me to find out sumthin' for ya?"

"Listen, Roland, I've found out someone from my past—and I hate this dude—has been rollin' big time. I need you to find him and see what he's up to. I stopped in to see Donnie—Donnie Paul—the other day and he wasn't giving up too much info. It was clear he knew the game Jarrett was runnin'."

"Jarrett? Jarrett, where do I know that name from?" He rolled his eyes in his head. "Oh, yeah, my boy. He's got it goin' on."

"So I hear, but I'm here to tell ya, I'll be shutting that show down." She paused. "Sounds like you know the real deal. Tell me."

Roland squinted his eyes. "Can I trust ya?"

"Of course," she lied.

"Jarrett, who sometimes uses Bryce now that he's perpetrating with new-timers, has a car operation, except it's not legal. He supervises a ring. They steal cars, strip them and sell their parts. Called a chop shop. That's how your boy is thrivin'."

The description was confirmed. It was the same scenario described by Donnie and Dillard. "Puhleeze, he is not hardly my boy. He's lucky to be livin' after doggin' my sister so bad." Terra expressed bitterness. "He doesn't deserve to be walkin' and breathin'. Vengeance is mine."

The waitress arrived with their meals.

"Those are some harsh words, Terra."

"And they're real, Roland." She sipped her glass of water. "They're a lot of car shops around. I'm sure you know where it's at."

"Look, mum's the word." He cocked his head to the side. "Unless you got some cash."

"Roland, we go way back. You gonna make me pay for the info?" She was appalled at his request. She was already prepared for the fact that you couldn't get something for nothing. "C'mon, bro."

He refused to budge. "That's how it is. I love ya, Terra, but my cash flow is low."

She frowned. "I'll see what I can do. I wasn't expecting this." *Maybe I can squeeze a little sumthin'-sumthin' out of Lamont.* Now that she was positive the Bryce she was familiar with was the same one married to Kyle, she could inquire about his shops. However, she didn't want to offer any clues about her agenda. Her prying could spark suspicion. And why were Donnie and Roland guarding?

Roland was aware how much hatred was in Terra's heart for Jarrett. Perhaps he should have broken the code and provided his whereabouts. He didn't want to see her do something she'd regret. She'd used the word *vengeance*.

He had a change of heart. He dialed Terra's cell number.

She picked up. "Hey, Roland."

"Thanks again for the breakfast. Listen, Terra, I was actin' greedy and selfish earlier. We go wayyy back so that's not cool. You're my girl."

Terra was silent.

"I don't wanna get paid," he advised. "I'll tell ya where Jarrett be hidin' out. He's got three locations, and the main one—where he does his dirt—is near Justin Street and Seventh. Called Jay's. He's usually there doin' his thang after-hours, understand?"

"Yes, I do. And Roland, thanks. I appreciate it."

"Just don't do nothin' stupid, sis. I ain't never liked to cross no women 'cause y'all can be some kinda vicious." Roland feared for Terra. She was bitter with a capital "B." He understood how close she and Toya had been, and he also was aware of Jarrett's notorious reputation as a womanizer. He wasn't acquainted with Kyle, but in his heart, he could only imagine the brutality Jarrett possibly displayed. He had four sisters and he dared anyone to disrespect them.

"I'm good, Roland. The deal is that I'll text you when I'm heading there." She clicked off the call.

CHAPTER 54
Terra

Waiting in the recreation center parking lot, Terra glanced in the rearview mirror. Kyle would be pulling up shortly. She'd told her to meet her after work and that there were youth in her neighborhood who were interested in dance. Kyle had expressed giving back to the community and wanted to volunteer.

When Kyle drove up, she spotted Terra, who was driving her grandmother's fifteen-year-old car. She parked and got into the car.

"Hi, Terra. This is awesome. I'm always interested in helping our youth." She looked at the rec building. "We going inside?"

"Yes, I had you meet me a little earlier. Our meeting with them is not for another hour or so," she lied. "I have somewhere else to take you." She started up the car and drove off.

"Where? I'm not trying to be funny, but I'm cautious about where I go." *And I really don't know you like that.*

"It's all good. I've hung out with you ladies enough to see you all like surprises."

"Well, that's true. I didn't expect any of this."

"Please hang tight. I'm not tryin' to disrespect my elders or anything."

Kyle laughed nervously. "So now I'm an elder? I don't have that much of an age difference."

Terra continued to make idle chat to distract thoughts of their destination. "The kids are so excited about meeting you."

"Likewise. You must be taking me for dinner or something. I'm starved."

"Well, we can do that, too." Terra turned on the street where Jay's was located.

"Hey, this is where my husband's shop is located." *This is a surprise all right, but what the hell is going on? How does she know about the shop or location? I never told her about Bryce's business.*

Terra parked on the side of the shop's lot away from the cars. "I'm sure you have a lot of questions."

"What's up with this? What's going on?" Kyle began to feel leery about Terra. She sensed that she was outraged, but she was clueless about the nature of the visit. "Listen, Terra, Bryce doesn't like me to make pop calls over here. Last time I did, he went off." She didn't feel comfortable enough to share her background with the young Terra.

"I bet he did."

"Why do you say that?" Kyle asked.

"Follow me." Terra reached over and grabbed her purse from the backseat. She opened the door, stepped out and closed it.

Kyle reluctantly complied. Terra was insistent on going inside the shop and Kyle feared what could happen to her alone. She had no idea about the nature of the visit, either. She opened the door and got out, following her to the shop's entrance. She took a deep breath. *Well, it can't get any worse. But I see she tricked me.*

The two entered the shop and everyone inside froze. A few of the workers recognized Kyle from her latest visit.

"Well, well, who do we have here?" Terra asked, staring at Bryce with evil eyes. "You didn't think you'd ever see me again, did you,

you son of a bitch?" she spat. "Look at you, up in here, perpetratin' like you a king." She looked at Kyle. "And you see who I brought along? Your *wife*."

Kyle stood quietly, fear implanted on her face.

"So let's get this all in the open. I want to make sure she hears everythin'." She looked at Kyle and turned back to face Bryce. "You ain't nothin' but a fake. Up in here pretending to repair cars. You stealin' cars. Yeah, that's right, I know *allll* about it.

"And I hear, *Jarrett*, that you supposed to be a Howard grad and all that jazz. Hell, you still a hood rat and the only reason you got cash is you hit the lottery."

Bryce was stunned and speechless.

Kyle, devastated by Terra's disclosure, wished she had a chair to lean on. She suddenly felt weak enough to faint.

"Sorry, Kyle, I didn't want to hurt you, but it was time for you to learn the truth. Your wannabe husband is Jarrett, not Bryce. He didn't go to Howard nor was he raised in a certain area of the city. He's a liar and a fake." She sneered. "Worse, he's the bastard who dated my sister, Toya. He misused and abused her and he's the reason she committed suicide. I vowed that if I ever crossed paths with him again…" She reached in her purse and pulled out a Glock. "That I'd not let my sister die in vain."

Sam and the other workers were brainstorming how to overtake Terra. Now that she'd pulled out a gun, it was more of a challenge.

Kyle observed with fright. She was disappointed to hear that he'd abused another woman and to the point of suicide.

Terra pointed the gun at Bryce. "So, you got any last words?"

Bryce trembled. He could see the shadow of someone entering the door. No one else was expected tonight. A crew had already arrived with the latest group of stolen cars. Slowly, a man lightly approached. Sam and the other workers also had observed his entrance and remained silent.

"I can't hear you, Jarrett…sorry, *Bryce*. I wanna hear your last words. You don't deserve to be alive. I ain't that acquainted with Kyle, but she's a lovely person and I'm sure you've abused her. So let me take you out of her life." Terra was enraged, her evil eyes glistening. "Okay, I'm waiting. No apologies will help ya. You shoulda thought about that when you were beatin' up on Toya… and probably Kyle. Humph, I betcha never thought it would go down like this." She thrust the gun further and aimed.

"Terra…" A voice from behind caused her chills. "Please, give me the gun."

Keeping in position, she looked straight ahead. "How did you—"

"I'd found the gun hidden at my place," Lamont advised. Roland had borrowed the gun from one of his cronies and given it to her as she'd requested. "I planned to question you about it. Then today I saw it was missing. You'd told me you were heading to the rec center this evening, so I drove around the neighborhood until I spotted your car. I was worried about you and your intentions."

"Oh, I see. You have no idea what this bastard did to my sister."

"I can see whatever it was, it caused you to lose it. Please, give me the gun." He spoke in soft tones to encourage her to release the weapon.

"No," she snapped.

"Listen, Terra, I love you," Lamont spoke with sincerity.

She froze with disbelief. *I love you?* No man had ever told her those words.

"Please, let it go," he encouraged, now closer.

She remained facing Bryce and never disconnected her eyes from staring at him.

"Terra, I truly love you," Lamont emphasized.

With those words including *truly*, Terra dropped the gun.

Lamont grabbed her from behind and gently by the waist. He turned her around and they embraced.

Suddenly, all eyes focused on the front door. Before anyone could grab the gun, several Metropolitan Police officers entered with a search warrant.

When Terra had texted Roland that she was en route to the shop, she'd also requested he alert police by calling at a specific time and reporting illegal activity at Jay's.

Payback is a bitch, she thought.

Kyle became overcome with emotion and collapsed.

Locked in a hug, Terra stared over Lamont's shoulder and her tears flowed. She didn't want to let go.

CHAPTER 55
The Wives

Several bottles of wine from Amber's collection sat on a cocktail table. She had invited Shayla and Kyle for an evening she'd called "Confessions: Part 2." It would be an opportunity to celebrate renewed sisterhood and update their statuses.

After Sonya's meal of shrimp and chicken pasta, steamed broccoli and garlic breadsticks, the girls kicked back to sample the wines. It was confessions night a la wine tasting.

Amber desired to share her latest news, although she was ashamed.

Sonya, followed by Topaz at her heels, trekked downstairs to the basement level. She ensured all the bottles selected were uncorked. The ladies were relaxed on a cozy sofa surrounding the table. After serving them mini pastries from a tray, Sonya headed back upstairs.

"Well, ladies, it's great to see you again. Please, help yourself to the wine. I personally selected some choices I wanted you to sample." She pointed to the bottles. Normally, Sonya would have served the wines, but Amber had indicated she needed privacy. She picked up a bottle of Riesling and poured three glasses. She handed one to Shayla and another to Kyle.

"Cheers to love, life and happiness." Amber held her glass up and the others followed, then they all sipped.

"We need these ladies hookups to keep our sanity and offer each other support," Amber said. "When we opened up to each other last time, I felt so rejuvenated." She tasted a mini pastry. "So it was time for a repeat. It was such a relief to pour it all out.

"So I thought we'd get together again…I have more to confess." She paused and then continued, "I never shared with you the fact that my habit got so bad that I borrowed funds from the Diamond Dreams account."

Shayla and Kyle were wide-eyed in disbelief about the foundation.

"Yes, I went there. And I kept it from Trevor. He's ecstatic about our youth, and I was scared how he'd react if he found out about the donations.

"Well, ladies, he discovered it," she informed. "You're aware of how compassionate I am about the foundation and our purpose. It was such an embarrassment. Imagine telling your husband you borrowed from your joint project to finance your latest shoes or clothes. I was one desperate chick."

"So, how did Trevor react?" Shayla asked.

"Of course he was pissed. Then he cooled down. I told him I'd taken part of the money, given it to Autumn's friend who's a pro gambler, and she'd doubled it. She was kind enough to turn it around for me and didn't expect anything in return. She didn't even want anything for her efforts.

"Now our account is back on track. Money is in the bank and we're moving forward."

"He didn't go off on you?" Kyle inquired, familiar with the consequences of dealing with a bitter husband.

"Well, Trevor is fairly low-key. Now, if I had told him I hadn't *replaced* the money, it would have been another story. He's usually in chill mode, but this was one time, I was tampering with his dream." Amber paused. "Believe me, it won't ever happen again. My hubby's the sweetest guy ever, but I don't plan to double cross him anymore."

Kyle had soaked up Amber's revelation intently. She'd had her own share of drama. "I can't believe how I could've lived under the same roof, married to someone with a fake identity."

Bryce was locked up without bond. She was mentally recuperating from the abuse she'd suffered.

"And what happened to my women's intuition? Here Bryce—excuse me, *Jarrett*—was a friggin' lottery winner, and I was thinking he'd earned his wealth from his damn mind.

"How foolish could I have been?"

"Look, Kyle, it isn't always easy to see through someone, especially if they're a skilled con artist," Shayla advised. "We both were wearing masks, I suppose. I had a stepdaughter who was my client, and I didn't have a clue we were related."

"Then Bryce was an abuser," Kyle added. She paused and unconsciously rubbed her leg. She was reminded of her physical injuries and visualized him striking her.

"If I'd only seen signs before we were married…," she continued, shaking her head.

"They're not always visible," Amber interjected. "And sometimes even if you do see nuances, you still may not see the whole picture. You can be sharp reading people, but you can be in the dark. So, Kyle, don't beat yourself up with the shoulda, coulda, woulda.

"Girl, it's even uglier now with the arrest thrown in the loop. And the beatings need to be addressed. I can't imagine how difficult this whole scenario is for you. If there's anything we can do, we're here for you," Amber offered.

"Thank you."

It had been two weeks since Bryce's arrest and Kyle was growing accustomed to his lockup. The home was lonely yet she was used to an emptiness with Bryce.

Kyle relished her sincere friendships. She'd also received a call from Erick, who'd left her a voicemail to offer his support. He said she was in his thoughts and he needed to speak with her.

Shayla poured wine into the glasses for another round. She sipped delicately from her glass. She'd decided she would end her affairs with Blaze and Wilson. After opening up to Amber and Kyle, it was best to expose her infidelity to Chad. He'd hidden parenthood and now it was in the open. She would reciprocate and share her innermost secret albeit a difficult one to reveal to your spouse, she thought. She wasn't sure how he would react. She loved Chad and was sad that she'd gone over the top with her affairs.

Her doctor had contacted her for a follow-up visit earlier in the week. He'd run various tests during her annual exam after she'd complained of sweating and fatigue.

She dropped her head, then raised it. She sighed.

"Ladies, when I went to Dr. Brown this week, he had some bad news for me…I'm HIV positive."

ABOUT THE AUTHOR

Charmaine R. Parker started writing fiction during early childhood. It included poetry, skits and short stories. She is the author of *The Next Phase of Life*. Parker has a bachelor's degree in fine arts from Howard University and a master's degree in print journalism from the University of Southern California. Born in North Carolina, she was raised in Washington, D.C. She is a former journalist who worked as a reporter, copy editor, production editor and managing editor. Charmaine lives in Maryland with her husband and daughter where she is working on her next novel. Visit the author on Facebook/ Charmaine Roberts Parker and Twitter @Charmainebooks. You may email her at charmainerparker@gmail.com

READER DISCUSSION GUIDE

1. How would you define a *trophy wife*?

2. If you consider yourself a "trophy," married or single, why?

3. If you could select one character with whom you identify the most, whom would it be: Shayla, Amber, Kyle or Terra? Why?

4. Which character is your favorite and why?

5. Should the wives have shared their secrets earlier in their friendship?

6. Should Shayla and Amber been honest with their husbands about their issues?

7. Do you know "trophy wives" (or single women in relationships) that have similar challenges as Shayla, Amber and Kyle?

8. Are women pressured to portray a certain image among their friends and spouses/partners?

9. Are women vulnerable when they select mates based on looks, status, background and finances?

10. Have you experienced deception from a mate? How did you become aware?

11. Do you or anyone you know have similar addictions as Shayla and Amber?

12. Do you or any women you know accept physical and verbal abuse like Kyle? Did they stay in their relationship or sever it after a period of time? Did they remain in relationship to maintain a specific lifestyle?

13. Should women open up to their friends about troubling issues? If so, should it be based on trust, length of friendship or another factor?

14. Should Chad have shared his secret with Shayla?

15. What are the consequences of Shayla, Amber and Kyle not sharing their secrets?

16. What are the themes or messages in the book?

17. What is your favorite chapter and why?

18. Is it a good idea for Terra to befriend Shayla, Amber and Kyle?

19. What lifestyle would you choose (or do you choose) in a wealthy marriage/relationship?

20. Does wealth guarantee happiness or success? How does it affect Shayla, Amber and Kyle?

If you enjoyed "The Trophy Wives," be sure to check out

THE Next
PHASE OF LIFE

BY CHARMAINE R. PARKER
AVAILABLE FROM STREBOR BOOKS

1

Pleasure 'n' paradise

Tai glanced at the nightstand clock: It was close to midnight. Eager to escape, she gingerly arose from the soft satiny sheets, peeping at her bedmate who was in a deep slumber. *I'm on this beautiful island and it's way too early for me to turn in*, she thought.

There was little time to worry about hooking up pieces for a sensual outfit; it would be quicker to grab a dress—one of her hot numbers. She pulled a fire-red jersey wrap sundress out of the closet and quietly headed for the bathroom. She analyzed the persona reflected in the mirror. Here she was in St. Maarten and confined in a hotel room with a grumpy ex-boyfriend. *Boring* wasn't the word for Vince; he was the king of Lazyville. After they'd had a rendezvous—a quickie—he had done the usual: drifted to sleep in record time.

Tai had buzzed him a few months ago on the relationship re-
bound. He immediately had agreed to take her to the tropical
retreat. She wasn't looking for love; only a travel escort.

She was still recuperating from the grave disappointment of a
no-show. Tai had celebrated her fortieth birthday with a big bash
when her longtime beau, Austin, decided to pull a disappearing
act. After envisioning them as a standout couple on her grand
night, when all eyes would be on them, he was nowhere to be
found. Tai was forced to celebrate her four decades solo. She had
spent months planning the party of 200 invited guests at the
Grand Hyatt in downtown Washington, D.C. Valé, her fashion
designer friend, had created a black and gold, form-fitting, one-
shoulder dress to show off the curves that she had managed to
maintain at her milestone age. Tai was proud that she had held on
to her youthful figure and had no problems flaunting it.

Throughout the evening, her guests had continuously inquired
about Austin. The duo had been joined at the hip like two peas in
a pod. Now, on her special night, he was ghost. Maybe her occa-
sional comments about turning forty being synonymous with
marriage had scared Austin. After all, so many brothers shied
away from the ring on the finger. However, Tai felt assurance that
Austin was ready to settle down after their five-year relationship.
She now presumed *commitment* wasn't in his vocabulary when it
came to a walk down the aisle.

Despite her constant calls, emails and texts, Austin had failed to
respond; she snipped her sweating-a-guy behavior. At forty, she
shouldn't chase after any man! Who the hell did he think he was
anyway? The chocolate- skinned, baldheaded and dapper attorney
was rolling in the looks and intellectual department. But the
disappearance proved that he lacked dignity and respect when it

came to their relationship. Pulling out on her with no explanation was surely immature. *Oh, well, it's his loss,* she thought. *Moving on…despite the pain and ongoing heartache. Can't let this man continue to play ping-pong with my emotions.*

Tai reached for the washcloth and freshened up, ensuring that the water ran lightly. She slipped into the little halter dress that lifted her 40-Ds and accentuated her curves. She dabbled on foundation and applied eye shadow and mascara, then searched her makeup kit for her favorite lip gloss. She sprayed on Halle Berry Reveal perfume and then turned to get a full-length view in the mirror on the bathroom door. She slipped into her black strappy heel sandals. The red dress complemented her honey complexion; she was pleased with her late-night look.

Tai peeped into their luxurious suite and Vince was like a statue. He had shifted slightly but not enough to awaken. *Boy, I must've put a whammy on him,* she thought. *He's sixty, but damn, he should have a little bit more stamina.*

Tai had dated Vince briefly when she was in her early thirties. Her associates, not her close friends, had considered her a gold digger. But she refuted, saying that she was attracted to Vince despite the age difference; it wasn't for his wallet. Yes, he was wealthy, a surgeon with a mansion in Beverly Hills and the ultimate bachelor. His sprawling spread was a fabulous six-bedroom resort with an indoor and outdoor pool, tennis court and a full gym. It was a fitness guru's paradise and Tai ensured that she took advantage of the amenities. She and Vince would work out on the weights and treadmill and then she'd whip up health-conscious meals in his huge gourmet kitchen.

Tai had met Vince during one of her business trips to L.A. when she was a marketing representative. The two became travel companions and their getaways were mainly on the West Coast: from bed and breakfast inns in Santa Barbara to shopping in Carmel to views of the Golden Gate Bridge in San Francisco. When Tai desired to escape to the islands after Austin's disappearance, she had thought of Vince. Now she was in St. Maarten at the fabulous Sonesta Maho Beach Hotel and he was snoozing in sync with the sounds of the flat-screen TV.

She tiptoed across the room and opened the door, being careful to close it securely behind her. She strutted to the elevator; feeling uplifted and ready for whatever was in store. When the doors opened, she stepped inside and headed to the lobby. The outdoor café beckoned.

Tai spotted a barstool, which she sashayed toward and pulled up to the bar. Scoping out the scene, she noticed that tonight's crowd was thin. It didn't matter; she was simply trying to chill and forget about the whole Austin saga. Sure, she was forty and eager now to find a "Mr. Right," if one existed, but meanwhile, she was in paradise.

"Hey, sweetie, what can I get you?" the charming bartender asked, flashing a Cheshire cat grin.

"I'll take a pomegranate martini. Please make it stiff."

"You bet."

The sounds of Maysa blared through the speakers. Tai loved neo-soul music; it always placed her in an upbeat mood. She absorbed the atmosphere on this moonlit night. A slight breeze was comforting and offered relief from the steamy sunshine that had blanketed the small island during the day.

It was Tai's first visit to the island known for being Dutch on one side and French on the other. Earlier that day, she and Vince had driven their rented Jeep through- out the countryside. They had heard about a nude beach on the French side where they stopped to take in the sights. Of course there were visitors who had no qualms about showing their bodies; no matter their shape or form. Vince had encouraged Tai to shed her swimsuit and join the others, but she wasn't following the old adage: "When in Rome do as the Romans do."

Singles and couples were scattered throughout the cocktail lounge featuring brilliant shades of turquoise, mango and fuchsia. The bright colors generated a feel of tropical living and created a lively ambience. Tai was enjoying the fruity flavor of her martini and was ready to order a second one. She stopped in her tracks when she locked eyes on a handsome islander. He commanded attention as his smooth cocoa complexion glistened under the low lights. His black button-down shirt showed off his well-chiseled chest. When he caught her look, Tai quickly turned her attention back to the bar scenery. She was slightly embarrassed but also pleased he had noticed.

"Hello, lovely, you sure are wearing that dress. It's on fi-yah." Tai jumped slightly as she was startled. The mystery man had made his way to the bar and was now overlooking her shoulder. "Hope I didn't scare you."

Tai turned and offered a sexy smile. "Oh, no…thanks for the compliment. I think you saw me checking you out."

"I did. What's your name?"

"Tai. And yours?"

"Carlton," he responded, rolling the "Carl" with his accent. Tai was admiring his full physique now that he was positioned close. "Care if I join you?"

"Please…"

Carlton sat on the barstool next to her. "What would you like to drink?"

"Well, I just finished a pomegranate martini." Tai made eye contact and edged closer. "But now I'd like a Sex on the Beach," she said slowly and teasingly.

"Hmmm…cool," Carlton responded. "Eric, the lady wants a Sex on the Beach. And I'll take Hennessy and Coke," he told the bartender.

"Got it. Will make it *real* sexy."

"Where are you from? Here alone?" Carlton inquired.

"I'm from D.C. and yes, I'm alone…for the moment."

Carlton raised his eyebrows in curiosity but he dared not barrage her with more questions.

Tai had never tasted the cocktail, but tonight she thought it was fitting. The name itself conjured up images of how her body was feeling; she was starting to heat up down south. She squirmed on her stool as she crossed her legs.

She sure looks luscious in that red dress, Carlton thought. His mind drifted to Coco Brown and the Phat Cat Players… *Caressing you so close… Sundress…*

"This is delicious. Wow, I've never tried it but was always curious." Tai was enjoying her newly discovered Sex on the Beach. She was relieved to have met Carlton as she didn't want to spend her last night "alone." She didn't mind being restless; just not lying in bed next to a knocked-out lover with a TV watching *him*.

"What do you do on the island? It's such a beautiful place. I can't imagine working here. I'd be stretched out on the sand, laid back and soaking up the scenery."

"Actually, I'm in law enforcement. I'm a cop." Carlton cleared his throat. "Mostly undercover." He stared into her eyes. "But we like to let our hair down, too."

Tai grinned and twirled her stool to face him. "Oh, I'd better behave." She smiled and took the last sip of her drink. Her mellow mood blended with the light jazz. Carlton recognized she was relaxed, and he didn't want the night to end.

"Let's take a walk," he suggested.

"Why not? That sounds cool. It's such a pretty night," Tai agreed.

Carlton helped her from the barstool, admiring her vision of beauty. Now he really could check out the dress he was singing about in his head.

Tai's and Carlton's shadows danced along the soft sand as they strolled barefoot. The waves of the turquoise sea played their own melody, offering a romantic breeze. They continued to a secluded sandy spot hidden below a cliff overlooking the moonlit landscape.

Wow, now this is what I call paradise, Tai thought, then exhaled.

Tai dropped her sandals and her tiny shoulder bag as Carlton embraced her tightly. They kissed ferociously and groped each other with intensity. Peeling off their clothes, they discovered irresistible passion. Their nude bodies meshed as they lowered to the sand. And the moon radiated a magical love potion.